CHIN MUSIC

CHIN MUSIC

Lee Edelstein

Sela House
Boca Raton, FL

First Edition
Printed in the United States

Interior Design by Five Rainbows Services
www.FiveRainbows.com

Cover Design by Rebecca Lown Design
www.RebeccaLown.com

Publisher's Cataloging-in-Publication Data

Edelstein, Lee.
   Chin music / Lee Edelstein.
     p. cm.
   ISBN: 978-0-9883434-0-5 (pbk.)
   ISBN: 978-0-9883434-1-2 (e-book: EPUB)
   1. Baseball—Fiction. 2. Mothers and sons—Fiction. 3. Coming of age—Fiction. 4. Ruth, Babe, 1895-1948—Fiction. I. Title.
PS3605.D451 . C55 2012
813—dc23

2012917218

"I swing big, with everything I've got. I hit big or I miss big. I like to live as big as I can."

Babe Ruth

PREFACE

JUPITER, FLORIDA
SEPTEMBER, 2010

THE SOUNDS OF CREDENCE CLEARWATER'S "BAD MOON RISING" FILLED the air as Bill Buck, a Classic Vinyl fan, started the car and pulled out of the near empty parking area. He hit a few buttons on the console and soon the ringing of a phone could be heard inside the car.

"Calling Mom," he said, before the boys could ask.

"Tell her I'm hungry," fourteen-year-old Michael called out from behind him.

Bill glanced in his rearview mirror, caught Michael's eye, and gave him a sarcastic look.

"Think she doesn't know?"

Beside him, sixteen-year-old Ryan chuckled.

When Susan answered the phone, Michael was the first to speak. "We're on our way home, Mom. What's for dinner?"

"Chicken Mama." One of their favorites.

"Great! I'm starving!" Michael crowed.

"Shocking!" Susan said, and then changed the subject. "How was the game?"

"We won," Ryan said.

"In dramatic fashion, I might add," said Bill.

"Can't wait to hear all about it. How far away are you?"

"Ten minutes," he said, as they rounded a curve in the road. Up ahead, the annoying traffic light, the one which took forever to change, blinked from red to green. "Maybe less."

"Okay," she said, then added for Michael's benefit, "Food will be on the table."

"Thank you, Chef Susan," he quipped.

"See you soon," said Bill, ending the call.

The radio returned and Jefferson Airplane's "White Rabbit" pulsed through the confined space of the car. For the moment, Michael sat quietly in the back seat.

"When's your next game?" Bill asked, looking at Ryan through the corner of his eye.

Ryan, star quarterback for his high school team, was lost in his thoughts, replaying the last-minute touchdown drive he had engineered to win the game. "Next Friday," he said, absentmindedly.

As they crossed the intersection, the song reached its crescendo and Grace Slick cried out commandingly, "*Feed your heaaaaad!*"

From seemingly out of nowhere, Ryan saw headlights, impossibly close, through his father's side window. His eyes widened and he felt a huge adrenaline pulse as he cried out, "Da..."

The speeding car hit them square on, front of center, with a force that drove their mortally wounded SUV dead right, halting their momentum far too suddenly. The crash unleashed forces that strained the safety features of their car to the limit and beyond. Ryan felt himself thrown violently to the right as everything telescoped in on him. His head smashed into a side strut and he felt an unbearable pain in his left leg. The car seemed to slide in slow motion, as if it would slide forever. Strangely, he seemed to hear a melody from far off, *Feed your heaaaaaaaaaad...*

Then everything went black.

CHAPTER 1

Iᴛ ᴡᴀs ᴛʜᴇ ᴍɪᴅᴅʟᴇ ᴏғ ᴛʜᴇ ɴɪɢʜᴛ ᴀɴᴅ Rʏᴀɴ ᴀᴡᴏᴋᴇ ʙᴀᴛʜᴇᴅ ɪɴ sᴡᴇᴀᴛ. It was the dream again, the same damn one. The one where he throws a pass to his wide receiver but instead of a football it's a key tumbling ever so slowly, like in slow motion, end-over-end, until it lands softly in his receiver's hands, except it's Michael who catches it in the end zone for the winning touchdown. Ryan throws his arms up in victory and goes charging down the field to celebrate with his teammates but he runs right into a hospital room where he suddenly finds himself in bed. His father and Michael are standing behind the doctor who is saying to him "you're going to make a full recovery."

Ryan sat up in bed, looked around his room, rubbed his face and tried to chase the dream out of the corners of his mind. He asked himself for the ten-thousandth time: *what had happened between the football field and the hospital? And the key...why the key?*

He had absolutely no recollection of the crash, didn't even remember getting in the car. For over two years since the accident all he wants to do is remember. After all the therapy he knows he may not ever remember, but, in his heart of hearts, he believes that if he *can* remember, then he will truly be able put it behind him.

He hasn't had the nightmare for some time and tonight he's able to shake it off without too much trouble. Another sign of progress, so his therapist Caitlin says. It wasn't until four months after the crash that the dream first appeared but, once it did, it wouldn't leave him alone, waking him from sleep three or four times a week, draining him of what little energy he could muster. The recurring nightmare fed his feelings of guilt and sent him into a tailspin. Finally, his mom forced him to see a therapist. After the first few visits with Caitlin, where he didn't say very much or want to know anything, he revealed the dream to her. She asked if he wanted the specifics of the crash, something he had avoided to that point, feeling that the basic facts—his father was dead, his brother maimed for life—were more than enough. Terrified, he said yes. So, quietly and softly, she told him. How the police estimated that the car that hit them was going fifty miles an hour; how their SUV was so accordioned by the impact of the collision that it took the rescue workers over an hour to get him out of the wreck; how his father died instantly; how it was a miracle that Michael had survived but with the loss of his left leg; how impossibly quick everything happened and how the cause of the accident was a drunk driver who had ignored the red light and had died en route to the hospital; how there was nothing Ryan could have done to change the outcome, a point Caitlin made for the first of what would be many times. For Ryan, hearing about it was one thing, actually remembering it another.

In that session, they agreed that he would tell Caitlin whenever he had the dream. Thereafter, they spent a lot of time talking about the nightmare and his desperate need to remember what happened. Caitlin talked with him about the symptoms of post-traumatic stress syndrome and survivor's guilt and his need to understand and recognize what he was feeling. She told him there was a real possibility that he would never remember any of the details of the crash. Mostly she talked about time and patience, being kind to himself, and how he was a blameless victim of a deadly crime. And that he would heal gradually but unevenly.

Though they talked about the dream, he kept his feelings to himself, not yet trusting the therapist, the stranger his mother insisted he start seeing. At the time, he fought his mom bitterly.

"It's Michael we need to be focused on," he insisted. "I'm fine, Mom. Don't worry about me!"

But it was Ryan she was most worried about.

Four months after the accident, Susan still had been reeling from the disaster that had struck them. With breathtaking suddenness everything had changed. Their idyllic life, as she longingly looked back on it, had been shattered like a delicate wine glass violently smashed to the ground. She felt overwhelmed.

Somewhere along the way denial gave up its stranglehold on her and she began to tentatively look forward. She tried her best to guide her children through the glass shards that littered their path but it was like walking through a mine field, not knowing where the mines were. In Ryan's case, it seemed that new mines would appear from seemingly nowhere.

After the numbness from the shock of having their father wrenched from their lives began to subside, Michael seemed to bounce back. He agonized over the fact that he would never become the elite athlete he had dreamed of but he quickly became focused on the monumental physical hurdles he would have to deal with. The challenge of overcoming his handicap and learning to walk again seemed to energize him. He threw himself into rehab with a singular focus and, amazingly, with good humor. Susan had yet to see an ounce of "Why Me?" in him.

Ryan was another story. She couldn't get a handle on him. After the first couple of weeks, when the dense fog that surrounded her in the aftermath of the disaster slowly began to recede, Ryan seemed lost and disoriented. While still on crutches from his broken leg, he had adopted an attitude of fierce protectiveness when it came to her and his brother. He bristled at anyone who interacted with them in a way that even slightly displeased him. He was moody and, at different times, angry and morose. This was followed, a couple of months later, by The Dream, as Susan thought of it. In the space of a few weeks, Ryan became visibly more despondent and started looking haggard and drawn. After much badgering on her part he shared the recurring nightmare that had begun to plague him. He was suffocating in what seemed to her an unwarranted state of guilt. As her concern heightened for his well-being she started to feel the paralyzing anxiety, helplessness, and panic that had overwhelmed her in the immediate aftermath of the crash. She felt herself spinning out of control. It was then that she stopped deluding herself into thinking she could handle the new normal by herself. She called their family doctor and asked him to recommend someone for Ryan to see.

"I worry plenty about you, Ryan," she said, when he protested. "You need help just as much as Michael but a different kind. With the assistance your brother is receiving he's working his butt off doing everything he can to walk. You need to be doing whatever you can to get this monkey off your back...and it's nothing you can figure out for yourself." She looked at him tenderly. "Ryan, this thing is weighing you down. I understand mourning your father and your sadness about Michael but what you're doing," she corrected herself, "what you're feeling is beyond mourning. It's survivor's guilt, and you've got a pretty good case of it."

He felt a flash of anger.

"Now you're a shrink! How the hell would you know?"

Susan maintained a veneer of composure.

"I talked to a shrink. Actually two shrinks. I told them about the last four months. Ryan, look at me." She paused until he did. "They both said the same thing. You should be seeing somebody."

"Sorry, not me."

She took a deep breath and continued.

"Listen Ryan, when was the last time I insisted you do something?"

"I don't know." He paused. "Maybe when I was seven or eight."

"Almost ten years. So, I guess I must feel very strongly about this. I *promise* you this will be a good thing. It won't be easy but Ry, please do your Mom a favor...just this once in a decade.

"God dammit, Ma! Just leave me alone!" he yelled.

Susan felt the room begin to swim around her. She reached out for something to steady herself as her outwardly calm demeanor disintegrated.

Alarmed, Ryan rushed to her and led her to the couch where she sat down.

"Mom, you okay?" he asked, fear in his voice.

Her distinctive blue eyes pooled with tears.

"I can't do it Ryan; I don't have the strength. I can't handle anymore loss." She began to sob. "I'm afraid. I can't lose you, too. I want you back the way you were before the accident!" she screamed, and then hugged him fiercely, holding him tightly as she wept uncontrollably into his shoulder.

Silently, Ryan held her.

Finally, she released him and took a moment to compose herself.

"I guess that's not possible. None of us will ever be the same." She paused. "But we've got to do things that will help us to move forward. Please do this for all of us," she said, softly.

So he agreed.

Over time he came to trust Caitlin and understand that she was a smart lady who had developed a pretty good handle on what was going on in his head. Now, a couple of years later, he still couldn't remember anything about the accident but it had begun to occupy a manageable space within him, a space that had enough room to enclose the dream on the increasingly infrequent times he had it.

Ryan yawned, lay back on his pillow, placed the dream in that space, rolled over, and, after a while, fell back to sleep.

Chapter 2

ST. PETERSBURG, FLORIDA
FEBRUARY, 1926

It was just after 1 PM, a slow time in Spud's Barber Shop. Spud methodically cut the hair of Tom Meany, a regular customer of many years. Bill Frawley sat tilted half way back in the second chair, reading the day's *St. Pete Times* as he awaited his next customer. The other barber swept the floor with a well-used broom.

Like most mornings at Spud's it had been quiet even though it was "the season", which swelled St. Pete's population from 37,000 to upwards of 60,000 residents. When yours is the third barbershop in a three barbershop town, it's never all that busy. This was particularly so for the barber who silently finished sweeping. After six months the hair cutter had yet to build much of a following, in spite of the fact that those customers who sat in the third chair walked out of Spud's with the best haircuts. Zel let out a discouraged sigh, then straightened the scissors and brushes that sat beneath the large mirror.

Spud tilted Tom Meany just short of horizontal. Using a pair of wooden tongs, he reached into the small steamer that sat behind the front counter. He extracted a hot towel, steam rising from it as he held it for a few seconds. With practiced grace, he took the towel in his left hand, put down the tongs, and tossed it back and forth. When the towel cooled a bit, he carefully wrapped it around his customer's face. Meany let out a long, soft moan as the steam drifted upwards.

Just then the door opened and there was a commotion as three large, well-built men walked into Spud's, the first two busily conversing with each other. The men towered over Spud, Bill, and Zel. They were loud.

"Can three guys get a haircut here without waiting?" boomed one of them. He had an oversized face and a big head of hair that badly needed trimming.

"Looks like two of us can," said the second, eyeing the three barber chairs, only one of which was occupied by a customer. He was taller and slimmer than the first, but just as noisy.

"I'll be done here in a couple of minutes," Spud said, not bothering to look up. "In the meantime, why don't two of you get started."

Bill Frawley, who was never in a rush, slowly pulled himself out of his chair and turned to the waiting men.

"Why don't one of you sit right here." He looked closer at the fellow with the big face. "Wait a minute," he said. "I know you." Bill's eyes widened as the guy started to laugh. "Babe Ruth! You're Babe Ruth!!" He started shaking Ruth's hand vigorously. "Babe Ruth, how the hell are you?"

"I'm great but I need a haircut. Look at this mop on my head!"

"Well, you can sit right here," said Frawley, as he pointed to his chair.

"What about my boys? How about their haircuts?" Ruth demanded.

"One of them can sit there," Frawley said, gesturing to the third chair, "and Spud here is done, too." Upon hearing Babe Ruth's name, Tom Meany had yanked the hot towel from his face and sat up in the still horizontal chair, staring silently at Ruth.

"Who's the third barber?" Ruth asked.

Angry at hearing this, Zel spoke up.

"I am. And you do need one. When was the last time you had a cut?"

The Babe, caught off guard, gave Zel a puzzled look and then broke out in a big grin. "A lady barber? A lady barber!!" he repeated. "I'll be a son of a bitch! I never seen a lady barber before. You really cut hair?"

"I do. And I can surely give you a better haircut than the last one you got!"

Kind of spunky, Ruth thought. *Good looking, too.* Never one to follow convention, he didn't hesitate.

"You're on, keed." He meant "kid" but that's the way Ruth pronounced it. He turned to the guy who was taller than him. "I got the dame, Meusel. You and Gehrig got the two guys."

Spud tried to intervene.

"You probably should use Bill or me, Mr. Ruth. We've got a lot more experience than Zel here. And you being an important person and all, you want to be sure to have a good haircut."

Ruth glared at Spud.

"Are you some kind of bum or something? Putting down your fellow barber? I'll use the lady...or we'll go somewhere else for our haircuts. That okay with you?" Ruth said, pointing his finger as he towered over him.

"Fine, fine, Mr. Ruth. Zel it is."

Spud turned to Meusel.

"I'll be glad to take care of you, sir."

"Nah, I'll go with this guy," Meusel said, pointing at Frawley. "You got Gehrig."

Gehrig, the third of the New York Yankees to enter Spud's, had yet to say a word. That fit his nature and his status as a second year player. Both Ruth and Meusel were veterans.

As the Babe sat in Zel's chair, she covered him with a smock, tucking it in around his thick neck.

"How short do you like your hair cut?"

"Make me look good, keed. Today's my birthday and the boys are taking me out later to celebrate. You give shaves?"

"Of course."

"Good. I'll have a shave, too."

"You got it," Zel said, as she got down to work. "How old are you?"

"Thirty-one," he answered. "A lady barber," Ruth chuckled. "Whadda they gonna think of next?"

One hour later, clean shaven and with neatly combed hair, Ruth looked in the mirror and pronounced himself satisfied.

"Best damn haircut and shave I ever had!" he boomed. "Let me see you guys," he said to Meusel and Gehrig.

They both turned to him and then looked at each other. Ruth laughed.

"I did better than either of you. You should have used the dame, too." He turned to Zel. "What do I owe you?"

"That will be one dollar for the cut and shave," Zel replied.

Ruth pulled out a wad of cash, selected a five-dollar bill, and returned the pile to his pocket. He held the bill by both ends, snapped it a few times making sure Spud and Frawley saw it, and handed it to Zel.

"Keep the change, keed." He looked at Gehrig. "We got a game tomorrow?"

"No Babe. No games for another couple of weeks," Gehrig replied.

"Right." He turned back to Zel. "Put me down for a shave tomorrow around four."

Zel, who couldn't believe Ruth had given her an astounding $4 tip, tried to remain cool.

"Tomorrow is Sunday and the Shop is closed. How about Monday?"

"4 PM?"

"Let me take a look." Zel walked to her appointment book that sat beneath the mirror. She opened to February 8th. The page was, like most in her book, empty. "Yes, I can fit you in at four."

"Well then, put me in your book at four each day."

Zel looked at Ruth questioningly.

"For a shave. My daily shave."

"You want a shave every day?" She had never heard of such a thing.

"Never shave myself," Ruth said, with a wave of his hand. "That's what barbers are for."

Zel's eyes got big. "Yes, sir. Four o'clock it is."

"Great. See you then. Thanks, keed."

With that, Babe Ruth, star slugger for the New York Yankees, Bob Meusel, starting left fielder, and twenty-two year old first baseman Lou Gehrig, were gone.

Zel turned to Spud and Frawley who stood staring at her.

"I've got to tell Horace," she proclaimed. "He's not going to believe this!"

CHAPTER 3

AFTER WORK, ZEL HURRIED DOWN THE STREET, HER MIND RUNNING IN different directions. Babe Ruth walking into Spud's was the most exciting thing to happen to her in the six months she had been living in St. Petersburg. Maybe it was the break she needed.

It had been a struggle for her, just as Spud had predicted when he reluctantly gave her the vacant third chair, which he only did to avoid having to cut the hair of that young hellion, six-year-old Jackie Dickerson. (Jackie's mother brought her son in every 4 weeks and Zel had the good fortune to ask for a job on Jackie's regular day. Thinking it would discourage her, Spud had immediately put Jackie in Zel's chair. It had only stiffened Zel's resolve.) Zel hadn't expected building a clientele to be easy, but not that difficult either. Apparently, the male population of St. Petersburg found a female barber to be downright revolutionary. But these were revolutionary times they lived in, what with women being able to vote and all.

She never planned on becoming a barber. But in 1918 the Spanish Flu struck and everything changed. The flu decimated her family, taking her mother and her older brother, Jimmy. Jimmy's death drained the life from her father, who had planned on his son joining him in the barbershop he owned. With just the two of them left, she pleaded with her dad to allow her to work alongside him. But he directed his anger over his terrible loss at her, and refused to consider the possibility. Eventually, her persistence wore him down, though, and she joined him. But her father never recovered from the loss of his wife and son and passed away a few years later. She carried on alone for a while but ultimately came to the conclusion that there was too much sadness for her in Columbus. One of her best customers had told her about St. Petersburg, Florida, where the local newspaper was given away free any day the sun didn't shine. She desperately needed sunshine in her life and the image resonated with her. So she sold the shop, the house, and all its belongings and used the money to bankroll her new life in the Sunshine City.

After six months in St. Pete she had developed a small following of customers and a growing cadre of youngsters whose hair she cut, but Zel had begun taking babysitting jobs on the side to supplement her meager income.

She pulled out of her purse the five-dollar bill Babe Ruth had given her. Four-and-a-half dollars of it was hers, the remaining fifty cents went to Spud, his half of the price of the haircut and shave. That meant a four dollar tip, far and away the biggest she had ever received. *That's equal to sixteen haircuts! And he has an appointment for a shave every day next week!* She wondered what his regular tip would be. Perhaps her fortunes had changed for the better. All she knew for certain was that she was going to give Babe Ruth the best damn shave he had ever had!

As she made her way home, Zel stopped to gaze in the window of Eleanor's Dress Shop. It was a fancy shop and featured dresses that she could only dream of. Her favorite was the yellow flapper dress displayed in the store's window. She loved that dress—she made a point of looking at it every day, even sometimes on her lunch break—and fantasized about wearing it out on the town to a jazz club or to one of the illicit but fashionable speakeasies where she would dance the Charleston, drink some hooch, and smoke cigarettes. But the price of the dress was $89, completely beyond her means. For a minute she stared at the yellow dress with renewed interest, then turned away, put the five dollar bill back in her purse, and continued on to Mrs. Albright's Boarding House, the place she called home.

It had been a tough six months for the Babe, too. Maybe the worst six months of his life. Not that he dwelt very long on anything of a negative nature. Truth was he didn't dwell on much at all. For him, it was always about *right now*. Nonetheless, he had to admit that the 1925 season had been pretty crappy, definitely the worst of his career. And he didn't have anyone to blame but himself. And maybe Miller Huggins—the flea!

The 1924 season had been easy, a piece of cake. He won the batting title by almost twenty points, hit nineteen more home runs than the next guy, and finished second in RBIs. A typical Babe Ruth season that included non-stop carousing and drinking. He had his problems with the flea, all five foot six inches of him, but as long as the Babe played his usual game, there was nothing the Yankee manager could do.

Nineteen twenty-five was another story altogether. First there was his wife, Helen, and her insistence that she meet up with him in St. Pete, at the start of spring training. As was his pre-spring training custom, he headed off to Hot Springs to the steam baths, the drinking, the eating, and the women. He ate himself into oblivion, ran wild, and arrived in St. Pete weighing over two-fifty and sick as a dog. With Helen keeping an eye on him he behaved, got better, and into some semblance of shape. But she cramped his style and made him cranky. When the team broke camp and headed north to play a series of exhibition games Helen returned to New York and he went crazy. Broads and booze, day and night. Huggins fumed.

All the revelry caught up with him in Asheville where, running a high fever with a major pain in his belly, he collapsed. A local doctor diagnosed the flu and a severe intestinal attack. He was ordered to rest—no baseball, ease up on the food, lay off the sauce—but, as his train pulled into Penn Station, he collapsed again. The only way they could get him off the train was to remove the window of his Pullman car so that four burly guys could hoist him out on a stretcher. Helen was there crying, reporters and hundreds of onlookers saw it all. Total chaos. He was Babe Ruth, so it was big news. They called it "the bellyache heard round the world."

He spent the next seven weeks in St. Vincent's recuperating and was practically foaming at the mouth to get back on the ball field. It was while he was stuck in the hospital all that time that he realized the physical act of playing baseball was as important to him as sex, eating, and drinking, but it wasn't until June 1st that he was back in the lineup and that proved to be too soon. He found himself struggling mightily, hitting two-fifty, just a handful of homers. People began to doubt him. Even Fred Lieb, that sportswriter who had coined the phrase "The House That Ruth Built" when Yankee Stadium opened two years earlier, was writing that his best years were behind him.

Then things got worse. He no longer could abide Helen and he let her know it. So she went and had a nervous breakdown. Just to complicate things, he fell in love with a classy widow named Claire. What a mess! Then there was the flea who ordered him to do a couple of things in a game that didn't make any sense to him so he went and did it his way, the right way, and he told Huggins to go fuck himself.

The flea didn't know shit about baseball anyway. Then Huggins really got pissed off and suspended him and fined him $5,000, ten times more than anyone else had ever been fined in baseball! Well, he's Babe Ruth, the greatest ball player that ever played the game, and there was no way he was going to stand for that kind of treatment. So he left the team and took a train to Chicago to meet personally with Judge Landis, the Commissioner of Baseball. Only Landis refused to see him. So he headed to New York to meet with the Big Cheese, Jacob Ruppert, the owner of the Yankees. But Ruppert sided with Huggins and so did Barrow, the GM. Licked, he crawled to Huggins and begged to be reinstated. It took nine days but the flea finally agreed to let him suit up and return to the lineup. Too little too late for the Yankees who finished the season in seventh place. Ruth vowed that 1926 would be different.

The first thing he did during the off season was get his personal life squared away. He separated from Helen and practically moved in with Claire and her family where he led a domestic, quiet lifestyle...at least while he was in New York. He worked out like a fiend at Artie McGovern's gym and got his body hard and his muscles strong. He reported to spring training in St. Pete weighing two-twelve and was in the best shape since his early years with the Red Sox. He couldn't wait for the season to start. Today, though, is his thirty-first birthday and he plans on celebrating. He and a few of the boys are going to find some dames and eat and drink themselves silly.

After Ruth dropped Meusel and Gehrig off, he headed to the ritzy new Jungle Hotel, and the suite that he secured for the duration of spring training. The joint wouldn't officially open for another four days, but he was Babe Ruth and they made an exception for him. He stopped the new Packard that he rented for the next two months and tossed the key to the valet, handing him a buck.

"Park it up front for me, keed. I'll be going out again a little later."

"You bet, Mr. Ruth."

As the Babe sauntered into the lobby, he rubbed his chin. *Damn good shave she gave me*, he thought to himself, and then chuckled. "A lady barber. Whadda ya know about that!"

CHAPTER 4

It was the height of the season and the streets of St. Petersburg were alive with activity. The city, like many others in Florida, had grown dramatically, riding the boom in Florida real estate that had been going full bore since the beginning of the decade. Just in the past year five new hotels had been built or were under construction, employing hundreds of people.

It was one of those construction people Zel was looking for as she bounded up the steps of Mrs. Albright's Boarding House. She passed Mrs. Hartley, sitting stiffly in a rocking chair on the covered porch, with barely a nod of her head. Hartley, who was in her sixties, was a bluenose and looked down on Zel and most other girls in their twenties. Such a shameful and rebellious generation!

Zel found Mrs. Albright in her usual spot, the kitchen, where she was toiling over a preparation of some sort.

"Mrs. Albright, what you making?"

"None of your business," Fanny Albright said, warmly. "Just a little something special for brunch tomorrow."

Mrs. Albright served her boarders dinner every day of the week, except Saturday night, when they were on their own. In its place she served a special Sunday brunch and it was that meal for which she was preparing her surprise.

"Have you seen Horace?" Zel asked.

"Took his automobile this morning out to that house he's building. Been gone all day." She stopped and dipped a finger into the mixing bowl and then licked it. "I think you're going to like this, Zel."

Zel loved Mrs. Albright. From the first day Zel arrived, Mrs. Albright had treated her more like a daughter than a boarder. She was warm and caring and supportive. No wonder she reminded Zel of Mama. Of course, Zel hadn't missed a weekly payment and hadn't fooled herself into thinking Mrs. Albright wouldn't mind if she did. After all, the boarding house was a business and, as nice she was, Mrs. Albright was first and foremost a businesswoman.

"Your cheeks are red, dear. And you've got this look in your eyes. What's going on?"

"I've got a new customer." Zel's eyes widened as she spoke.

Mrs. Albright put down her mixing spoon and looked at Zel.

"You look like you're about to burst. Out with it!"

"Babe Ruth."

No further explanation was needed. Everyone knew the name Babe Ruth. He was simply the most famous person in America.

Now it was Mrs. Albright's eyes that got wide.

"Babe Ruth? You're kidding!"

"Nope. Gave him a cut and a shave and he made appointments for a shave every day next week," she beamed. "He says he never shaves himself. That's what barbers are for."

"Really!"

This *was* surprising news and Mrs. Albright found herself momentarily at a loss for words. She returned to mixing her concoction then paused and looked shrewdly at Zel. "How does he tip?" Mrs. Albright, the businesswoman.

"The biggest tip I ever got!"

"Good for you, honey. You were due to catch a break."

Zel looked at the clock on the wall.

"I've got to get going. Babysitting for Mrs. Dickerson." She headed to her room but stopped before leaving the kitchen and turned back to Mrs. Albright. "Don't say anything to Horace about Babe Ruth. I want to tell him myself."

"Don't know when Horace will be back. You know him, he might stay out there right through tomorrow. I won't say a word, though." She put down her mixing bowl. "What are you doing about dinner?"

Zel shrugged.

"You go get yourself ready and I'll make something up for you to take with you to Mrs. Dickerson's."

"Thanks, Mrs. Albright. You're the cat's pajamas!"

Mrs. Albright rolled her eyes. This flapper generation and their lingo!

CHAPTER 5

ZEL HAD A HABIT OF SLEEPING LATE ON SUNDAYS AND BY THE TIME SHE made her entrance into the dining room, brunch was well underway. Horace was nowhere to be seen. Disappointing.

Back in her room after brunch, Zel sat down at the small table that doubled as a writing desk and opened the journal she had kept since her arrival in St. Petersburg. Zel was no churchgoer, not since Mama and Joey died, but she religiously tended to her journal each Sunday, recording the highlights of the past week. She was thrilled with this week's highlight! Babe Ruth, a customer! A lucky break at last. She flipped to the next blank page of her journal and began writing.

Afterwards, she removed a folded piece of heavy duty paper from the table drawer, and opened it. It was her bank book and inside was the five dollar bill the Babe had given her. She checked her bank balance. It stood a little over half what it was when she arrived in St. Petersburg.

After getting settled at Mrs. Albright's, Zel had sat down and carefully calculated what she needed to earn to make ends meet. The Boarding House cost $9 per week which included her room, dinner every night except Saturday, Sunday brunch, and facilities to do her laundering and ironing. She needed an additional seventy cents per day to cover her daily

expenses: breakfast, lunch, a Dr. Pepper, an occasional picture show, and miscellaneous items like toiletries and the
chocolate candy she craved. Zel forced herself to set aside
another $1 per week for emergencies and to replace the shoes
and clothing she wore out. The total came to $14.90. She set
her weekly earnings goal at $15. But, after six months, she
had yet to reach her goal. Not even once.

She got paid half the price of a cut or shave plus tips.
This was Spud's standard arrangement with any barber who
worked in his shop. She had figured that, at a price of fifty
cents a cut or shave, half of which was hers, and an average
tip of a dime, she needed some combination of forty-three
shaves or haircuts to reach her goal. In her six day work
week, that meant seven customers a day. Zel was averag-
ing four a day, half of them children where the tips weren't
as good. That was why she had begun babysitting several
months ago.

But Babe Ruth, a regular customer? That could change
everything. Based on how he tipped her yesterday, it wasn't
unreasonable to think he would hand her a dollar for his
daily shave. That meant twenty-five cents to Spud and seventy-five cents to her, which would get her very close to her
weekly goal.

Zel laughed as she thought about how Horace would react when she told him about her new customer. Horace had
become a valued and loyal friend. In her first week at Spud's,
when she had nary a customer, it was Horace who showed
up one day for a haircut, though he barely needed one. She
had given him a tough time, not wanting anyone's chari-
ty, but he stood his ground. The next day several of his fellow construction workers showed up for haircuts, too. That
evening at dinner when she confronted Horace, he seemed
sincere when he said it was nothing more than some of the
men he worked with needing haircuts and asking him where
he got his.

"Nothing wrong with me telling them it was you," he had challenged her.

Zel wasn't sure she believed him but they kept on talking. Afterwards, they went for a walk and he bought her a Dr. Pepper. Soon they were going for walks every evening

She learned that Horace was an avid baseball fan and it was all he could talk about when his favorite team, the Pittsburgh Pirates, made it to the World Series that October and came back from a three games to one deficit to defeat the Washington Senators. While Horace's loyalties lay with the team from Pittsburgh, his favorite player, like so many other fans, was a New York Yankee—Babe Ruth—whose accomplishments he followed closely.

She couldn't wait to tell Horace about her newest customer!

CHAPTER 6

I<small>T WASN'T UNTIL AFTER SUNSET ON</small> S<small>UNDAY THAT</small> H<small>ORACE'S BEAT-UP</small>
Model T came chugging up to Mrs. Albright's. He was dog-
tired but excited, too. The house he was building was coming along nicely and he could see its completion was now
just a couple of months away.

He had a surprise for Zel that he planned on giving to
her the following Sunday, Valentine's Day; that is if he could
sneak it into his room without her seeing it and if he could
contain his enthusiasm. He wasn't very good at keeping
surprises under wraps, particularly when it came to Zel.
He hadn't told a soul about his biggest secret—his plans to
quit his construction job and start building houses on his
own, once he saved enough money to get started. But he
told Zel all about it during one of their evening walks. She
loved the idea and encouraged him not to wait too long. That
was one of the things he liked about her—she was so positive and confident and hardworking and a little crazy, too.
Zel seemed to love the Roaring Twenties vibe that was in
the air. Horace knew she imagined wearing flapper dresses,
dancing the Charleston, and sneaking into speakeasies to
drink bootlegged liquor. But her practical side and limited
funds allowed her none of those. He loved how she longed to

be a flapper when she wasn't anything like that at all. Yes, she talked like a flapper, throwing around all the jazzy new expressions of the day—none of your beeswax, you're the berries, that's copacetic—stuff like that. But the new lingo, which he himself used on occasion, did not a flapper make. She didn't run around town, thumb her nose at authority, and surely didn't lead a hedonistic life. In most ways, she was just like him—hardworking, earnest, and with her feet firmly on the ground. She was also beautiful and he was completely captivated by her fiery spirit, her resolve, and courage. This was a woman who, at the age of twenty-three, sold the family house and business, packed up her belongings, and ventured a thousand miles from Columbus, Ohio, to St. Petersburg, Florida. When she shared her sad story with him at the end of one of their first evening walks, Horace felt his heart melting. *What gumption she possessed!*

Their friendship grew and their evening strolls became the highlight of Horace's day. He just wished he could work up the nerve to give her a kiss and tell her how he felt. Well, he now had a plan for how that might happen and this was one plan he had no intention of sharing with her. It included the gift he had made for her which he tucked under his arm as he headed up the front steps of Mrs. Albright's Boarding House. Now if he could just sneak it into his room.

"Horace!" Zel called out to him, as he entered the front hallway.

Damn.

"How's the house coming along?" Zel asked.

"Another two months and it should be finished," he said, a gleam in his eye. "Can't wait to show it to you. Maybe we can make a picnic of it. We'll get Mrs. Albright to pack us a lunch, drive out there, and spend the day. What do you say, Zel?" He talked fast while easing the gift he had made for her to his side where, hopefully, she wouldn't notice it.

"That's jake with me, Horace." Zel could feel her face flush as she prepared to give him her big news. "I've got something to tell you, too. I've got a new customer..."

She paused.

"And?"

"...who goes by the name of Babe Ruth."

Horace craned his neck forward and looked at her suspiciously.

"Says you! You're joshing me."

"I'm leveling with you, Horace."

"Swear you're telling the truth!"

"I swear."

Zel described Ruth's surprise appearance with his two teammates, the Babe's selection of her to cut his hair and shave him, and his desire for a shave every day the following week.

Horace had but two questions.

"When is his appointment on Monday?"

"4 PM."

"How long will the shave take?"

"A half hour."

"Good. Schedule me for a haircut at 4:30."

Zel looked him over.

"Horace, you don't need a cut for at least another week."

"Doesn't matter. I'll be there early for my appointment, about 4:15."

"Horace,..." Zel started to say, but he interrupted her.

"As a matter of fact, put my boss down in your book for 5 PM."

Zel looked at him, puzzled.

"He's a big baseball fan. It's a chance to meet Babe Ruth. He'll jump at it." Horace went to smack his hands together, his house plans and Zel's Valentine's gift forgotten for the moment. "Babe Ruth. I'll be damned!"

Zel smiled quietly. *Babe Ruth is going to be good for business.* Then she noticed the wooden box in Horace's hand.

"What you got there, Horace?"

Horace tried to hide the box but it was too late. He could feel his face flush.

"Oh, it's nothing. Just something I was working on."

Zel could read Horace like a book. By the blush on his face, it was something of importance that he didn't want her to see.

"Can I see it?" She didn't wait for his answer but walked up to him and took it out of his hand.

Horace shifted uncomfortably.

"Aw, Zel. It's supposed to be a..."

"Horace, this is beautiful!"

It was a carefully constructed wooden box, about one inch high, twelve inches long, and a few inches less than that wide. There were brass hinges and a small latch that secured the top to the bottom. The top of the box was deep mahogany in color and had, at its center, an intricate, inlaid carving of the letter Z. Zel flipped the latch and opened the top. The inside of the box was empty but was lined with a smooth fabric, lighter in color than the outside of the box.

Zel looked at Horace.

"This is beautiful," she repeated herself. "But what is it?"

Horace squirmed. "It's supposed to be a Valentine's Day present."

"For whom?" she asked, innocently.

"For you." He sighed. "There goes my surprise. I was going to give it to you next Sunday, on Valentine's Day, but I guess you can have it now."

"Why thank you Horace." She hesitated. "It's a handsome box."

By the way she spoke Horace could tell she didn't understand its purpose.

"It's a box to keep your journal in, Zel. You're always telling me how you write in it every Sunday so I figured it must be pretty important to you. If you keep it in here," he said, pointing to the box, "it will stay nice and safe."

Zel was touched.

"Horace, that is so thoughtful of you. Thank you so much!"

She lovingly closed the box, put it on a nearby table, and gave Horace a big hug with both arms, squeezing him tightly.

Horace was overcome. This was the closest they had ever been to each other. He felt dizzy. He didn't know what to do next. Should he hug her back? Kiss her? When it came to intimacy, he, who was so confident in all other aspects of his life, was at a loss.

The moment passed.

"Oh, it's just a little something. No big deal," he spluttered.

Zel was pleased as punch.

"I'm going to my room and put my journal in it right now." She turned to leave. "See you tomorrow at 4:15. And thanks for not waiting until Valentine's Day to give me this," she said, as she carefully held up the magnificent box he had made for her. *What a special friend Horace is*, she thought.

Horace let out a long sigh as he watched her dash up the stairs.

CHAPTER 7

ZEL WAS RELIEVED AND NERVOUS WHEN BABE RUTH SHOWED UP MONDAY afternoon for his shave. Relieved that he kept his appointment; nervous that he would be satisfied with the shave she gave him. It got her nerves jangling thinking that the most famous person in the entire country would be sitting in her chair; it was a once-in-a-lifetime opportunity. But she quickly found herself relaxed and comfortable with her favorite new customer. The Babe made it easy. For all his popularity and fame, he turned out to be a regular Joe. He talked a blue streak and seemed to go out of his way to put her at ease. He told her about the bad season he had in 1925, how he was determined to have a great year in 1926, and went on at great lengths about all the hard work he had done to get himself in shape. It reached the point where, after he was lathered, she had to ask him to stop talking so she could shave him. And he handed her $2 after every shave. A dollar and a half tip, which put her over her $15 per week goal. Finally!

When Horace walked into Spud's at 4:15 on Monday he could not believe his eyes when he saw Babe Ruth sitting in Zel's chair as she carefully shaved him. Zel swelled with pride as she introduced him to Ruth. It was the first time she had ever seen Horace speechless. Horace shook Babe's hand energetically as he stumbled over his words.

"Nice to meet you, keed," said Ruth, laughing.

Every evening thereafter, Horace's first words to Zel were "how was the Babe's shave today?" Zel found herself surprisingly pleased by Horace's increased attention.

The day before Valentine's Day, the Babe showed up with a present of his own for Zel. It was a brand new baseball which he carefully signed his name to using Spud's pen. Spud was not the least bit happy but Zel was overjoyed. She let it sit on the shelf in front of her mirror until the ink dried. Then she carefully wrapped it in a towel and put it in her purse.

By the following week, Zel noticed that the almost universal resistance to being cared for by a lady barber had begun to crumble as several regulars asked her for a shave or cut.

"So, keed," Babe asked her that Saturday. "When should I get my hair cut again?" Although he had an appointment six days a week, Ruth never called Zel by her name. It was always "keed." It took her a while but she finally realized he had no idea what her name was or, it seemed, anyone else's.

"How often do you usually have it cut?"

"Who the hell knows. Whenever I get a chance."

"If you're asking me, a man of your stature and fame should have his hair cut every two weeks. You don't ever want to be looking sloppy." She paused. "Like when you first came in here."

Ruth was pleased with her answer.

"Yeah, yeah. I know. So, when would that be?"

Zel looked at her appointment book.

"Actually, that would be today."

He had a hot date in about an hour.

"Can't stay any longer today; somewhere I gotta be. Let's make it Monday." Babe paused and looked at her through the mirror that faced him as he sat in her chair. "How's the barbering business these days? You make a good living?"

Zel hesitated. How truthful should she be? Better to let him think she was successful rather than just getting by.

"Business is fine." She smiled back at him in the mirror. "And getting better since you became a customer."

"Ah, it's nuthin'. You're good!" Babe looked at the customers being worked on by Spud and Frawley. "These guys give you a tough time? Being a dame and all?"

She hesitated again.

"Come on, keed. You can level with me."

"They've been slow to come around," she said quietly, so the others couldn't hear.

"I'll bet," Ruth replied, speaking softly, too. "Ah, they're just a bunch of huckleberries. What do they know!"

"Well, a few of them have begun to see the light since you became my customer," she said, as she carefully placed a steaming towel over his face.

Ruth groaned.

"I can do better than that," he said, his voice muffled by the hot cloth. After a minute, Zel removed the towel. "Monday," he said. "We'll show them Monday."

Ruth hopped out of Zel's chair, pulled a disorganized wad of bills out of his pocket, selected two singles, and handed them to her. "See you Monday, keed." Then he winked at her. "Look good!"

As he walked towards the front of the shop a chorus of men called to him, "Take care, Babe."

"See ya, boys!" he said breezily, as he exited the door.

CHAPTER 8

JUPITER, FLORIDA
JANUARY, 2013

SEE THE BALL, HIT THE BALL.

See the ball, hit the ball.

See the ball, hit the ball.

It had become Ryan's mantra in the batter's box and out, a metaphor for his life, particularly when his thoughts got jumbled and he found himself starting to look inward and back. See the ball, hit the ball. Keep it simple, uncluttered, and looking forward. It seemed to be helping.

Baseball.

A compromise he had agreed to with his mom and Caitlin.

Sports—football, basketball, baseball, lacrosse—had been a huge part of his life before the accident. Football was his favorite, but after the crash it was impossible to step back on that field. In fact, he wanted nothing to do with sports at all. But it bothered Mom, and Michael, too. After a while they started to push him ever so gently to resume playing. If football was too difficult emotionally, then he should choose another of his old favorites.

"It's time to get back on the horse, Ryan," Caitlin had encouraged.

"Not football," Ryan said adamantly.

"It doesn't matter which sport it is, Ryan," she said gently. "Some sport though. You're a competitive guy and an athlete. Those traits are part of who you are. Playing a sport, any sport, will allow you to rediscover those parts of yourself. Give it some thought. When you feel you're ready, pick one. Okay?"

"I'll think about it," he said, grudgingly.

"Good. It would be another step forward for you."

Ryan sighed. He was so tired of people telling him to move forward. His mom. Michael. Caitlin. His teachers. He wanted to "move forward" but it wasn't that simple. He wasn't unhappy hanging out in his room, reading, doing his schoolwork, playing video games. It was easy to be there, not thinking about anything, not caring about anything. Not scared that everything that mattered was going to be swept away in an instant.

When his mother brought up trying out for a team again a few weeks later, Ryan exploded and yelled that it was his life. Susan's face had fallen and tears pricked her eyes. Remorse flooded Ryan. What had he done? He'd just yelled at the one person he loved more than anyone else. He knew his mom just wanted to help but he hadn't been able to control his reaction. Without another word, he turned and fled to his room. Laying on his bed, he'd thought about the year and a half since the accident and wondered what had happened to that time. When Susan knocked on his door later, he was sheepish. He apologized for yelling. She sat on the edge of the bed next to him like she had when he was a small child.

"I just want you to be happy again, Ryan."

"I know." And then Ryan had taken a step forward and told her he would try baseball. He didn't have any special love of baseball, but it was the middle of the season. He could play immediately before he might have a change of heart.

Michael was thrilled when Ryan told him he had talked with the baseball coach, Coach Carruther, about playing and how the coach immediately added him to the team. Michael had reacted very differently to the accident from Ryan. He was overwhelmingly relieved that he had survived. He was sitting right behind the driver's seat when the other vehicle smashed into them at fifty miles per hour. But for the fact that it hit their SUV front of center Michael would have died just like his father. The rescue personnel determined that the airbag did its job, saving his life, while the doctors who worked on him thought it miraculous that he emerged unbroken except for his left leg, which was crushed beyond repair and had to be amputated halfway between his knee and hip. Unlike Ryan, Michael was able to mourn his father's death unencumbered by guilt. He wept and grieved while his heart broke but after a while he began to focus on the momentous task that lay ahead of him—learning to walk under decidedly adverse circumstances. His determination to overcome the fate that had befallen him emerged early and never wavered. Not once had he looked back or felt sorry for himself.

Michael recognized that it was a step forward in Ryan's recovery when Ryan started playing baseball and he immediately became his brother's biggest fan and cheerleader. This helped Ryan persevere through the first couple of awkward weeks as a new member of an established team. Ryan struggled to find his timing in the batter's box, but he was a gifted athlete and his defense was superb. It seemed that he had a natural instinct in the field. He knew where a ball was going the moment it left the hitter's bat. It was nothing he had to think about. He always knew what to do when a ball was hit to him—the quickest route to get to the ball and where to throw it when it reached him. And his arm was something special. His throws were laser beams—powerful, precise, and on target. Ryan found playing defense to be effortless. His head stayed clear and when a ball was hit his way, he simply took off after it. No thinking, pure reaction.

Hitting was another story. His mind filled with all sorts of thoughts once he stepped into the batter's box. Not all the time, but it didn't seem to be anything he had control over. When his head was clear and he felt able to concentrate on the pitched ball, he could sock it. Coach was constantly telling him to clear his mind and just "See the ball, hit the ball."

Ironically, Coach's mantra seemed to be helping more when he was out of the batter's box, out leading his life, not playing ball. There were longer and longer stretches when he was able to get outside himself and just be himself, the way he used to be, enjoying the people and the scene around him. His mom had noticed there were more frequent smiles on his face, occasional laughter in his voice and far less of the depression, brooding, and sadness that had smothered his joy of life. She hoped he had turned some mental corner and was starting to make steady progress. She wasn't shy about telling him how happy it made her to see him taking these steps. Meanwhile, Caitlin kept him grounded with her warning that progress would be a "two-steps-forward, one-step-back" process. Lately, he had been moving in one direction—forward.

Not so the case in the batter's box, where results continued on a hit or miss basis.

He had begun to have spectacularly successful ball games interspersed with miserable performances. Four for five with a couple of extra base hits one day, zero for four with three strike outs the next game. There seemed to be no rhyme or reason to his hitting and it drove Coach Carruther crazy. That's why Coach had him here today for extra batting practice.

"See the ball, hit the ball," the Coach repeated to him. "That's all you gotta do, Ryan. Keep it simple and your swing will take care of the rest."

Easier said than done.

CHAPTER 9

TWO YEARS AFTER THE ACCIDENT SUSAN WAS FEELING GOOD ABOUT THE progress the Buck family was making.

Michael was simply remarkable. He had adapted to the loss of his leg without missing a step. She shook her head at the simile but it was the truth, and a testament to his determination to make the most of the life that he was so appreciative to have.

Ryan was a lot more problematic. She still had sleepless nights over him. While he had emerged from the crash in much better physical shape than Michael, it turned out that he was a lot more damaged than his younger brother. Caitlin had an explanation—different personalities, different emotional makeup, and, most significantly, a different perspective on what occurred. Michael saw himself as a victim who was lucky to be alive. Ryan viewed himself as a contributing cause of the accident.

"But that's ridiculous!" Susan had exclaimed, at the time.

"Not to Ryan," said Caitlin. "It's very real to him."

"Please help me to understand. I need to understand," she pleaded.

Caitlin shifted positions and took a gulp from the ever present mug of coffee she kept within easy reach.

"Part of it is easy to understand. His father and brother were at the game to see him play quarterback. In Ryan's mind, if he wasn't playing there wouldn't have been any accident." Caitlin took another sip of coffee. "But there's more. Ryan has an undefined sense of guilt that he is unable to identify. It causes him unease and, at times, great anxiety. But what the exact nature of his guilt is, he doesn't know and neither do I."

That conversation was over a year ago, and Susan kept coming back to it even now.

Today, Susan was having one of her periodic sessions with Caitlin to get an update on how Ryan was progressing. Her mug in hand, Caitlin settled into her spacious armchair as Susan started the conversation.

"Ryan seems to be doing really well the past couple of months. I'm feeling optimistic."

'You should be. He definitely seems happier and more comfortable with himself. How is he at home?"

"Good. He's relaxed and actually pleasant most of the time. There's a lot less of the watchdog personality and he even fights with his brother on occasion; in a healthy, normal way. And his appetite has come all the way back. He and Michael eat more than three horses do."

Caitlin smiled. "All encouraging signs." She took a sip from the mug. "I just need to caution you that it would be very normal if Ryan regresses and takes a step or two backwards."

Susan got a pained look on her face.

"Caitlin, please tell me the worst is over."

"I believe it is. Ryan is in a lot better shape. He's more knowledgeable about what he and the rest of you have gone through. He has insight." Another sip of coffee. "But there are issues he still has to face and come to terms with."

"The dream?"

"It's much more contained than it was. Ryan has made real progress in being able to manage it, for lack of a better word. But there's always the possibility that he will remember something about the accident that his mind has so far repressed. If that occurs, it will be something he will have to deal with."

"You've been working with him for two years. What do you think? Will he ever remember the accident?"

Caitlin paused and gathered her thoughts.

"Sometimes an event or action can trigger recall, causing a flood of repressed memories to suddenly reappear. Our minds have a tendency to let us remember the unthinkable when we are finally at a point where we can handle the news." She shrugged. "Having said that, there's really no way of knowing."

"What should I be doing?"

"Doing?" Caitlin thought for a moment. "You should be enjoying your children." She took another gulp and shifted gears. "What about you? How's your business going?"

"Paying all our bills and keeping our heads above water," Susan said, cheerfully.

After the accident she had successfully developed her own business as a headhunter. It allowed her to be there for her boys and meet the family's day-to-day financial obligations which included home care for her father. But it didn't take into account the extra expense of a new prosthetic leg which Michael would soon need. She hadn't yet figured out how she would pay for those expenses.

"Have you found any time for yourself?"

"For myself?"

Time for herself was nothing she had given a thought to, unless you counted her work. She didn't think that was what Caitlin meant. Susan interpreted Caitlin's question as a roundabout way of asking about her social life, as in "any interest in dating", a subject Caitlin first introduced a few months earlier. But that was the furthest thing from Susan's mind. Her entire being was focused on her children, who were her entire world. Besides, Bill would always be her man.

"We've settled into a nice routine the past couple of months," she reflected. "That makes me happy."

"You've all worked hard to get to this point. Enjoy it...and keep on working."

CHAPTER 10

ST. PETERSBURG, FLORIDA
1926

At 4 PM on Monday, Babe Ruth walked into Spud's Barber Shop with a photographer from the *St. Petersburg Times* in tow.

Zel had heeded his casual admonition to 'look good' and had put a touch of make-up on and wore her best barber's frock, even though she had no idea what the Babe had in mind.

As Ruth made himself comfortable in Zel's chair, the photographer got right down to business. He staged a couple of photos of Zel cutting the Babe's hair, then he had them switch positions, with Zel in the chair and Ruth holding a pair of scissors, pretending to cut her hair. Zel couldn't stop laughing and the photographer had to take a few extra shots until he got one he could use. Finally, he took shots of the Yankee slugger lathered up and ready for a shave, one of them with a cigar in his mouth. Then, he was gone. The whole thing hadn't taken more than fifteen minutes.

Zel loved every minute of it. It was exciting and a break from her daily routine.

"What was that about, Babe?"

"That guy's a pal of mine. He's gonna give those photos to his editor and see if they'll put a story in their paper about you being my barber and all. That should get you a bunch more customers."

Zel was overwhelmed. Here was this very important man going out of his way to do that for her. *Babe Ruth...he's the berries!!*

That Sunday, Zel wrote in her journal about her favorite customer and what a dream he was.

The next week, early one morning, the photographer showed up at Spud's, looking for Zel. He had a large envelope in his hand.

"These are for you," he said, all business. "The Babe thought you might like them."

Zel pulled two photos out of the envelope. One was a picture of the Babe pretending to cut her hair as she sat in her chair. The other was the picture of her with the straight-edge in her hand, about to shave a lathered Ruth who was sitting straight-faced with a big cigar poking out of his mouth."

"These are the cat's meow!" she said. "When will they be in the paper?"

"Not gonna happen," the photographer said. "The editor put the kibosh on them. But he said he's gonna give you a blurb at the end of one of the spring training stories this week." He shrugged. "Sorry lady, it's the best I could do."

Zel nodded her head and thanked him.

"Let the Babe know I tried. Okay?"

She nodded again as he exited the shop.

Zel looked at the photos and carefully returned them to the envelope. She put the envelope safely away and turned back to business. She had a customer waiting.

As February turned to March, spring training games began in earnest. The story about Zel finally appeared at the end of a recap of the day's game. It was just a paragraph and spoke about how the Great Bambino, one of Ruth's colorful nicknames, had chosen a lady barber to cut his hair and shave his face while he was in St. Pete. She was mentioned by name as was Spud's shop. The next day she had seven new customers and it continued that way for the next two weeks. All of a sudden Zel found herself busier than Spud or Bill Frawley. Her appointment book was full for the next month.

Any nervousness she had around the big man had long since disappeared. Ruth had a million stories he shared with her and she, in turn, told him about her life, her friend Horace, Mrs. Albright, and even Lady Bluenose. They had become friends and she idolized him. He, in turn, loved bestowing favors on her. One day he handed her two tickets to a spring training game over the coming weekend.

"Why don't you bring your friend along," the Babe said, referring to Horace, as he lit up a cigar. "Best seats in the house and I'll hit a home run for you." He handed her two bucks and rubbed his chin. "You give a helluva shave, keed."

That night Zel showed Horace the tickets.

"Front row seats!" Horace exclaimed. "It's a Sunday game so I'll just work on the house Saturday. I'm not going to miss this."

He had put himself on a tight schedule—finish the house no later than the end of March. Horace wanted to see if he could keep on track which would be important when he became a full-time builder. But front row seats to see Babe Ruth and the New York Yankees! The hell with the schedule!

—

Not only were the seats in the first row but they were adjacent to the Yankee dugout. The ballplayers weren't more than ten feet from where Zel and Horace sat.

Zel recognized the two Yankees who had accompanied the Babe the first time he entered Spud's and pointed them out to Horace.

"One of them is Bob Meusel," he said, excitedly. "He's a star. Plays the outfield, just like the Babe. The other guy is Gehrig, I think. He's the first baseman. A newcomer."

Just before the game started Ruth walked over to them.

"How do you like the seats, keed?"

"They're the berries, Babe!" Zel smiled from ear-to-ear. "Thanks a lot!"

"Ah, it's nuthin."

"Babe," Horace interjected. "Zel says you're going to hit a homer for her today."

"Gonna try, keed. Gonna try." He gave a wink and then headed out to right field.

"Zel, everyone is looking at us," Horace said, as he glanced around. "Bet they're wondering who we are!"

Zel gleamed. "We're friends of the greatest baseball player in the world! That's who we are. He's the bee's knees!"

The Babe came to bat in the eighth. The pitcher wound up and threw a ball that almost took Ruth's head off. The Yankee star had to dive out of the way and was left sprawling on the ground, covered in dirt. Ruth stood up, dusted off his uniform, glared back at the pitcher, and dug in. On the next swing he hit a towering fly ball that carried well beyond the centerfield fence. The Babe played to the crowd as he slowly circled the bases. As he crossed home plate he took off his cap and waved it to his legion of fans who cheered him loudly. They had come to the ballpark to see him hit a home run and he had just delivered.

Ruth, hat in hand, kept waving all the way to the dug-out. Then he caught Zel's eye and tossed her his cap. She caught it on the fly as the fans' cheers got louder. Unsure what to do, she stood and curtsied to the Babe, then waved to the crowd and put his hat on her head. Ruth pointed to her and, with a big smile on his face, gave her a bow and then headed into the dugout. What an experience!

When the game ended, Zel and Horace remained in their seats as the rest of the fans trickled out of the ballpark. After a while, the Babe came over.

Zel called out to him. "Thanks for the cap, Babe!"

"What a homer, Babe," Horace said, shaking Ruth's hand vigorously.

"That pitcher went headhunting. Guess he didn't know chin music brings out the best in me. Glad I knocked it out of the park for you," he said to Zel.

"Do you think I could just hold your bat, Babe," Horace asked, tentatively. "Maybe take a swing? I've always wondered what it would feel like."

Ruth chuckled. "Sure, why not."

He disappeared into the dugout and popped out with it.

"Here you go, keed. Knock yourself out."

Horace took the bat from him, gripped it tightly at the handle with both hands, and, with a wondrous look in his eyes, carefully swung it back and forth. Horace was strong; fit, too. But the bat was heavier than he ever imagined. He looked at Ruth with awe. It was astonishing to him that anyone could swing this massive club fast enough to hit a fast-ball thrown by the likes of Walter Johnson.

"You like it?" Ruth asked.

"Like it? It's, it's..." Horace struggled to find the right word. "It's amazing," he said, reverentially. Reluctantly, he handed the bat back to Ruth. "Thanks for letting me hold it, Babe."

"Why don't you keep it, keed. You seem to get a lot of pleasure out of it."

"I couldn't," Horace protested.

"Sure you can. Besides, I got two dozen more just like that one."

Horace didn't know what to say. "Thank you, Babe. Thank you," he spluttered.

Afterwards, as Zel and Horace walked back to Mrs. Albright's, she with her cap, he with his bat; they both had smiles on their faces.

"I'll bet we're his two biggest fans in the entire country," Horace said.

"I am for sure," Zel replied. "What's chin music, anyway?"

"When a pitcher throws a ball at the batter's chin or head. Usually makes the batter think twice about getting too comfortable in the batter's box. Doesn't seem to work with the Babe, though."

"You can say that again!"

CHAPTER 11

WHILE JUST A MONTH EARLIER ZEL'S WORK WEEK SLOWLY HAD DRAGGED on, her days were now so busy that, before she knew it, the week had flown by. She was now seeing upwards of a dozen customers a day and, because her tips improved as well, clearing $35 a week; not sufficient for her to buy that yellow flapper dress she loved but enough that she was able to start saving real money. She was riding high and she owed it all to Babe Ruth.

So, it was a big letdown for her when the Babe announced at the conclusion of his shave one afternoon, that he would be leaving the end of the following week. Spring training was coming to an end and the Yankees were heading north in ten days. Zel had known this was going to happen but it snuck up on her a lot quicker than she expected.

"Well then, Babe," she said, gathering her thoughts, "we better schedule your last haircut before you abandon us. Don't want your New York fans up north to see you looking scruffy."

"I'm gonna miss you, keed. You've taken good care of me."

"Not any better than you've taken care of me."

Zel forced a smile on her face as she penciled him in for a cut the following Tuesday.

Babe watched her in the mirror as she stood over her appointment book.

"Now don't go getting sad on me," he said. "You know, we've had such a good time that we oughta celebrate, not get down in the dumps. Let's have a party! You're always talking about how you want to go dancing and to a speakeasy. Well let's do it!"

Zel perked up.

"I'll arrange for everything," he said. "We'll have music and food and booze, all in my suite."

"Not a speakeasy?"

Ruth got a pained expression on his face.

"I can't go out in public, I'll get mobbed! People don't leave me alone. Believe me, it'll be a lot better if we can do it in my suite. It's a big place." He watched her as she seemed to hesitate. "Oh, and bring along that friend of yours, the guy I gave the bat. He seems like a good Joe."

"Horace?"

"Yeah, him."

Even though Zel feared life would be shades duller when her favorite customer left town, she couldn't dwell on it. She was too excited about the prospect of the party the Babe had just outlined.

"Sounds jake to me, Babe. I'll let Horace know." *But might not three be awkward?*

Ruth reached in his pocket and pulled out his usual disheveled wad of bills. He grabbed two dollars and handed it to her.

"Thanks for the shave," he said.

Then he dug around in the pile and pulled out another bill and handed it to her. It was a hundred dollar bill, the first Zel had ever seen. "Take this and get yourself that yellow dress you're always talking about. You can wear it to our party and be a real flapper."

Zel was astonished.

"Babe, I can't," she said, emphatically. She extended the hundred back to him.

"Sure you can. Don't worry about it. There's plenty more where that came from." Then he got a stern look on his face. "But there's one condition."

"What's that?"

"You have to use it to buy that dress. No saving it like you do with all the other money I give you. We got a deal?"

Zel couldn't keep the smile off her face.

"It's a deal. Babe, you're the bees knees!"

He smiled and got a twinkle in his eye.

"Yeah. That's the way I like it. See ya, keed," he said, as he turned and headed out the door.

CHAPTER 12

A FEW MINUTES AFTER 8 PM ZEL RAISED HER HAND AND KNOCKED ON the door of Babe Ruth's suite at the sparkling new Jungle Hotel. She was dressed in the yellow flapper dress she had coveted for so long but never ever imagined wearing. On her head was a white cloche accented with a thin yellow ribbon that perfectly matched her dress. She was the embodiment of a flapper.

Earlier in the week, before she could even mention Babe's invitation, Horace had told her he would be working the entire weekend and she decided on the spot not to say a word about the party to him. She had wrestled with whether or not to tell him. She knew Horace would jump at it but the idea of dining alone with Babe Ruth, the star of the New York Yankees, was thrilling! But Horace's work schedule had made her decision easy. When Ruth had come for his haircut, she informed him that Horace would not be able to make the party. But Zel reassured him that she had no intention of passing up what was sure to be an exciting evening. After all, how many chances would a girl like her get to dine and drink in a suite at the swanky Jungle Hotel?

As the Babe settled into her chair for his final haircut before heading north he asked Zel what she liked to drink.

"Rum and Dr. Pepper, my favorite."

Ruth let out a belly laugh.

"Glad I asked. I'll make sure we have the necessary ingredients!"

Knowing it was to be the Babe's last haircut, Zel had planned carefully. While he was busy talking to her, she took several fingers-full of his hair she had just cut and quietly placed them into an envelope she had brought along specifically for that purpose. She wanted something that was a physical remembrance of the famous Yankee slugger who had been her customer and who had done so much for her. She carefully set the envelope aside.

That was Tuesday.

It seemed longer than usual for Saturday to roll around but here she was, standing outside his suite. Zel adjusted her hat, squared her shoulders, and knocked again.

When the door opened, there stood Babe Ruth in a maroon smoking jacket and a drink in each hand. The scent of bay rum floated in the air as he greeted her.

"Keed," he said, as he looked her up and down. "You look great in that dress. Best hundred bucks I ever spent!" He gave her the drink he held in his left hand. "Rum and Dr. Pepper, just like you ordered. Come in and make yourself at home."

Zel felt magical as she glided into the suite. But as Babe closed the door behind her, a fleeting thought passed through her mind, *he remembers what I drink but never remembers my name...*

CHAPTER 13

A KNOCK, KNOCK, KNOCKING ON THE DOOR SLOWLY INVADED HER SLEEP.

"What?" Zel, said sleepily. "Who's there?" she said, louder.

"Zel, it's me, Fannie Albright. It's 10 AM. I wanted to make sure you're all right. Not like you to sleep this late, even on a Sunday. Everything okay?"

Groggy, Zel rolled on her back and tried to sit up.

"I'm fine, Mrs. Albright. I guess I needed the extra sleep."

"Get in late last night?"

"Not particularly," she lied. "Just feeling a little lazy this morning."

Zel hadn't told a soul last night about her dinner with Babe Ruth. When it was time for her to leave for his hotel she had snuck out the side door of Mrs. Albright's. Getting back in was less of a problem. It was so late that everyone was sound asleep.

"You're entitled, dear," Mrs. Albright said, sympathetically. "Just didn't want you to miss brunch."

"Thanks, Mrs. Albright," Zel called out. "I'll be down in a bit."

Zel collapsed back on her pillow. She felt exhausted, not a bit of energy in her. As she lay there, her head began to swim. Her memory was a hazy jumble. She couldn't even remember how many drinks she had last night. She gave a shudder. What a crazy night!

With great effort, she pushed herself up on her elbows and looked around her room. The yellow dress hung carelessly over the chair by her writing desk. Her cloche was nowhere to be seen. Zel moaned to herself as her head began to clear and her recollections of the prior evening became sharper. She shuddered.

"What have I done?" she said, softly.

She shook her head as she examined her feelings. Shame, remorse, amazement, and exhilaration flooded her. She couldn't believe how she had acted but underneath was the thrill of the experience.

Zel hauled herself out of bed, staggered a bit to the washbowl, splashed water over her face, and brushed her teeth. That helped. She felt almost human.

She took her yellow dress off of the chair and carefully hung it in her closet. She started to get dressed but, preoccupied, stopped and sat on the edge of her bed. After a few minutes, she moved to her chair, pulled out the wooden box Horace had made for her, opened it, and removed her journal. *What should I say? How shall I write it?* She turned to a blank page, paused for a moment, and began writing.

By the time Zel made it to brunch practically all the food was gone. It didn't matter though because Horace had unexpectedly showed up and he was jumping with excitement.

"Zel," he said, beaming. "I've got a surprise for you!"

"Horace," she said. "What are you doing here? I thought you were spending the weekend working on your house."

She wasn't expecting to see Horace and she felt self-conscious when he looked at her. Could he tell she had been out last night without him? It wasn't like they had an agreement but Zel had a strange feeling she couldn't quite identify fluttering her stomach and heart.

"Zel, come with me. I've got a picnic lunch all packed and waiting in the Ford. There's something I want to show you!" Horace was practically bursting at his seams.

"It's finished?"

"Uh-huh," he nodded, enthusiastically. "The house is done!"

Zel knew this was a very big moment for Horace. He had been laboring hard for months to reach this point. As tired as she was, it wouldn't be right for her to decline. *Besides, it will keep me busy and my mind off other thoughts, which will be a good thing.* She screwed up her strength.

"Okay," she smiled. "Let's go! I can't wait to see it!"

They headed northeast out of town, a twenty minute ride in Horace's Model T. Horace was really wound up. He talked a blue streak all the way there, explaining in great detail the many considerations that went into completing his house, what he had learned, and how he intended to use his knowledge when he got into full-time building.

When they arrived at their destination, Horace leaped out of the car, ran around to the other side, and opened Zel's door before she could move a muscle. With a flourish, he bowed.

"Welcome to my castle, fair maiden," he said, gallantly.

"Why, thank you Horace. You are a true knight in shining armor," she said, mustering a smile and playing along with him.

"Please, let me show you the way."

He took her arm, guided her up to a white picket fence and opened the gate. They walked up a flagstone walk at the end of which, Horace bowed again.

"My humble abode awaits you."

He gestured to the front door with a sweep of his arm.

Zel walked into the house and marveled at Horace's achievement. The house had two bedrooms, a sitting room, kitchen, bathroom, and laundry room. It was electrified and had indoor plumbing. A modern house in all respects. The finish work was impressive.

"Horace, this is quite an accomplishment! First class in every way. I just love it!"

Horace glowed with pride at Zel's comments.

"It sits on an acre of land and it will be easy to expand the house in the future. You know, add another bedroom or two."

Horace guided her out the back of the house, spread a blanket on the grass, and took out their lunch. It was a beautiful late-March day, perfect for a picnic. They sat quietly and ate their sandwiches, soaking in the peacefulness of the country.

Zel was glad she had come. The fresh air made her feel better. Out of the city the horizon seemed far off and the sky went on forever. Whatever concerns she had seemed small and insignificant out here.

"I guess this means you'll be leaving Mrs. Albright's and moving into your new house," Zel said, taking the last bite of her sandwich.

"Probably next week sometime."

"You've been an excellent fellow boarder, Horace. A good friend, too. I'm going to miss you and our walks and talks." She reached over and patted his hand. She felt that strange feeling in her stomach again, like a fluttering butterfly. Was she nervous? Sad? She wasn't sure. "I guess this means I'll be buying my own Dr. Peppers from now on."

Horace looked at her and gripped her hand tightly.

"Zel."

His face flushed and he stopped.

"Zel, I love you. I've loved you since the moment we first met, eight months ago. Not only do I love you but you're my best friend, too. Our walks and talks are the highlights of my day." He paused for a moment. "All the while I've been working away out here I thought it would be perfect if the two of us left Mrs. Albright's together and moved into this house as man and wife."

He stood up and then knelt on one knee.

"Zel, give me the honor of buying you Dr. Peppers for the rest of your life. Marry me!"

Zel's head swam. The sky began to spin. She reached out to steady herself but all she got was a handful of air. She turned chalk white and started to sway as the blood drained from her face. The fluttering in her stomach became a flock of butterflies beating to get out. She felt completely overwhelmed.

Horace looked at her with concern.

"Zel, are you all right? You look pale."

Zel tried to smile and reassure him but before she could utter a word she fainted dead-away.

CHAPTER 14

As Susan wandered down one of the seemingly endless aisles in the cavernous Convention Center, she was having misgivings about the snap decision she made that morning. Over breakfast, while flipping through the newspaper, she had read an article about the National Sports Memorabilia annual convention that was taking place at the Orlando Center. On an impulse she jumped in her car and drove to Orlando, an old baseball card carefully nested in her handbag. In need of extra funds, she decided to find out what she might get for it.

Preoccupied, the two-and-a-half hour ride flew by as she drove without conscious thought. The decision to sell the Babe Ruth memorabilia that had been in her family for generations was, in her mind, as controversial as the items themselves. It was an issue she had wrestled with for quite some time. Once again, she weighed the pros and cons of selling them. On the one hand they were a direct link to her great grandmother, Zel, a woman she greatly admired. Although Zel died the year before she was born, Susan felt as if she knew her well. Zel's journal, which she had read numerous times, had brought her great grandmother to life.

Zel was a favorite of her mom, as well, which made her decision to sell the memorabilia feel like a betrayal. That was a
definite con. On the other hand, the memorabilia were not
without controversy. For one thing, Grandma Annie had an
entirely different opinion of the Ruth items, not that she ever
talked about it. But it was clear by the set of her jaw and the
faraway look in her eye, that, whenever the subject of Zel,
St Petersburg, or Babe Ruth came up, Annie wasn't happy.
And, she had kept the Ruth artifacts and Zel's journal hidden away. It wasn't until after Annie passed that Susan got
her first glimpse of them.

   It all came down to the interpretation of one particular
entry in the diary. Susan and her mom read it one way. Her
dad and Grandma Annie read it differently. Over time, it
had become a major source of friction between her parents.
Susan shuddered as she recalled the fight that was seared
into her memory, the one she had overheard when she was
twelve years old. Her moralistic father, in need of money and
with no attachment to the memorabilia, had seethed at her
mom one evening. "You and your fancy airs about Zel and
Babe Ruth. You're afraid to face the truth! Your grandmother
was nothing but a whore, a cheap whore at that! Gave herself up for what? A bat and ball? Those Ruth items are nothing more than the wages of sin. We should be rid of them!"
To this day, Susan couldn't decide whether she was more
shocked by how her father had spoken to her mom or by the
accusation he had made. Either way, after that incident, she
never thought of him in the same way. Selling the memorabilia would, in a way, remove the dispute that had strained
family relationships over many generations. These reasons
were the pros. But the biggest pro of all was the money the
sale of the Ruth memorabilia might hopefully bring. Michael
would soon outgrow his prosthesis and need a replacement.
She was determined to get him the best one available. But
the cost of the device and the training and physical therapy

that went with it was staggering. She was doing well enough to more than cover their living expenses but between meeting Michael's needs and the infuriating costs of caring for her father, she wasn't close to having the necessary funds. Maybe the Ruth items would get her there. According to the article in the paper, The National Sports Memorabilia Show attracted all the major dealers in the business. She thought it was a good place to start.

But the massive exhibition hall was overwhelming. There were hundreds of booths featuring all sorts of sports memorabilia. Card dealers were everywhere, busily hawking their wares to the thousands of collectors who had descended on the place. She didn't know where to begin. As she turned down another aisle she felt a wave of emotion. It was the "beleaguered feeling" that would occasionally wash over her since the accident.

"Can I help you Miss?" asked a middle aged gent. He stood behind a couple of tables that were filled with baseball cards. "You look a little lost."

Susan smiled weakly. She had been wandering around the giant hall for an hour and this fellow was the first person to say a word to her.

"This place...it's a little hard to know where to begin."

"Well, what brings you here?" he asked, helpfully. "What are you looking to buy?

"Actually, I'm a seller, not a buyer."

"And what might you be selling?"

Susan reached into her handbag and slowly pulled out the plastic baggie that held the old Babe Ruth card. She held it up for the dealer to see.

His eyes flared for a brief moment.

"Mind if I take a closer look?"

Susan handed him the baggie.

He carefully opened it and gently removed the card, letting it rest on the flattened palm of his hand. He picked up a magnifying glass and methodically examined the card, paying particular attention to the four corners. After a moment he looked up at Susan.

"You serious about selling this?"

She nodded her head.

"It's in pretty good shape although the corners could be sharper," he said, nonchalantly. "I happen to have a customer who's looking for a Babe Ruth card...and you look like a sincere person." He looked at her thoughtfully. "I'll tell you what; if you want to sell it right now I'll give you...," he paused for a moment as he watched Susan lean in closer to him with a look of heightened interest. "I'll give you $5,000 cash."

"Five thousand dollars!" she exclaimed. "Seriously?" It seemed like a ridiculous amount of money for a baseball card.

The dealer took a roll of money out of his pocket and offered to pay her on the spot.

"We got a deal?" he said, as he started counting out hundred dollar bills.

From behind her came a gravelly voice that had a decidedly New York accent.

"You don't wanna do that."

She turned and saw that it belonged to an older man, maybe in his seventies, she guessed. He was short with bandied legs; maybe five-four, not as tall as her. He had a deep suntan and wrinkles that looked like they had been etched into his face. His bushy gray hair needed trimming and he wore khakis and a white golf shirt that didn't fit him all that well. His glasses were the only stylish thing about him—black frames that were the current favorites of a much younger set. Surprisingly, he had a muscular build for a man his age.

Intent on her conversation with the opportunistic card dealer, Susan hadn't seen him standing nearby, so his words startled her.

She froze him with a stare.

"Do I know you?"

Her tone of voice made it clear that she didn't appreciate the intrusion.

He looked at her impatiently.

"If you knew me you wouldn't be selling *that* card to *this* guy," he said, jerking his thumb towards the card dealer, who silently had begun to fume.

Tightlipped, the card dealer said, "This is private business. I'll be with you in a few minutes." He continued counting out hundreds, as she watched him closely.

But the funny looking man persisted.

"Lady, do you have *any* idea what your card is worth?"

The dealer stopped counting and turned to him.

"Mister, this is none of your business. Leave my exhibit area. Now!"

The old guy edged up to the card dealer, puffed himself up to his full height, like a bantam-cock, and glared at him. Then he turned back to Susan whose posture had stiffened.

"Lady..."

"Go!" she said, emphatically.

He shook his head in disgust. Then he opened the convention program he was holding, flipped through it until he reached a certain page, pulled a card out of his pocket, jotted something on the back, and handed it to her.

"Go to PSA, booth 718, before you take any of this thief's money. *Don't be a schmuck!*"

Susan felt her face turn crimson but before she could respond he turned and walked away.

"What a bitch," Sam Frank thought to himself, as he walked away.

A half hour later, he sat listening to Chuck Bernard, General Manager of the New York Yankees, as he discussed his interest in sports memorabilia. Bernard was a baseball card collector, just like Sam, and he had taken a day away from spring training to have a fan session at the National Sports Memorabilia show.

As he spoke, Sam got the sense that Bernard was almost as big a nut about vintage cards as he was—just last week Sam had plunked down $24,000 for a 1915 Honus Wagner. It was graded 8.5 by PSA, the leading sports card grading company, which made it one of the three or four best of that card in existence. He beat out one other determined bidder in an internet auction that lasted into the wee hours of the morning.

Sam's ears perked up when Bernard mentioned that one of the sets he was building was the 1915 Cracker Jacks. A few minutes later, the moderator asked him how he purchased his cards.

"Auctions. Usually internet auctions from trustworthy companies," Bernard answered. "They're efficient and reliable, and a particularly good way for me to buy cards."

"Why is that?"

"When I have to deal with someone face-to-face and they recognize me, it becomes harder to negotiate a good price."

"You could always throw in a few Yankee tickets as part of your offer," the moderator kidded.

Bernard laughed.

"Unfortunately, it doesn't work like that."

"Can you share a recent card purchasing experience with us?"

"Sure, just had one last week. I was bidding on card number 68 of the '15 Cracker Jack series—Honus Wagner. Graded 8.5. Very hard to find in that condition. I went back and forth with another bidder but lost out. I'm kind of kicking myself for letting it get away."

Sam was stunned. That was the card he had just acquired. Chuck Bernard, GM of the Yankees, was the other bidder! *Son of a bitch!*

When it came time for questions from the audience, Sam raised his hand and eventually the moderator called on him.

"Mr. Bernard. I'm the other bidder."

Bernard looked puzzled.

"What do you mean?"

"The Wagner card. From last week. I'm the guy who out-bid you." Sam shrugged his shoulders.

The audience started to laugh and so did Bernard.

"Oh you are!" he boomed. "Sir, I'd like to see you when we're done with this! And bring that card with you!"

"We can talk." Sam replied, as the crowd laughed harder.

Afterwards, they did talk. Bernard wanted to know if Sam, too, was building a Cracker Jack set. Sam explained that his goal was different...to collect each member of three very exclusive clubs—500 home runs, 3,000 hits, 300 wins. Bernard protested as to why Sam had zeroed in on Wagner's Cracker Jack card, the one he wanted.

Sam shrugged again.

"It's a first class card."

Bernard nodded.

"Sorry I let it get away. Don't let the grandkids play with it; maybe I'll buy it from you someday."

"No grandkids to worry about," he said, softly.

Sam went on to tell Chuck Bernard that as a kid he had never been a very good athlete, so he had harbored a dream of someday becoming a general manager of a major league team. When Sam asked him how he got started Bernard said that his first assignment was as an assistant scout. From there, over a dozen years, he listened a lot and worked his way up to the position he now enjoyed.

"I know a few things about baseball myself," Sam said. "I should. Been to more than my share of games, starting with the Bums at Ebbets Field. My dad took me to see my first ballgame there when I was eight years old. We were big Dodger fans so I never thought much of your team back then.

You guys were too damn good." He shrugged. "But now I root for the Yankees." Then he got a gleam in his eye. "How about making me a scout, Chuck? Unofficial like. So I can feel like I'm on my way to dream fulfillment? Know what I mean?"

Bernard laughed. This odd character had an engaging personality.

"Sure, why not!" He pulled a business card from his pocket and handed it to him. "This has my office and cell numbers on it. If you find a red-hot talent call me on the office line. If you ever want to sell the Wagner call me on my cell."

"It's a deal," Sam said, smiling broadly as they shook hands.

Then Bernard was gone, back to spring training. The regular season was less than six weeks away.

As Sam walked back onto the convention floor, he checked his phone. There was a new text message, sent five minutes earlier.

"took ur advice. visited 718. psa graded card 9. no what its worth? sorry." It was signed "stupid ass."

He laughed as he read it. *Maybe not such a bitch after all.* He had a very good idea what the value of that particular card was, so he texted her back.

"60,000 or so." He signed it "smart ass."

A half-minute later, he heard back from her.

"65,000!! u no ur stuff. coffee?"

"ok"

"meet me at 718. susan"

"c u there. Sam"

CHAPTER 15

S<small>USAN WAS ALL APOLOGIES.</small>

"I can't thank you enough. What a fool I was!" She took a sip of her coffee. "Sorry I was such a witch back there."

Sam noticed that her look had changed as much as her demeanor. For one thing, the ponytail she had been wearing was gone. Her chestnut hair now hung loose to her shoulders which made her angular face look softer, less severe. She had prominent cheekbones and a strong chin. Her eyes were the most expressive part of her face. They were an amazing shade of blue that seemed to change color in tandem with her mood. Earlier, when she was upset with Sam's unexpected interruption, they were a cool, icy blue. Now they were a deeper, warmer tone.

Sam chuckled. "It's not exactly Sotheby's out there," he said, gesturing with his thumb towards the Convention floor. "*Caveat emptor*, as we used to say in the old neighborhood."

"Where exactly is the 'old neighborhood'?"

"Paris, France," he said, sarcastically. "Can't you tell by my accent?

"New York?"

"Close. Brooklyn. Flatbush to be specific."

"Well, I'm glad you spoke up. You saved me from making a terrible mistake. $65,000! I had no idea a baseball card could be so valuable. I actually thought the $5,000 was a ridiculous offer." She paused and looked directly at him. "I usually do my homework but not this time. How stupid of me!"

He brushed off her chagrin with a wave of his hand.

"Should be the worst thing that ever happens to you."

Susan nodded. "You're right about that."

"If you don't mind my asking, how do you come to own such a valuable card?"

"My great grandparents were big Babe Ruth fans."

"I happen to be a big Babe Ruth fan myself. Got any more cards like that lying around?" he kidded.

"As a matter of fact, I do. And a bat, a hat, and a signed ball."

His eyes widened.

"You're kiddin' me."

She shook her head.

"Go on!" Sam said, skeptically, stretching out the last word, as he waved his hand.

Susan smiled, and changed the subject. "So what are you doing here other than saving damsels in distress?" she asked.

Sam explained that he had come to the convention to check out the scene and add a card or two to the collection he was building.

"I used to be big in this stuff. But now I'm retired so I just play around."

Susan, who had been playing idly with the card he had written on earlier, held it up.

"Everything Baseball. What is that?"

"That was my company, from when I was in the memorabilia business."

"You know all about this?" Susan gestured towards the convention floor.

"Just baseball. I don't go in for the other sports." He jerked his thumb towards the exhibit area. "There's a lot of crap out there."

Susan giggled. This fellow didn't pull any punches.

"Can I ask you a question?" she said.

"Why not?"

"Suppose you had some Babe Ruth items; a few cards, a bat, a signed ball, a hat...."

"A cap," he said. "We call it a cap."

"A cap. How would you go about selling them so that you got the most money for them?"

He shrugged his shoulders.

"I'd call a few friends, tell them what I had. Then I'd send the right item to the right guy to be graded and authenticated. I'd check their provenance and then put them up for auction."

Susan sighed anxiously.

"Suppose you didn't know anything about memorabilia," she said. "And you didn't have any friends in the business and didn't have the slightest clue as to what provenance even means. And it was very important that you sold everything for the most amount of money possible. What would you do then?"

"I'd get myself some help. That's what I'd do."

"I live in Jupiter," she said. "How about you?"

"Boca."

"Not far."

"Forty-five minutes, give or take. Why?"

"How retired are you?"

"Completely."

"I don't think so."

"How's that?"

"For one thing, you're here at this convention 'just playing around'. And you're looking to buy a card or two for whatever it is you're collecting." She paused. "Let's say I wanted to engage your services to determine the value of my other Babe Ruth items and help me sell them. What would your fee be?"

"Not so fast," he said. "First of all, this kind of thing isn't what I used to do. I only bought and sold my own stuff.

Secondly, you don't even know me. I could be just like that card dealer back there," he said, pointing in the direction of the guy's booth. "A goniff." He paused. "Like we used to say in the old neighborhood."

"Goniff?"

"Flatbush for thief. Actually, it's Yiddish but that's another story."

Susan took a sip of coffee, leaned forward, and spoke in a quiet but firm voice.

"This may be more than you need to know but, that crooked card dealer notwithstanding, I'm not what you would call a very trusting person." She reached in her handbag and pulled out the 1933 Ruth card, now safely encased in a plastic holder that included a unique identifying label showing a grade of nine. "But if you were a 'goniff' you would have offered me $6,000 for the card back there." She stared at the card for a moment and then looked at him. "I'm holding $65,000 in my hand that says you're an honest man. *Am I wrong?*"

She watched his tan face darken a shade. *He's blushing,* she thought.

"No, you're not. I'm right up there with Abe Lincoln," he said, dryly. "Always gave people a square deal." Then he got a pained expression on his face.

"Something the matter?" Susan asked.

"Nuthin' serious. My shoulder, I think I strained it patting myself on my back just now."

"Very funny."

"All I'm saying is here I am vouching for my own honesty. Maybe you should check me out independently."

"Trust me, I will. I'm going to google you and Everything Baseball, too," she said, all businesslike. "Assuming you check out, does this mean you'll help me?"

"Maybe. I've got a few more questions, though."

"Fire away."

And so began a three hour conversation.

CHAPTER 16

I̲T̲ ̲W̲A̲S̲ ̲C̲O̲M̲P̲L̲E̲T̲E̲L̲Y̲ ̲O̲U̲T̲ ̲O̲F̲ ̲C̲H̲A̲R̲A̲C̲T̲E̲R̲ ̲B̲U̲T̲ ̲S̲U̲S̲A̲N̲ ̲F̲O̲U̲N̲D̲ ̲H̲E̲R̲S̲E̲L̲F̲
pouring her heart out to this odd and strangely disarming
fellow who, in addition to having saved her a small fortune,
proved to be an attentive listener, as well. "The anti-Dad,"
she reflected, thinking of her aloof father and what a hor-
rible listener he had always been.

When Sam asked, "Tell me again how you came to own
the Ruth memorabilia?" she spent an hour recounting how
Great Grandma Zel was Babe Ruth's barber during spring
training in 1926. She went into enough detail that he questioned how she knew so much. So she told him about Zel's
diary. That's when he asked if he could read the diary. She
knew then that he would help her even as she got anxious
about sharing the contents of the diary. No one outside the
family had ever read Zel's journal.

But the conversation didn't stop there.

"After all the years in your family and the ties to your
great grandparents it's gotta be a tough decision to sell these
things," he said.

"It's something I've wrestled with for quite some time," she
said, earnestly. "But I need the money to buy a state-of-the-
art prosthetic for my youngest son along with the training

and physical therapy that goes with it." She shrugged. "That's the deciding factor."

That led to another hour's discussion as she shared with Sam the tragedy her family had endured. It wasn't really a discussion. She talked, he listened—attentively and without disruption—which made her feel all the more comfortable. So unlike Daddy who had recoiled when, in a moment of weakness, she had tried sharing her pain and sorrow in the aftermath of the accident. When she finished, Sam surprised her with his response.

"Your loss is so different from mine."

She tilted her head and scrunched her eyes.

"Explain."

That led to another half hour's conversation where he did most of the talking and she the listening.

It had been over twenty years since he had lost his wife to breast cancer. "A lifetime ago," he said. They had contended with her illness for nine years, the last three from when she was re-diagnosed, after seemingly having been cured, to when she lost her fight. "A very different experience than yours. Easier in a lot of ways," he reflected.

She began to protest but he stopped her.

"It's true," he said. "Yours was like 9-11, out of the blue, completely unexpected. Not to make less of my loss but we at least had time to prepare, time to say what we needed to say, not leave anything on the table. And," he emphasized, "it was just the two of us. We didn't have kids to care for and worry about."

Susan could feel a pervasive sadness about Sam as he spoke, as if the two decade old events were still fresh in his mind. She imagined this was the way it was—a hole in your heart that never heals.

"I'm sorry for your loss," Susan said. She hesitated for a second. "Family?"

He shook his head.

"No brothers or sisters," he said. "The rest are all gone"

"Have you found love in your life?"

It was a very personal question, normally far too private to be asking a person you had just met, but Susan found the question popping out before she could stop it. She was amazed at her boldness. What was it about this odd man that invited such familiarity?

"Oh yeah," he said, with a peaceful smile. "Frankie was the love of my life."

Susan was struck by his response. She meant "since you lost your wife" but realized, by his answer, that there had been no one else.

"Don't get me wrong," he elaborated, "I'm not a hermit or anything like that. There have been more than a few girl-friends..." his voice trailed off. "But no one serious."

Sam was struggling with turning seventy. It had led to much introspection on his part, very out of character for him since he wasn't a guy who ever did much in the way of soul-searching. But lately he found himself spending a lot of time thinking about the decisions he had made, par-ticularly in the years since Frankie's death. When he did, an old Neil Diamond song title kept popping into his head, "Solitary Man." The lyrics didn't apply, but the title...at sev-enty, that's the way he was feeling.

Now he pulled himself out of his momentary reverie and took a sip of the Root Beer he had purchased when Susan suggested lunch midway through their conversation. He felt a connection to this new woman. A fatherly need to look out for her.

"Your boys, how are they doing?"

Where to begin? As she composed her response she glanced at her watch.

"Oh my, we've been talking for hours! I've got to get going. How my boys are doing will have to wait for another time, although I can tell you they're always hungry."

"That's a good sign."

"I guess, unless you don't have dinner ready for them. Then they can get pissy. Teenagers," she said, that one word explaining a lot. She gathered herself. "So, what do you think? Will you help me?"

No hesitation.

"Of course I will. Can't let you go screwin' things up. This is too important."

"What will your fee be?"

He looked at her in a way that made her feel like a fool.

"I told you I'm retired. My fee charging days are over. This one's on the house. Besides, I always made it a point not to charge friends."

"We're friends?"

"Feels that way, doesn't it?"

"It does," she said, seriously. This was *so* unlike her but she was struck by how personable this little man with the big personality was.

Shifting back to the task at hand, he said, "Next step would be for me to see the other Ruth pieces and read that diary."

"I can bring them to you..."

Sam stopped her with a raised hand.

"The less you move your valuable merchandise the better. How 'bout if I come to you?"

"I don't want to put you out any more than necessary."

His hand went up again.

"I assure you, the forty-five minute ride is not an issue."

She thought about how the boys might react to this character and how he might react to them. No problem with Michael; Ryan on the other hand...

"Okay. One evening this week, after dinner?" Before Sam could respond, Susan continued, "Fair warning! One of my boys may not be all that friendly."

"Should I wear a batting helmet?"

Susan laughed.

"A can of pepper spray might be better."

"Okay," Sam said, chuckling. "You're on."

They traded contact information and settled on a date.

As Susan headed toward an exit sign, she heard Sam call out to her playfully.

"Try not to make any more bad deals on your way out!"

She turned back towards him, gave him a wry smile, and flipped him the finger.

She could still hear his full throated laughter as she reached the exit door.

CHAPTER 17

THE BALL CAME TO RYAN ON ONE BOUNCE. HE CAUGHT IT WITH HIS momentum going forward and in one smooth motion transferred it from his glove to his throwing hand and whipped the ball toward third base. It was a strike and the runner, had there been one, would have certainly been out. Ryan jogged in from right field, grabbed a bat and waited his turn in the batter's box. The lighted field was a hubbub of activity as Coach Carruther, with the help of his two assistants, put the team through a full practice. They had lost their past three games and he wasn't happy with their level of intensity. So, practice it was.

There was one player ahead of Ryan before his turn to hit. As he stretched and took a few swings, he thought about what awaited him and Michael after practice. Mom had invited some expert to look at the old Babe Ruth things that had been in the family for years. When he had asked why, she was a bit mysterious but finally told him she wanted to sell them so that she could get Michael a new leg but to keep that information to himself.

Ryan didn't like strangers in their house. He still felt the need to watch out for mom and Michael. But if this expert could help mom get the most money for those Ruth pieces, it would help Michael that much more. So Ryan decided he might give the expert the benefit of the doubt, once he was convinced the guy was for real.

Ryan wasn't so lost in his own guilt and recovery that he wasn't aware how hard his mom worked to get her business off the ground. He heard her typing on the computer late at night and saw the circles under her eyes in the morning. He knew she was trying not to burden him, or his brother, with financial problems. He also knew that his dad had been the main provider and that what was left of his life insurance wasn't going to last much longer. He wondered if he should get a job. Help out. But his mom discouraged him every time he brought it up. She said she wanted him to enjoy being a kid. There was plenty of time for working later. That was part of why he'd decided to start playing baseball. She was working hard and he thought maybe it would make her a little happier to see him trying too.

Ryan stepped into the batter's box and took a couple of pitches. For whatever reason, his head was clear and he was seeing the ball well. He swung at the next pitch and hit a scorching line drive that flew over the fence in right field. On the next pitch he hit a towering fly ball to right center that cleared the fence by thirty feet. It was a blast that everyone on the field stopped to watch.

"Bombs away!" Michael bellowed, from his seat in the stands. "Back-to-back home runs for Ryan Buck."

Ryan ignored his brother's cheers. The homers didn't mean a thing. It was just batting practice.

Afterwards, he and Michael split a pizza and then headed home.

CHAPTER 18

JUPITER, FLORIDA HAS MORE THAN ITS SHARE OF FANTASTIC BOATING enclaves where multi-million dollar vessels are as common as palm trees. Fabulous golf havens featuring spectacular courses dot the landscape. Susan, on the other hand, lived in a non-descript community of what looked like three- and four-bedroom modestly landscaped ranch homes. The houses were neat and well maintained. Solid middle class.

Not the kind of homes that house a baseball card worth $65,000, Sam thought, as he turned onto Susan's street. Then he chuckled. *But that's nuthin'!* He had spent some time the past few days researching the market for Ruth memorabilia. A Babe Ruth cap was a true rarity. If it was the real McCoy, Susan was going to be shocked when she found out how valuable it was.

His encounter with Susan had stuck with him for more reasons than the exciting baseball artifacts she possessed. Their lengthy conversation, completely spontaneous, had covered a lot of personal territory, both hers and his. Never the shy retiring type, he nonetheless found himself telling her things he hadn't shared with anyone in a long time. Just like that. And her story had touched him. After all that she had been through, her upbeat personality, perkiness, and sense of humor showed that she was resilient...and tough, too. She had his admiration.

He was intrigued by the Ruth items as well as the connection between her great grandmother and the Big Bam, one of Ruth's many nicknames, and he was excited to see the memorabilia. Combine that with why she needed the money and he felt himself already committed to helping her maximize their value.

It was exactly 8 PM when he knocked on her door.

Susan welcomed Sam to her home. She was excited and a bit anxious, too. As she led him through the house, Sam paused to look at a faded yellow dress in a shadow-box picture frame that hung from her living room wall. Unusual.

"This is interesting," he said.

"It's a flapper dress, from the 1920's. It belonged to my Great Grandma Zel," Susan explained. She decided to leave it at that, for now.

They continued into the dining room where an old cardboard carton, a bat handle protruding from the top, sat on the otherwise empty table. She reached in, pulled out a cloth sack and handed it to him. He opened it and carefully removed a baseball, holding it gingerly on the seams. The ball was white and in pristine condition. Rotating it revealed a bold Babe Ruth signature.

"This is beautiful," he marveled. "It's in fantastic condition."

"I love his signature. His handwriting is so graceful, almost feminine," Susan said.

"He was a kid who grew up on the streets until he was sent to reform school. It's amazing his penmanship is so clear and precise," he said. "It's the most famous signature in all of sports."

He put the ball back in its sack, pulled the bat out by its handle, and read the name that was etched into the barrel.

"A Babe Ruth bat," he said. Over the years, he had held a few other Ruth bats and it was always special.

Sam clutched it, stepped away from the table, and swung it a few times. It was an electrifying feeling...holding in his hands a bat that the Great Bambino once held in his.

"Heavy, isn't it?" Susan said.

"It is. He must have been very strong." He allowed himself a moment to imagine the Babe swinging this club in earnest. Then he put it aside.

The next item Susan pulled from the box took his breath away. He had spent a lot of years in the memorabilia business and, at one time or another, owned just about everything worth collecting, but he had never held one of these. It was an old Yankee cap, not nearly as substantial as current day Yankee standards. Sam picked up the navy blue flannel cap by its flat brim and lightly ran his fingers across the intertwined NY of the Yankees' logo on the front of it. He turned it over and, sure enough, embroidered inside was 'G H Ruth'. Sweat stains were visible throughout the interior. Sam had no doubt that he was holding a cap that Babe Ruth had worn and toiled in.

"What does the G H stand for?" Susan asked.

"George Herman was his given name. But everyone called him Babe."

He gently put the cap down.

"We're going to want to put this in a special container," he said. "It's very valuable."

"As valuable as the card?"

"You might say."

Sam reached in his back pants pocket and pulled out a folded piece of paper. He opened it and showed it to Susan.

"Susan, last year a Babe Ruth cap sold for over $500,000. Of course..."

Susan gasped and grabbed the paper from him. She quickly scanned the article.

"This changes everything!"

Her face flushed as she grasped Sam's arm. There was relief in her voice.

"This means Michael can get the best equipment and training and…"

"Wait." Sam had a troubled look on his face.

She stared at him.

"What? What's the matter?"

"I was about to say this cap," he pointed to the article, "was a game-used cap. Although yours shows signs of being worn, we don't know for sure if Ruth actually wore your cap in a game."

"That's important?" she asked, incredulously.

"It has an impact on its value. That's where your great grandmother's journal may be helpful."

"Zel's diary," Susan said.

She reached in the carton and pulled out a leather-bound, weather beaten journal. She held it in her hands.

"Zel's diary," she repeated.

"May I?" Sam asked, as he extended his hands.

Susan hesitated for a moment, gave an inward sigh, and then handed the diary to Sam.

He carefully opened the journal.

"You've read this?"

She nodded. "More than once but not since the accident. Can't say I remember the specifics about the cap."

"Hmmm," he said. "Let's hope the diary provides a clue as to how Zel came to own it."

"That's important, too?"

"Definitely. If Zel wrote about Babe Ruth and how she and Horace came to possess the Ruth items, it could show provenance. That would be significant."

"That's the second time you've used that word." Susan tilted her head and gave him the squinty-eyed look. "Explain."

"The diary may provide the back-story of how the cap and other items came into their possession. Put them in historical context. That's called provenance. And provenance is all-important. If the diary can shed light on how Zel and Horace came to own these things then each item becomes unique. Your Ruth cap will be distinguished from all other Ruth caps; the same for the bat and ball. As such, they become more desirable and collectors will be willing to pay more for them. I'll need to read this," he said, holding up the diary, "to be sure."

Susan nodded. "I understand." *A half-million dollars for the hat,* she thought. *By all means, read the diary. I just wonder what you'll think about that one entry.*

Sam smiled. "What else have you got in that carton?"

Susan pulled out a manila folder. But before she could open it a horn honked twice outside.

"That's the boys," she said, putting the folder aside as she headed for the front door. "By the way, don't be put off by Ryan. He's rather protective of me around strange men."

Sam hung back, suddenly not sure what to do with himself.

"Here they are," she said, as the door opened.

Although Sam would not realize it until much later, that first time he laid eyes on Ryan Buck would become an indelible memory. He was about six-foot-three, slender but solidly built, and looked older than his eighteen years. He wore a baseball uniform that needed washing. He carried his glove in his left hand as he held the door open with his right. His younger brother had a slight but noticeable hitch to his gait as he walked through the door and announced in a loud, enthusiastic voice, "We're home! I'm starving!!"

"Didn't you go out for dinner?" Susan asked.

"We split a pizza," Michael said. "I'm still hungry."

Susan rolled her eyes and changed the subject.

"How was practice?"

"Great! Ryan really beat on the ball. You should have seen it, Ma, he hit two homers. Big shots, too!"

"Boys, I want you to meet Mr. Frank. Sam Frank."

Michael looked Sam up and down and got a bemused look on his face.

"You're the baseball card expert, right? Hey, you've got two first names," he said.

"I guess I do," said Sam, a puzzled look on his face. It was something he had never thought about.

Susan continued with the introductions.

"This starving guy here is Michael. The home run hitter is Ryan."

"Aw, Ma, it was batting practice. It didn't mean anything," said Ryan. He sounded annoyed.

"Well, in any event, go get washed up. We're doing things in the dining room that require clean hands. You might want to join us. I think you'll find it interesting."

They both headed to their side of the house. Sam got a smile from Michael and not a hint of recognition from Ryan.

"He looks like Yoda with glasses," Michael whispered mischievously to Ryan, as they headed to the bathroom.

Sam thought the boys' physical appearance seemed to mirror their demeanors. Michael, with the lighter personality, was fair skinned with curly light brown hair, while Ryan was swarthy with hair that was dark brown and wavy. Though they both had brown eyes, Ryan's were a dark chocolate brown, Michael's more like milk chocolate. But, given their differences, it was easy to tell they were brothers. They had the same spread noses and both had lips that were full to the point of almost being puffy. Each was handsome.

As Susan and Sam returned to the dining room, she shared with him that she had yet to tell the boys how valuable the Ruth memorabilia was.

"I didn't think they would believe me so I decided to wait until our expert was present," she said, as she patted Sam on the back. "By the way, I haven't told Michael yet what I plan on doing with the money so mum's the word."

"I was thinking about that. Doesn't your health insurance cover the cost of an artificial leg?"

Susan laughed, sardonically.

"Sure. Enough to get a peg-leg like you see in old pirate movies." She gave a resigned sigh and continued. "A high-performance leg prosthesis can cost upwards of $70,000. It's filled with microprocessors to make walking easier and more natural. It takes careful fitting, close follow-up, and lots of hard work on Michael's part."

"I had no idea."

"There's more. Michael's sixteen and he's growing like a weed. Prosthetic legs have a limited life."

"I'm beginning to understand." Sam was feeling very stupid.

"Where were we?" Susan said, as she carefully opened the folder and nodded to Sam. "Take a look."

Inside were three more Babe Ruth cards, also from the 1933 Goudy series. Ruth was such a star that he commanded four cards in the set. Each looked to be in excellent condition.

"These are beauties," he said.

A magnifying glass and tweezers appeared in Susan's hand.

"Do you want to check the corners?" she asked.

Sam looked up at her.

"Aren't you the fast learner."

"I paid attention at booth 718. I saw how they did it."

"Huh?" Michael said, as he joined them.

"Technical stuff, Michael," Susan said, mysteriously. "I'll explain later." She pulled out her laptop and started typing away.

Sam had the magnifying glass glued to his eye as he peered intently at card number 53, a picture of the Babe from the waist up with a bat on his shoulder, set against a yellow background. It was the hardest of the four Ruth

Goudeys to find in top condition. He gently put it down and, in turn, carefully examined the other two cards.

Susan and Michael, who had been chatting quietly, turned their attention to him as he put the last card down.

"What's the verdict Holmes?" Michael asked.

"Holmes?" Sam said, but before Michael could respond, he got it. "Oh yeah, Sherlock Holmes." Sam stared at him through the magnifying glass, speaking in his finest Brooklyn accent. "Well, Watson, they all seem to be in excellent shape but we still have to send them out for professional grading." He turned from Michael and stared at Susan through the glass, a la the fictional detective. "Impressive items you have here, lady."

"How do you determine their value?"

This came from Ryan who had silently entered the room.

"Take a look here, Ryan," Susan said. She turned her laptop to face him. It showed PSA's website. "This is the company that grades cards. They also list the value of every card."

It was clear that this time Susan had been doing her homework, Sam observed.

Ryan took command of the laptop and quickly figured out how to navigate through the website as Michael looked over his shoulder.

"Ryan, look up what these others are worth," said Michael, impatiently.

"We don't know what grade they are, Mike," said Ryan.

"What do you think, Holmes?" Michael said.

Sam rubbed his chin as he contemplated Michael's question. "A grade of eight for each card is a safe bet."

"Okay," Michael said. "Look them up, Ry."

Susan wrote the card numbers on a piece of paper and handed it to Michael who called them off to Ryan.

"Number 53."

"Hold on. That would be $40,000.

"Holy shit!" Michael cried out. "Number 149."

"Thirty-three thousand dollars!"

"Number 181."

"Seventeen thousand five hundred dollars!"

Michael did some quick adding and announced, "If they get grades of eight that's $90,500! What was the number of that other card, Mom, and what grade did it get?"

"Number 144 and it's a nine."

"Sixty-five thousand dollars," Ryan said, as he stared at the screen.

"Sixty-five thousand dollars!" Michael said, disbelievingly. "Let me understand this. One baseball card is worth $65,000? Those old Babe Ruth things are worth that kind of money?"

The boys were familiar with the various Ruth pieces but Susan had never told them about Zel's diary. Why give further life to the controversy that had bedeviled the family for so long?

As the resident expert, Sam jumped in.

"It's because of the condition they're in. Number 144 was graded a nine out of ten which makes it one of the best examples of that card in existence. Superb condition and the fact that it's a Babe Ruth card makes it very valuable. As far as the other cards, I'll help your mom fill out the paperwork so she can send them out to be professionally graded. Then you'll know for sure."

Ryan, too, was stunned by the value of the cards. He knew the Ruth items had been in his mom's family for many years but, when she told him why she needed the money, he was okay with her decision to sell them. He knew the memorabilia was authentic but what about this weird looking guy? Could Yoda be trusted with such valuable assets?

"Are these prices for real?" Ryan asked, skeptically. "I mean, do people actually pay these prices? Or are these like 'list price' which no one ever pays?" He looked up at Sam who was standing on the other side of the table. "Where do these prices come from?" he challenged.

Sam answered, calmly.

"It's a fair question. These are actual market prices. PSA tracks auction sales as well as other sales that are made public. Prices fluctuate but that's true for all collectibles—art, stamps, coins. Baseball cards are no different. Ultimately, it comes down to supply and demand. Fortunately, Babe Ruth is the Vincent Van Gogh of baseball memorabilia. Every collector wants to own something Babe Ruth, especially high end stuff." He pointed to the cards. "Like these."

"How do you know so much about baseball cards?" Michael asked.

Sam chuckled.

"That's a long story. I'll give you the five minute version. I grew up in Brooklyn, New York. My parents owned a candy store on a street named Kings Highway."

Michael got a confused look on his face. Sam realized an explanation was required.

"There was a candy store back then every two or three blocks. It's where people came to buy the paper, pick up a pack of cigarettes, have a cup of coffee, an egg cream, a malted."

"An egg cream? That sounds gross," Michael said.

"It's a drink. It sounds funny but it tastes real good. And it doesn't have any eggs or cream in it." Sam smacked his lips and nodded his head. "Nuthin better than a chocolate egg cream!" He paused. "Where was I?"

"Your parents owned a candy store," Susan said.

"Right. Well, I started working in the store when I was ten. That would be 1952, the same year Topps came out with a set of beautiful baseball cards. I loved baseball and I was a big Brooklyn Dodger fan. I used all the money I earned to buy those cards. At the end of the season I convinced my father to keep the unsold packs rather than return them. From then on I started collecting all baseball cards. I bought lots of old cards, some that went back before the turn of the century." He looked at the boys who were listening intently.

"I'm talking the other turn of the century, the 1880s. Paid practically nuthin for them. Not that I thought they were a good investment. I did it because I had a real passion for them. In 1957, when our heroes abandoned us and moved to LA, most of my friends gave their Dodger things away— to me. I built up quite a collection. When baseball memorabilia started to take off, I had what everyone was looking for. I started selling a few things, buying others. Cards, bats, balls, everything baseball. Somewhere along the way I turned it into a business. Called it Everything Baseball. Wound up making a lot of money. Guys thought I was this brilliant businessman. I wasn't. I did it because I loved it." He shrugged. "Turned out I stepped in shit and got lucky."

Michael laughed, Ryan rolled his eyes, and Susan turned red.

"What's your all-time favorite card?" Michael asked.

"That's an easy one. It's a Lou Gehrig card from the 1933 Goudey card series, same set as your Ruth cards. It was my father's card that he collected as a kid. It was the only one of his that survived. My grandmother threw all the others away. To me it was a miniature work of art on a cardboard canvas; not in great shape, but I thought it was a little jewel. The fact that my father had actually bought it when he was a kid and had kept it over the years made it very special to me. I still have it." Sam reflected. "I've had lots of cards that were a lot more expensive but none that were more special than that one card of my Dad's."

He paused and looked around the table. Michael stared at him with a sad expression on his face. Susan's eyes were full and ready to brim over. Ryan looked angry. Sam suddenly realized that he was talking to two boys who had lost their dad not all that long ago.

"Did your father collect cards?" he asked, softly.

"Don't know," Ryan snapped. "I never got the chance to ask him." The bitterness in his voice was painful to hear.

"I'm done here. I've got homework to do." He rose abruptly from the table and left the room.

Sam was a tough guy but he cringed.

Susan could see the pain on his leathery face.

"It's okay," she sniffled.

"Don't worry about Ryan," Michael said, reassuringly. "He gets like that sometimes."

Sam wanted to find a hole and crawl into it.

But then Michael changed subjects. "How long will it take?"

Preoccupied, Sam didn't understand what Michael was asking.

"What?"

"To get the other cards graded?" Sam shook his head, as if to clear his mind.

"It's fast. You'll ship them FedEx overnight and should get them back in a couple a days."

"$155,000!" Michael exclaimed. "That is if you're *right* about them getting grades of eight." Michael eyed him. "How sure are you?"

A challenge, Sam thought. "Sure enough to make you a bet."

"A pizza?"

Never one to back down, he said, "I heard you say you were hungry when you walked in. Sounds like one pie won't be enough so let's make the bet two pizzas."

"Cool! We can't lose. If you're wrong we get to eat. If you're right, we're rich! Wonder what we're gonna do with all that cash?"

"Don't be getting ahead of yourself, Michael," Susan said. "I have plans for that money. Now, you go find yourself some dessert while Mr. Frank shows me the paperwork to get these cards out tomorrow morning."

Michael gave Sam a big smile and headed for the kitchen.

Sam turned to Susan.

"I screwed up. Sorry."

"You didn't do anything wrong. It's a sensitive subject. Ryan overreacts sometimes. Believe it or not, he's a lot better than he was. Don't take it to heart." She smiled, encouragingly. "How about you show me what I have to do so that I can send these cards off to be graded."

An hour later, as Sam was completing the paperwork, Ryan entered the room.

"Getting kind of late, Ma."

"We're just finishing up, Ryan. Why don't you hit the sack?"

"In a while."

Sam still had an uncomfortable feeling and he felt he had to say something to Ryan.

"Ryan, I was insensitive before. I didn't mean to say anything that was hurtful."

"I know," Ryan said. "Long ride home?" His tone made it clear that he had had enough of Sam Frank for the evening.

Sam sealed the envelope he had just finished addressing.

"As a matter of fact, I'm done."

Susan walked Sam to the door, as Ryan headed back to his room. She carried the diary in one hand.

"Sorry about Ryan," Susan apologized. "He can still get a little funky." She sighed. "I can't wait for the old Ryan to reappear. I'm seeing more and more glimpses of his old self but," she shrugged, "we still have a ways to go. You okay?"

"I'm fine. I feel bad for him. It must be tough."

"Maybe you should have worn that baseball helmet after all."

He held up his hand to stop her.

"No need for any helmet." He made a fist and knocked his head a few times. "This head has gotten pretty thick over the years."

"I want you to know how much I appreciate you coming here tonight." She paused. "I completely understand if you don't..."

He stopped her.

"Hey, cut it out. I got to hold a Babe Ruth cap. Never did that before. It was a thrill. Besides, I like the idea of helping Michael to get what he needs."

Susan rubbed a hand gently over the worn cover of Zel's diary. She took a deep breath. "Here," she said. She handed the journal to Sam. "Let me know what you think."

"Okay," Sam said, eagerly. "Let's hope Zel mentions the Sultan of Swat."

"Who?"

"One of the Babe's nicknames."

"Oh." Susan wasn't concerned about that. She knew the journal would show provenance, or whatever it was Sam called it. What she really wanted to know was Sam's reaction to that one particular entry that, for the past few days, had been more and more on her mind. She just knew it would come up for further discussion.

Susan's evening wasn't quite over after Sam left. As she walked towards her bedroom, she noticed the door to Ryan's room was half-open. Ryan was sitting at his desk, looking at his computer.

"What ya doing, Ry?" she asked.

"Facebook."

She entered his room, put her hands on his back and started gently massaging his neck.

"Can you believe how valuable those old cards are? It's crazy, isn't it?"

"It is. I'm glad. It'll make things easier for you."

"It can make things easier for all of us. The cap could be worth a fortune."

"This guy. What do you know about him?"

"I googled him and his company—not much but what's there is all good. He's a real character but he's nice and he knows about baseball memorabilia. He's excited about the Ruth stuff."

"What's in it for him?"

"Nothing." She shrugged. "I offered to pay him but he refused. I don't think money is an issue with him." Susan wrestled with a thought. "I think he's lonely." She recounted Sam's story to Ryan.

He was quiet for a while before he spoke. "Do you trust him?"

She paused.

"He's a character but I think he has character."

"That's not what I asked."

"Trust him? Let me put it this way..." She told Ryan how he had saved her, a perfect stranger, from making a $60,000 mistake and how, after hearing her story, he had agreed to help her. "So yes, Sam Frank has, in a short period of time, established an unusual level of trust with me and if he is willing to help us sell the Ruth objects, I'm prepared to accept his generosity. You know how important the money is." Susan swung her son's swivel chair around, so that he was facing her. "You think you can cut him a little slack?"

Unwilling to be convinced, Ryan gave a shrug.

"I guess. Let's see what grades those other Ruth cards get. See if he really knows what he's talking about."

"Fair enough." Susan tousled her son's hair. "And now I'm going to bed."

CHAPTER 19

THE NEXT MORNING, SAM MADE HIMSELF A BOWL OF CEREAL AND A GIANT mug of coffee and sat down to read Zel's diary.

A couple of hours later, he put the diary down, made a fresh cup of coffee, and sat back to contemplate all that he had read. The hairs on the back of his neck were standing on end!

All of the Ruth memorabilia in Susan's possession had been accounted for. For their immediate needs the diary was more than complete. It was dynamite! Showing provenance wasn't going to be a problem. But, there was now an issue that loomed much larger.

He got up from the kitchen table, walked into his library, and pulled a paperback from one of the shelves that lined the room. He spent the next half hour searching for one particular paragraph in the book. Finally, he found it and read it over twice. His suspicion was confirmed. Unfortunately, he thought, there was no way it could be proved.

He called Susan but got her voice mail. Frustrated, he left a message that he had finished reading Zel's diary and that she should call him as soon as possible.

Susan didn't return his call for several hours and when she did it wasn't the diary that was on her mind.

"Can you talk?" Sam asked.

"I'm wading through resumes."

What was that about? "Explain," he said. He pictured the squinty-eyed look on Susan's face the times she had asked that of him.

"Hey, that's my line," she said. "I'm trying to fill a position for a new client."

"You're a headhunter?"

"Some call us that. I prefer self-employed recruiter."

"Sounds more professional," he agreed. "Any particular industry?"

"Pharmaceutical sales. Several of the major pharma companies are clients. A few of them call me on a regular basis."

"Doing it long?"

"Way back when, a headhunter recruited me to work as a sales rep for a pharma company. After Bill died I needed to find a job where I could make a living working at home, so that I could care for the boys. I contacted the person who originally recruited me. He was very gracious and took me under his wing. Taught me what I needed to know and even gave me a few accounts. After a couple of years at this, I think I've gotten pretty good. My clients keep coming back to me and the money's good enough that I can pay the bills, put food on the table, and have no credit card debt." She paused. "No small feat given how my boys eat."

She continued. "I never thought I would have my own business, much less be self-sufficient. Very satisfying." She thought for a moment. "Tragedy stretches you in lots of different ways."

"Yeah, tragedy can make a regular Gumby out of you."

She laughed.

"Good description—Gumby. Michael's a Gumby. Ryan's just beginning to get there." She took a deep breath and steered the conversation to why he had called her. "Zel's diary. Did you read it?"

"I did. We need to talk."

"Does it show provenance?" she asked, dutifully.

"In spades. You're gonna get maximum value for the cap, bat, and ball. She also writes about a couple of photographs of her and Ruth. Any idea about them?"

"No," she said, genuinely puzzled. "I've never seen any photos. What about the cards?"

"The diary ends in January, 1927. The cards weren't printed until 1933 so there's no mention of them." He paused. "There's something else."

A chill shot down her spine. "What?"

"We need to go over it in person. There's something I gotta show you."

"You're being mysterious."

"Sorry. It would be better if I could show you what I found and then we talked about it. When can we get together?"

But Susan needed to know more. The thrill of knowing that the Ruth memorabilia would materially change their finances was offset by the anxiety she felt that the old, troublesome question might be raised, once again.

"At least give me a hint."

Sam thought about it and decided it wouldn't do any harm to whet her appetite a bit.

"Annie. We need to talk about Annie."

Here we go. "Grandma Annie? What about her?"

"That's all you get over the phone. What's your schedule like?"

"I'm up to my eyeballs with resumes and I'm on a deadline." Susan paused and when she continued her voice became animated as she momentarily put thoughts of the diary aside. "This new client, they've finally given me a shot. They asked me to send them candidates for a vacant sales territory. I'm determined to find them a few fantastic people. This could be a big opportunity for me! Can you give me a couple of days?"

"Hmmpf." He had what qualified as blockbuster news but Sam could hear the excitement in her voice so he relented. "Ahh, Zel's diary's been sitting around for eighty-five years. I guess it can wait a few more days."

Yes it can. "Well then, how about lunchtime Friday?" Susan said. "I should be done with my work by then."

"Good by me. See you then."

Susan felt excited and uneasy as she hung up the phone. But right now she didn't have time for valuable memorabilia or contentious diary entries. She returned to the pile of resumes that sat on her desk.

Susan called Sam the next day and informed him there were now two items on the agenda for Friday. The first was reading Zel's diary. The second was to find out the grades of the other Ruth cards. She had received an email that the graded cards would be in her hands by Friday afternoon.

"Michael asked if Holmes could be there when we open the FedEx package," she said.

"Holmes? I got a permanent nickname?"

"Seems that way. He hasn't forgotten the bet you two made."

"Ryan's okay with it?"

"Actually, Ryan agreed. I think his exact words were 'let's see if this guy knows what he's talking about.'"

"Is that so?"

"I'm afraid it is. You've been challenged."

Sam felt a testosterone rush.

"Challenge accepted," he replied, without hesitation.

"Sure about that?"

"Absolutely. I wanna be there when they see that *I* know what I'm talking about."

"Oh my," she said, with an exasperated sigh. "You boys are all the same...no matter what your age. Ryan's playing ball in the afternoon. It's a home game so he should be here by 6:30. We'll eat around seven and then open the FedEx box. Care to join us?"

He had no plans.

"Sounds good."

"Better bring along pizza money. In case you lose your bet."

"Better let your boys know dinner is gonna be on them," he replied.

She sighed again.

CHAPTER 20

SUSAN HAD SANDWICHES WAITING WHEN SAM ARRIVED SHORTLY AFTER noon. They talked as they sipped on Diet Cokes.

"When was the last time you read Zel's diary?" he asked.

Susan thought.

"Maybe three or four years ago. Before the accident." She did that often—view past events in terms of having taken place either prior to or after the crash.

"You should read it again. The parts about the bat, ball, and cap will be all the more meaningful to you. Terrific stuff! In terms of provenance, you couldn't do better."

She sighed. "There are parts of Zel's diary I know very well but not the ones about the memorabilia."

Oblivious to the angst Susan was feeling, Sam continued. "For now though, I want to focus on three entries."

He opened the diary to the first page he had bookmarked but first he set the scene.

"Zel's initial diary entry was written a few days after she moved from Ohio to St. Petersburg, Florida. Once she arrives in St. Pete, her entire focus is on finding a job, hopefully as a barber which is what she knows how to do. Well, it only takes her a week to find work but then she really struggles. The only good thing that happens to her over the next six months is the friendship she develops with Horace who lives

at the same boarding house. Then one Saturday afternoon
Zel gets a big break. Babe Ruth and a couple of his teammates walk into her shop and she winds up giving him a
haircut and shave. He becomes a regular customer and they
become friends. One day he brings her the baseball which
he autographs; on another visit he gives her two tickets to
a spring training game where he hits a homer and winds
up tossing Zel his cap and giving Horace the bat. As spring
training comes to an end, just before he's ready to leave for
New York, he invites Zel to a party in his suite. Read this."

Susan's stomach knotted as she looked at the open page.
It was *the* entry, the thorny one that had divided her family
for generations. Although she knew the entry by heart, she
pretended to read it, word by word.

Sunday, March 28, 1926
    It is almost noon as I write this. I did not
rise from my bed until almost 11 AM, surely a
record for me.
    Last evening I dined with Babe Ruth in his
suite at the new Jungle Hotel, the swankiest
place in town.
    This past Tuesday, Babe came by the shop
for his usual shave. When he talked about our
party, I gave him the bad news that Horace
was unavailable. He would not be back from
working on the house until Sunday evening.
Babe got sad when he thought I would cancel
on him and there would be no party. I could
not let my very best customer who had treated
me so grandly be disappointed. So I told him
I would come anyway. He immediately started
planning our dinner by asking me what I liked
to drink. I told him my favorite is rum and Dr.
Pepper. He thought that was funny but assured

me I would have it. I asked him if we could dance the Charleston and he laughed again but promised me that, too. Then, to my complete astonishment, Babe gave me a hundred dollar tip (one hundred dollars!!) with the condition that I use it to buy the flapper dress I had been telling him about and wear it to dinner Saturday night. I ran out right after work and got that yellow dress in the window, the very one I had been looking at for months. I hurried home, put it on, and danced the Charleston to imaginary music in front of the mirror in my room. It was so exciting!

Finally, Saturday night arrived. Zel Hitschnik, modern day flapper, knocked on Babe Ruth's suite door with a case of the heebie-jeebies. I was about to have dinner with the most famous man in America, the man whose hair I had cut and face I had shaved for the past six weeks. Babe greeted me wearing a red velvet smoking jacket. He had a drink in each hand and he gave one to me. I smelled the bay rum he wore as I floated into the room.

First thing I did was drink my rum and Dr. Pepper to quiet my nerves. I could feel the liquor and I quickly found myself relaxing as I walked around Babe's hotel suite. It had a dining room, a sitting room, a bedroom, and two bathrooms. It was magnificent.

Babe told me the butler would be up shortly to serve us dinner. We were eating steak that evening. He made me a second drink and poured himself another scotch.

Over dinner, he once again talked about the upcoming baseball season and how, after a bad

time last year, he was determined to have
a great season in 1926. I was amazed at how
much he ate and drank. He finished two steaks
before I was half way through mine and he must
have had at least six drinks. I myself was on
my third drink, which, I must say, made me
very happy. By dessert, which was chocolate
ice cream (my favorite!), we were both
laughing and joking and having a fine old time.

After dinner, Babe moved the furniture off
to the sides of the sitting room and turned
on the Victrola. Suddenly, the sounds of the
Charleston filled the room. We both kicked off
our shoes and started to dance. We didn't stop
for over an hour, except to fill up our drink
glasses and change records. There I was in my
flapper dress, a drink in one hand, cigarette
in the other, dancing the Charleston with none
other than Babe Ruth. I was the cat's meow!

I think it was right about then that he
kissed me. A man of big appetites, Babe kissed
the way he ate and drank–heartily. I pushed
him away and told him the bank was closed. He
asked if he could have some cash. I told him
I'd give him a check. We both laughed and had
another drink.

The Charleston kept playing and I didn't
leave his suite until after 1 AM. Babe smoked
two cigars that evening.

As I write this the day after, I am feeling
many things. Things that I cannot put into
words, other than to say it was the most
memorable night of my life. Babe is gone,
already on his way north. He is, without
doubt, the most unique person I have ever met.

As I sit here and write, I doubt that I will ever see Babe Ruth again and, I realize, I am all right with that.

Susan looked up at Sam. Her mind was swirling. How should she react? Should she let him lead her or should she open up to him? Share with him the multigenerational dispute Zel's words had caused. But before she could speak, Sam continued.

"We'll come back to this entry. There are two more I want you to read." He turned the page. "This one was written the following Sunday."

April 4, 1926

I have decided to marry Horace Phillips.

I was not expecting this but, now that I have made the decision, I am growing comfortable with the idea. Last Sunday afternoon Horace surprised me with the announcement that the house he had been building was finished. He invited me to see it. He had packed a picnic lunch and, though I was exhausted from the night before, we took his automobile to see his completed home on the outskirts of town. It is a homey place that he has built with two bedrooms, a sitting room, a nice size kitchen, is electrified, and has indoor plumbing. It sits on an acre of land. Horace explained that he built it in a way that it would be easy to expand the house in the future.

Over lunch, I ventured that he would soon be leaving Mrs. Albright's and moving into his new home. He said that was the case. I told

him he had been a good fellow boarder and
that I would miss him as well as our walks
and talks. I joked that I guessed I would be
buying my own Dr. Peppers from now on.

It was at that point that Horace confessed
his love for me. He said that he had been in
love with me from the moment we first met and
our walks and talks were the favorite part of
his week. He was quite sincere and endearing
as he spoke. Finally, he got on one knee and
offered to buy me Dr. Pepper for the rest of
my life. He told me that, as he completed work
on the house, all he could think about was how
perfect it would be for the two of us to leave
Mrs. Albright's together and move into his
new home as man and wife. He then asked me to
marry him.

He caught me quite unaware and I swooned
from my fatigued state. I had not seriously
thought of Horace in this way. When my head
cleared I realized that he would be a good
provider. He was a nice enough man and I
believed him when he told me he loved me.
Given my situation, I realized it made great
sense for me to accept his proposal.

I said yes! I do not know who was more
surprised by my answer, him or me.

Horace jumped for joy and gave me a big kiss,
our very first. "When shall we do this?" he
asked. Since the house was waiting on us, I
told him the sooner the better. We decided
we would get married next Sunday, the 11th of
April. And so we shall.

I think I could grow to love him.

"That's when great grandpa Horace popped the question," Susan said, noncommittally.

"There's one more entry I want you to read. Zel wrote it about nine months later." Sam turned to the last entry he had marked. "Take a look."

January 2, 1927
> *We have a New Year's Day baby. Little Anna Judith Phillips was born yesterday. The birth went well but it was exhausting. However, I could not let this momentous event go by without noting it in my journal.*
> *We will call her Annie.*

"The diary ends a month later," Sam said. "Between a full work schedule and tending to the baby, Zel writes that she no longer has the time for her journal."

Susan closed the book.

"Annie," she said. "You wanted to talk about her?"

Sam shook his head. "Not her. Her parents."

Susan didn't hesitate. "Her parents are Horace and Zel!" she said, adamantly.

Sam was taken aback by her tone. He had struck a nerve. He paused and looked at her keenly. "Is this a touchy subject?"

"No!" She snapped. She rose from the table and started to pace around the room.

Sam eyed her, wordlessly. Obviously, it was a very touchy subject.

Susan sat back down. "Do we really have to go into this? Don't you have the proof you need to show provenance? Is this really necessary?"

Sam shook his head, as if he was trying to clear cobwebs. "Susan, would you mind telling me what's going on here?"

She took a deep breath and let it out slowly. *He's trying to help me. What's the point in not leveling with him?*

"I know where you're going with this, Sam. It's a road my family has gone down for eighty years or so." She paused. "Did Zel sleep with him. Could Babe Ruth be Annie's father?"

Susan proceeded to tell him the conflict Zel's entry of her evening with Babe Ruth had caused her family. How it had weighed heavily on her parent's marriage. The contentiousness it had caused over the years.

"The truth is Zel's words are ambiguous. I've read that entry fifty times and I keep coming to the conclusion that nothing happened between them. My mother saw it the same way. My father thought Zel was a cheap whore. He actually called her that! Damn him!" She paused and gathered herself. "I give Zel the benefit of the doubt. I think she was a great lady."

Sam chose his words carefully.

"I agree with you, Susan. I think Zel was a very special person. I read her journal and felt tremendous admiration for her. As we used to say in the old neighborhood, 'she had balls'!"

He paused. "But I also think she slept with the Babe."

Susan shot him a look but Sam continued.

"Before you jump down my throat, hear me out. I've got some information that you may not be familiar with. Can I show you something?"

"What!"

He flipped to March 28th in the diary, sat next to her, and pulled out a typewritten page he had worked on the night before with the help of an article he found when he googled '1920s slang'. "I took Zel's entry and replaced the 1920s lingo with their non-slang meaning. The paragraph now reads: 'I was very stylish! I think it was right about then that he kissed me. A man of big appetites, Babe kissed the way he ate and drank—heartily. I pushed him away and told him no kissing or making out. He asked if he could have a kiss. I told him I'd give him a kiss later. We both laughed and had another drink.'"

Susan got huffy.

"That's hardly conclusive!" She tossed aside the page he had given her. "I could picture being in that situation and saying something like that myself just to keep that big oaf at bay."

"I know." He paused for a second. "But there's more."

"What!" Susan definitely did not like the direction the conversation was going.

"Read the next two sentences. Out loud."

She stared at him for a moment with steely eyes. Then she read.

"The Charleston kept playing and I didn't leave his suite until after 1 AM. Babe smoked two cigars that evening."

"Okay," Susan said, "so she stayed late. That doesn't mean she slept with him."

"No, it doesn't. But let me show you something."

He had brought with him the paperback he had consulted after he first read the diary. He put it on the table.

"Because of his legendary stature, many books have been written about Babe Ruth. New ones are published all the time. In my opinion, this is the best of them." He handed it to her. "It was written in 1974 by Robert Creamer, a respected journalist, who interviewed many of Ruth's teammates while they were still alive. He writes about Ruth's exploits on and off the field." He paused. "Susan, Babe Ruth was an extraordinary individual, a man defined by excess. He did everything to extreme, from eating to drinking to hitting home runs and striking out. He was overindulgent and extravagant in everything he did. He was no different when it came to sex. He was the most famous person in America and he used it to his advantage. The man did not fathom the concept of moderation and was a force of nature unlike anyone before or since." He flipped to page 321. "Read this."

Susan took the book from him and read aloud the passage he had highlighted.

> Meusel was half asleep when Ruth came in with a girl, went into his room and made love to her in his usual noisy fashion. Afterwards he came out to the living room of the suite, lit a cigar and sat in a chair by the window, smoking it contemplatively. When he finished the cigar he went back into the bedroom and made love again. And then he came out and smoked another cigar. In the morning Meusel asked, "How many times did you lay that girl last night?" Ruth glanced at the ashtray, and so did Meusel. There were seven butts in the tray. "Count the cigars," said Ruth.

"He screwed the girl seven times?" Susan said.

"That's not the point. It's that he smoked a cigar after each time. Look what Zel wrote."

Susan handed the paperback to Sam, picked up the diary, and read out loud what was, to Sam's thinking, the key sentence in Zel's journal, "Babe smoked two cigars that evening."

She looked at him.

"Why would Zel write that in her journal?" Sam asked.

Susan sat silently.

After a minute, she spoke.

"So, you think Zel slept with Babe Ruth that night?"

The defensive tone in her voice had dissipated. The possibility was settling in.

"Twice."

Susan sat back pensively and stayed that way for some time. Sam could sense her mind working, struggling with this new piece of information.

Finally, she spoke and what she said indicated that she had thought the situation through to what was a logical possibility.

"You know what this means." She didn't pose it as a question.

Sam gave a slight nod of his head.

"If you're right, that would mean..." She paused to stare at him with her distinctive blue eyes that had suddenly gotten very wide. "...that I could be the great granddaughter of Babe Ruth."

CHAPTER 21

THE KITCHEN GOT VERY QUIET AS THE POSSIBILITY SUNK IN.

"But, there's no way to prove it," Sam finally said. "It's a question without an answer."

Agitated, Susan got up and walked into the living room. After a minute, Sam followed.

He found Susan staring at the faded yellow flapper dress.

"When I was seven or eight, Grandma Annie would let me play dress up when we visited her. She'd take me into the attic and let me put on her old shoes and hats, scarves and dresses. One day I found this," she said, pointing to the framed dress. "It was off by itself, behind a pile of old books. My grandmother flipped out when she saw me in it. Made me take it off and go downstairs. I didn't see it again until after Annie died and my mother sold their house. Mom liked the idea of me framing it like this and hanging it here."

Susan walked to a bookshelf and pulled out what looked to be a photo album. Past generations were very much on her mind.

"I keep talking about my family. Want to put some faces to the names?"

Sam sat next to Susan as she opened the cover and turned to the first page.

"Great Grandma Zel and Great Grandpa Horace," Susan said.

Printed neatly beneath the photo, were the basic facts: Zelda Hitschnik Phillips 1902—1-9-69 and Horace Phillips 1899—8-3-47.

Sam gazed at the faded, sepia-toned photograph.

"That's a nice picture. They're smiling and they look happy. You never see anyone smiling in these old photos. Zel was a looker."

Susan turned the page and there were more pictures of Zel and Horace and then a few with them and a baby.

"That's Annie," Susan pointed. "Their only child."

"Well hello Grandma Annie." *I wonder who your real daddy is.*

Susan flipped through a few pages of Annie growing up. Then there was a picture of another couple. The neatly printed captions included their dates of birth and read: Anna Phillips Porter 1-1-27—12-5-93 and Ralph Porter 8-8-23—5-18-97.

"And this is Grandma Annie and Grandpa Ralph. I was their only grandchild and they spoiled me rotten."

There were several pages of Annie and Ralph at various ages and in a variety of locations. Apparently Grandpa Ralph was a dedicated fisherman because there were lots of pictures of him holding up his prize catch of the day. After a couple of pages, Annie and Ralph were joined by a little baby of their own.

"That's my mom, Sylvia Porter Coster."

She flipped through more pages that traced her mother through elementary school, high school, and as a young woman.

Sam looked on, silently.

Susan finally got to a page that showed a picture of her mom and dad. It read: Sylvia Porter Coster 10-14-46—10-6-04 followed by Frank Coster 2-23-39—.

"Mother and father." She paused. "Mom was a real sweetie pie. Dad, not so much."

Sam looked at her questioningly.

The startling possibility of Annie's parentage momentarily receded in Susan's brain as she got lost in talking about her father.

"Daddy came up short in the emotional department," she said, with a sigh. "He never seemed to have much time for me. Made me feel like I was a burden." She paused. "He could be mean and hurtful to my mom and he would say terrible things about Zel. He always wanted to get rid of the Ruth items, hoping to make a couple of bucks. I'm sure he had no idea what they were worth." She shook her head. "He was always so self-centered."

Sam noticed there was no date of death for Susan's father.

"Is he still alive?"

"Sort of. He has dementia," she explained. "Its gotten pretty bad. Most of the time he doesn't recognize me when I visit him."

"Is he in a facility?"

"No. He lives at home." Susan elaborated. "Their long-time housekeeper agreed to move in. It's a good arrangement. She gets a place to live for free plus I pay her, but a lot less than if I had to bring in professional help. Isabel knows him well and takes good care of him." She shook her head. "Better than he deserves."

"You have strong feelings when it comes to your father."

Susan's jaw clenched.

"He never reached out to us after the accident. Very disappointing." She shook her head. "If it was up to him, we wouldn't have the Ruth memorabilia. He wanted to sell it all after mom died." She flipped to the end of the album where there was a pouch that was part of the inside back cover. Susan pulled from the pouch some old, discolored envelopes and a folded document. She put the envelopes aside and opened the document. "And he would have if it wasn't for this." It was titled The Last Will & Testament of Sylvia Porter Coster. She turned a few pages and pointed to a paragraph. "Thank God Mom was smart enough to include this in her will."

Sam glanced at the paragraph. "I leave to my daughter Susan all of my jewelry, the family album, Zel's diary and box, and all Babe Ruth memorabilia, including the bat, cap, ball, cards, and photographs."

"What about the photographs?" Sam said, pointing to the will. "Zel mentions them in her diary and here, too,"

"Don't know. They never showed up. Father insisted they were nowhere to be found."

Sam pointed to the yellowed envelopes Susan had removed from the pouch.

"What's in those?"

Susan got a quizzical look on her face. She put her mother's will aside and picked up the envelopes. She couldn't recall their significance. None of them were sealed shut, so she opened one and peeked inside. What she saw jogged her memory.

"Now I remember. I guess because she was a barber, Zel kept hair clippings of her family—Horace, little Annie, and herself." She handed one of them to Sam.

Written on the outside in faded ink was the name "Annie." Sam looked inside and saw blond hair clippings. He carefully looked inside the other two envelopes. For the second time in two days, he felt the hairs on the back of his neck stand on end.

"What?" Susan said, as she saw the intense look of concentration on his face.

"I gotta find something." He reached for Zel's diary and started flipping through it. "Give me a minute."

Susan watched as Sam's eyes quickly scanned the pages. Finally, he stopped and craned his neck forward as he deliberately read through one of Zel's entries.

Susan jumped when he slapped his palm on the coffee table.

"Read this!" he said.

Sunday, March 21, 1926

Babe informed me that a week from today he will be heading north with the rest of the team. Spring training is coming to an end.

Even though this was no surprise I got sad with the news and I suppose my face showed it. Looking at me through the mirror, Babe said we should have a party to celebrate his last days here. Knowing my desire to go dancing and to a speakeasy, he said he would arrange for music and hooch in his suite. We could dance, drink, and dine, all in his room. Because of his popularity, Babe said, this was the only way he could enjoy himself without swarms of well-wishers pawing him to death. He told me I should bring "that nice fella" along and we would make a time of it.

As Babe sat in my chair for his last haircut I decided that I would keep a lock of his hair as a memento of having such a famous person as a customer. I secretly took a few fingers-full of his hair as I cut it and silently slipped it into an envelope. Later, I placed the envelope in my journal box for safekeeping.

I fear life will be shades duller when my favorite customer leaves town. I will follow his exploits closely and hope that he has a stellar baseball season. I believe I am his number one fan.

Susan looked at Sam, questioningly.

Sam held up the two envelopes that contained hair snippets of Horace and Annie.

"Here we have hair samples of Annie and Horace, her supposed father. Zel put a hair sample of the other possible father in a safe place. That begs a question."

"What?"

"Where is Zel's journal box?"

CHAPTER 22

"DNA HAIR ANALYSIS?" SUSAN QUESTIONED. SHE HAD TAKEN A MINUTE to process what Sam had said. "Do you know about that?"

"Not a thing but you can bet I'll find out what we need to know."

Unbelievably, it seemed that it might be possible to determine who Annie's father was. That is if Susan could put her hands on Zel's journal box.

"Without the box we don't have anything," Sam said. "Any idea where it is?"

Susan frowned.

"Not really." Her face became a mask of concentration. "I remember a box with the letter 'Z' carved on the top." She smiled as a memory surfaced. "I called it the 'Zippety-do-da' box, after the song. It was very distinctive. I think it was in Grandma Annie's attic, along with lots of other old things." She frowned again. "But that was a long time ago."

"What happened to everything when Annie's house was sold?"

"Grandpa Ralph lived longer than Annie. When he died, my parents moved whatever they kept to their house. We stored some boxes in our attic, too." Susan grimaced. "Most of it they got rid of."

"Think it still exists? Maybe it wound up in the garbage."

She thought for a moment and then shook her head.

"No. Mom would have kept it. I'm positive of that. She loved Zel and everything connected to her." She paused. "Let me give it some thought, Sam."

Susan looked at her watch.

"Oh my, look at the time. We're missing Ryan play. Want to go see a baseball game?"

In the ten minutes it took them to get to the field they talked about one of the ramifications of the Babe possibly being Annie's father. If it were true, that meant Ryan and Michael were his great, great grandsons.

"You gonna tell them about this?" Sam asked.

Susan was definitive.

"No way. Too many ifs to even go into it. For one thing, I'm still not 100% convinced that anything really happened that night. Even if Zel did sleep with him, the only way we could possibly prove it is with Ruth's hair clippings and we don't know where they are or even if they exist at this point." She paused. "I've never shared the contents of Zel's diary with the boys. I wanted to put an end to the whole controversy. That now may be more difficult than I thought but I don't need to be sharing any suspicions that their great, great grandmother had a one night fling with the Sultan of Sweat, or whatever it is you call him."

"The Sultan of Swat."

"Whatever. No, the whole thing is pretty flimsy." Her mind made up, she continued.

"No Sam, let's keep this to ourselves. Not a word to the boys. Let's move ahead with selling the Ruth pieces while I try to remember where Zel's box might be."

"Susan, there's something you need to understand about Zel's diary. If you want to maximize the value of the Ruth items, other people will have to read it. This is nuthin' you're going to be able to keep quiet."

"Explain."

"We're going to have to send certified copies of the diary to the auction house we select. They'll most likely insist on reading the original at some point."

Susan got a pained look on her face.

"There are all sorts of forgeries out there," he explained. "We're going to be using prestigious companies and big dollars are involved. People are going to insist on whatever original documentation is available. The good news is Zel's journal is fantastic. Each of the items is going to sell for a lot of money. And if there's proof that the Babe was Annie's father, the sky's the limit." He paused. "But at some point Ryan and Michael are going to learn what's in the diary."

This is getting complicated, Susan thought. She felt pressured.

"We'll cross that bridge when we get to it," she said. "For now, no mention of the diary to the boys." She sighed. "I've got to think this thing through."

CHAPTER 23

BY THE TIME THEY GOT TO THE GAME IT WAS THE START OF THE FOURTH inning. Ryan was in right field, and his team was ahead by one run. The first batter up for the other team lined a shot into the gap between left and center that turned into a triple. The next batter hit a high fly to medium right. As Ryan settled under the ball, the runner on third tagged up and took off for home as Ryan caught the ball and threw. The ball flew like a guided missile—one bounce and into the catcher's mitt. The catcher applied the tag as the runner slid. It was close but the umpire called him out. With two out and no one on base, the next batter hit a long fly over the left field fence for a home run. Tie ballgame.

There were less than a hundred spectators, mostly students and, Sam imagined, parents of the ballplayers. At his request, they sat behind first base, towards the back of the stands, where they would be inconspicuous. He wasn't sure how Ryan would feel about his being there and he didn't want to be a distraction.

The game stayed tied until the bottom of the sixth when Ryan, a lefty, came to bat. He took the first two pitches for strikes. Sam watched closely as he dug in. The next pitch was over the plate but this time Ryan swung...a quick, fluid stroke. The ball rocketed off his bat and, in seconds, flew over the center field fence...way over. It was a blast that made the other kid's home run look puny by comparison. What a swing! It was short, compact, and powerful—his homer would have gone out of most major league ballparks. Susan cheered wildly as Ryan circled the bases. When Ryan's team held their opponents scoreless in the seventh Sam and Susan scooted out of there and headed back to her house.

While it was just a couple of innings, Sam was struck by Ryan's ability. His throw was powerful and accurate. His swing was compact and he generated surprising power. *The kid can play,* Sam thought, as he felt another chill run down his spine, *and he could be the great, great grandson of Babe Ruth.* He decided he needed to find out just how good a ballplayer Ryan might be.

Back home, Susan had phone calls to make and pizzas to order so she shooed Sam off to the family room where Michael, who had gotten home from school, was engrossed in an incredibly violent video game. His eyes never moved from the TV screen as his fingers and thumbs moved in spastic hysteria over the controller he held in both hands.

"Holmes," he called out. "Back again?"

"Watson. Good to see you."

"It's pizza night and the only question is who's buying?"

"You and your brother better bring your money to the dinner table," Sam said, smiling. Unlike around Ryan, he felt completely relaxed with Michael.

"Sound pretty sure of yourself. Actually, if you win the bet, we'll get Mom to pay. She'll be able to buy lots of pizzas if your prediction holds up."

Michael's body moved in a jerky rhythm as his fingers kept tapping away. Sam guiltily looked to see if he could notice his prosthetic leg as he sat on the couch. But, if you didn't know, you wouldn't know.

"You any good at that game?" he asked.

"Above average. I can kick Ryan's ass and I beat most of my friends. Except Louie. No one beats Louie. That's okay because Louie has no life. No life, no girls, just video games." Michael's eyes didn't move from the screen as he talked.

"You have a girlfriend?"

Sam wasn't sure if this was the right thing to bring up given Michael's handicap but before he could feel badly about having asked the question, Michael responded.

"Sort of. There's a girl I like, just moved here from Chicago. But I've got to go slowly with her. I need to see that she's okay going out with a guy who only has one real leg."

Hearing him say that was jarring but Michael said it matter-of-factly and it didn't seem to weigh on him.

"Is that a problem with girls?"

"Depends upon the girl. A few really get freaked out by the idea. Others feel sorry for me. I don't like either of those types. But there are some who are totally cool about it. I'm not sure which category this girl falls into. Until I figure it out, I move slowly." Michael continued to mow down enemy fighters as he talked. "Speaking of girls," he lowered his voice conspiratorially, "I set Ryan up with one."

"A good looking guy like Ryan needs your help?"

"Not really. But he hasn't gone out with anyone nice in a while and there's a girl who is perfect for him. She's smart, she's got this really big heart, and she's a babe. That's a pretty unusual combination."

"Why don't you go out with her?"

"Too old; she's seventeen. Besides, I'm going out with her younger sister, Katie."

"Oh?"

"Maggie's a perfect match for Ryan. They'd be great together."

"He takes your recommendations when it comes to girls?"

"Are you kidding? He'd never take my advice about a girl." Michael paused the game and looked up at Sam. "He doesn't know."

Sam looked at him quizzically.

Michael explained. "Katie and I figured it out. She mentioned to Ryan that her sister likes him. I told Maggie that Ryan likes her. They already started talking."

Sam laughed and then threw Michael a compliment.

"You've got a terrific sense of humor, Michael. You keep things light. You've been through tough stuff and you're still smiling. You're an optimist at heart and optimists go far in life."

Before Michael could respond, the doorbell rang and Susan called out, "Pizza's here."

Ryan, who had come home directly from the game, was already seated at the table. He was relaxed after a steaming hot shower but he felt himself tense up when Sam entered the room. It was creepy, someone else joining them at the dinner table, even if it was only for pizza.

"First pizza, then report card time," Michael chirped.

"I don't understand," Susan said. She had ordered two pies—one with everything on it for the boys and one plain cheese.

"Time to get our grades. Actually, the grades Babe Ruth gets," Michael explained.

"Ah, the FedEx package. Exciting, isn't it!" Susan's cheeks glowed with anticipation.

"There's always drama when you get a card back that you sent out for grading," Sam said. "Your heart always beats faster as you open the box and unwrap the bubble pack."

"You still standing by your prediction? You can change your mind if you want," Michael said.

Ryan had yet to acknowledge Sam's presence but now he turned his gaze on him as Sam seemed to deliberate. *Let's see if he waffles,* Ryan thought.

"No. I like my forecast. Two eights, with the red Ruth maybe getting a higher grade. You boys are paying for this dinner."

Ryan finally spoke.

"We'll see." he said, curtly.

There wasn't a lot of talking as Ryan and Michael dug into the two pizzas, which seemed to disappear before Sam's eyes.

"You win today?" Michael asked his older brother, as he chewed on a piece of crust.

"Four to three," Ryan replied.

"Close game," Michael said.

"We beat a decent team."

"You do anything?" Michael asked.

"Threw a runner out at the plate."

"Get any hits?"

"Two for three."

"Sounds like you had a pretty good game," Michael concluded.

"Not bad," Ryan said. Then he changed the subject. "What about you?"

Not a word about his home run. Sam looked at Susan but she paid him no attention.

"Math is killing me," Michael moaned. "It's torture."

"What kind of math you studying?" Sam asked.

"The really tough kind."

Ryan couldn't resist busting his brother's chops.

"That would be all math for Michael. I don't know if division and subtraction is considered math but he had trouble with those."

"Not true! I did fine with math until algebra. Then it got very boring...and very mysterious." He laughed at himself. "I suck at math. I really do. But I don't care."

Susan had a quiet smile on her face.

"We know math's not your thing," she said. "And science isn't your favorite, either."

"Nope. I'm more a humanities kind of guy," Michael said. He sounded pleased with his answer.

"Humanities?" Ryan said.

"English literature, romance languages...you know, humanities."

"What romance languages do you know?" Ryan teased.

"I love French."

Ryan grimaced. "Since when?"

"Since Miss Ferrie started teaching it." Michael pronounced her name "furee," with the accent on the last syllable.

"Ah, now we're getting to it," Ryan said. He had a big grin on his face. "Miss Furry got your attention, yes, yes? Or should I say, 'Oui, Oui."

"It's feree, not furry, you dick head," Michael replied.

Susan jumped in.

"Okay, that's enough. Shall we move on?"

"Oui, oui," Ryan answered, at which point Michael gave him the finger and Susan sighed. She gave Sam a cross-eyed look.

"Dinner is officially over," she announced and turned to Sam. "Time to see if PSA agreed with you."

The anticipation grew as they cleared their plates and moved back to the now spotless dining room table. Susan produced the FedEx box.

"Who wants to open it?" she asked.

Michael spoke. "You open it Mom. After all, these originally belonged to your great-great-great-great grand somebody or other."

"That would be great grandmother Zell and great grandfather Horace." She gave Sam a quick look.

"Open it, Ma," Ryan chimed in.

"OK, here we go."

She tugged the string on the side of the FedEx box, pulled out a handful of bubble wrap, and then a small cardboard box. She opened the box, gently removed the three cards, and held them facing her, like she was playing three card poker. She stared at the cards.

"I've got a pretty good hand." She smiled. "And I know who won the pizza bet."

As she turned her hand down, to reveal the front of the three cards, she announced, "Hope you brought your money, boys."

She laid the cards on the table. There were two grades of eight and one grade of nine, the red Ruth. Sam's prediction was correct.

"Whoa baby!" Michael exclaimed. "Hold on a minute!" He looked down, as if he was thinking. "That's $150,000!"

"You seem to be pretty good with that math," Ryan said.

"Did you memorize what they're worth?" Susan said.

"Nah." He revealed a small sheet of paper he had been holding in his lap. "I just kept what we did the other night." He turned to Sam. "Holmes, your reputation remains intact."

CHAPTER 24

OVER ICE CREAM SUNDAES, VERY LARGE ONES FIT FOR THE OCCASION, a more relaxed Ryan expressed his amazement at how valuable the cards were. It *was* hard to believe.

"Their excellent condition aside," Sam said, "it's a testament to Babe Ruth that these cards are so valuable. After all, he's the greatest baseball player of all time." Sam was unequivocal in his statement.

"What makes him the greatest?" Ryan challenged. "What about Cobb, Williams, Mays, or Pujols? What makes you so sure he's the best?"

"You left out Gehrig, Aaron, and Musial. They're all great players. But head and shoulders above them all is Ruth. Let me tell you why."

Sam spoke passionately as he warmed to the subject.

"While all those players are Hall of Famers, none had the impact on the game that Ruth did. The Babe changed baseball forever. Before him, the home run was an oddity, an accident. Nobody *tried* to hit home runs. They played what was called 'inside baseball'—get on base with a walk or single, advance to second or third on the hit and run, and score on a sacrifice or well-placed ground ball. Pitching, defense, and low scoring were how the game was played.

"Through 1919, the most home runs hit in a season were 29 and that was by Ruth when he was a part-time hitter. In 1920, no longer pitching, Ruth hit 54 home runs, more than all but one team. And his homers were monster shots like no one had ever seen before...into bleacher seats that had never been reached; over fences that had never been cleared.

"The fans went wild. Everywhere the Babe played, there were sellout crowds. The baseball owners saw this and they decided home runs were a good thing and the strategy of the game changed. All because of Babe Ruth."

Sam could see he had the attention of the Buck family who were absentmindedly eating their ice cream as they listened intently.

"The Babe's emergence couldn't have happened at a better time for baseball which was reeling from the Black Sox scandal of 1919."

"The Black Sox?" Susan asked. "Isn't it the Red Sox or the White Sox?"

Ryan chimed in. "The 1919 Chicago White Sox. They threw the World Series to the Cincinnati Reds. The players involved were banned from baseball for life for doing it. Shoeless Joe Jackson was one of them. They called the team the Black Sox."

"Ryan's right," Sam said. "Baseball was the primary sport of America in those days and it was wildly popular. Suddenly it found itself under a dark cloud of suspicion. The Babe lifted that cloud and had the fans cheering for more. He was an engaging and entertaining extrovert who the fans loved and who, in turn, loved them back."

"What about his stats?" Ryan asked.

"They're hard to refute. He's number one, two, or three in virtually every power category—home runs, rbi's, home runs per at bat, slugging average. But in addition to all the slugging, he had a lifetime batting average of .342. That's in the top ten of all time. He has the highest OPS in baseball history and is second in on-base-percentage. And if you're into sabermetrics, the Babe is number one all-time in WAR."

Susan, who was not the baseball fan her sons were, was lost in the jargon.

"Could you translate that for a normal person?" she said.

Sam looked at Ryan and nodded in deference to him.

"It means he didn't just hit home runs. Babe Ruth was an all-around great hitter."

Michael, who, for a change, had silently been taking in the discussion, spoke up. "What about Ted Williams? Isn't there a case to be made for him as the best hitter of all time? If he hadn't missed all those years fighting in wars, his stats would be better than Ruth's."

Sam stared at Michael for a second and then turned to Susan.

"Your boys know baseball."

"I taught them everything they know," she quipped.

"Sure you did, Mom," Michael said. "What does OPS stand for again? I forget?"

Susan hesitated, but just for a moment.

"It stands for Obnoxious Person and Smartass...which you are, you OPS."

"Good answer." He laughed, and turned back to Sam. "What about Williams?"

"You won't get an argument from me that Williams was one of the greatest hitters of all time...right up there with Ruth and Cobb and a few others. You could say the same for Gehrig whose career was cut short by ALS. But with Ruth there's more. You know that he started his career as a pitcher?" he asked, looking at both boys.

"For the Red Sox," Ryan said.

"Correct. Do you know his pitching stats?"

"Not the specifics," Ryan said.

Michael shook his head as he ladled a final spoonful of ice cream into his mouth.

"In 1916, he won 23 games and pitched nine shutouts. That's a record that lasted thirty years. He beat Walter Johnson five out of six times that season and led the Red Sox to the World Series, which they won for the second year in a row. Overall, he won 94 games and lost 46, one of the best win percentages in baseball history. And he's in the top twenty of lowest earned run average of all time. To put that in perspective, his career ERA is right there with Mariano Rivera's. The great closer for the Yankees," he added, for Susan's benefit. "He won almost 100 games by the time he was 24. If he had stuck to pitching, he would have been one of the greatest of all time."

The boys listened attentively.

"Babe Ruth was the most popular person in the country in the 1920s. At least he was until 1927 when Lindbergh flew across the Atlantic. And even then, Ruth recaptured America's attention when he hit his 60th round tripper to break his own home run record for a season. It's over seventy-five years since he played his last game and his numbers and popularity remain astounding.

"He was the total package: greatest slugger of all time, superb hitter, one of the finest pitchers in the game, the most popular player, and a showman supreme. With that, I rest my case. Babe Ruth: greatest baseball player of all time."

Sam looked at both boys and then at Susan. All three stared at him. He noticed their sundaes were long since finished while his had melted down to a soft glob floating in a small pond of chocolate swirl.

"Sorry," he said, sheepishly. "Got a little carried away there."

"You really are passionate about Babe Ruth," Susan said.

"I've read a lot about the Babe and I'm passionate about baseball in general," he said, quietly. The intensity had left his voice. "I just love the game. Always have, ever since I was a little kid. It started with collecting cards in the candy store and hasn't stopped yet."

He paused for a moment to reflect and think about what he was about to say. He spoke slowly, looking at the boys.

"Your mom already knows about this. I lost someone myself a long time ago—my wife. It was a long illness followed by a slow downward spiral. I did all I could to help her through that situation. She was my total focus." He shook his head. "But I couldn't do anything to protect her." He paused. "Baseball kept me sane during that time. I played in a fantasy baseball league and each of those seasons, planning for the draft, choosing my lineup each week, following my players, adjusting my roster, those things kept me from going crazy." He sighed. "I believe that.

"Baseball is part of me. It's a place I keep going back to," he said, pushing the remaining melted ice cream around with his spoon.

There was silence in the room.

Finally, Sam looked up.

"I wanna say something to the three of you. I'm sorry for your tragedy. When I think of the sudden and senseless manner in which you lost your Dad, your husband...," he looked at Susan, as his voice trailed off. "I don't walk in your shoes, we hardly know each other, so I won't presume to understand the pain and suffering you have had to endure. But I am familiar with the loss of someone who is loved deeply. I know how difficult that can be. You are moving forward with your lives in productive ways. You have my admiration."

Silence ensued and lasted a minute or so. It was Michael who spoke first.

"We went to a bunch of baseball games with Dad," he said. There was a slight smile on his face. "Spring training and a few regular season games. They were fun."

"Their Dad loved baseball," Susan said. "Of course, he loved basketball and football and lacrosse and just about every other sport, too."

"Not soccer, Mom," Michael protested.

"He thought soccer was boring," Ryan said, quietly. "Football was his favorite, but baseball was a close second."

Susan and Michael got up from the table carrying their empty dishes. She patted Ryan on the back as she headed for the kitchen.

"He loved watching you play both. It made him very happy."

"Yeah," Ryan replied. There was bitterness in his voice.

He rose from the table, grabbed his empty bowl and, without acknowledging Sam's presence, headed into the kitchen, leaving Sam alone at the table.

It was a Friday night and both boys had plans after the pizza and card reveal. As they helped their mom with the dishes, Sam could hear the conversation as she asked them for details.

Michael was off to his friend Louie's to play video games and would be home by eleven. Ryan was going to the movies.

"By yourself?" Susan asked.

"No, Ma, not by myself."

"Share, please."

"I've got a date."

"Nice. Anybody I know?"

"Nah. She's new in town."

Michael leaned out the doorway and gave Sam a quick wink.

Susan wasn't finished cross examining Ryan.

"Does she have a name?"

"Maggie. Her name is Maggie."

"Well, I hope you have a good time with her."

When Susan reemerged from the kitchen, Sam announced that it was time for him to go, too.

"We owe our new found fortune to you," she said, as she walked him to the door.

Sam stopped to look at the faded yellow dress in the frame that hung on the living room wall. He stared at it a moment and shook his head.

"You should thank Horace and Zell. They're the ones who get the credit. And thank the generations that followed for not throwing those things away. Which reminds me, I need to finalize sending the bat, ball, and cap out for authentication. I'll make some calls tomorrow."

They agreed that they would meet again the following week, at which time Sam would arrange to ship out the items.

"In the meantime, you need to think about where that box might be," Sam said

"Will do, Mr. Frank." She gave him an army salute. "Thanks for being there for us."

He walked to his car, turned, and saluted back.

"My pleasure, Mrs. Buck. Dismissed!"

It wasn't until almost 2 AM that Ryan got home but Susan was still up. Actually, she stayed up until he returned.

"You're home late. How was your date?"

"Good."

"Think there will be a second date?"

Ryan frowned.

"Ma, what are you doing up? It's late. Go to sleep. I'm fine."

"I know you are, Ry. Just wanted to know how your evening went."

He paused.

"Yes, there will be a second date. We already made one." Ryan changed the subject. "What's the next step with the Ruth stuff?"

"Sam will be back next week to send the cap, bat, and ball out for authentication and to tell me more about which auction house we should use." She paused. "So how are you feeling about him now?"

He wasn't a bad guy but even though Sam Frank knew about baseball, Ryan remained skeptical. He ran his hand through his thick, wavy hair. "I can't figure out what's in it for him."

"Does there have to be something in it for him?"

"There usually is, isn't there?"

"I think it may be nothing more than he's lonely."

Ryan shrugged.

"Whatever. I'm hitting the sack. 'Night Mom."

He gave her a peck on the cheek and headed to his room thinking, *Why don't you just ask him, Mom?*

CHAPTER 25

THAT NIGHT, RYAN HAD THE DREAM AGAIN. BUT FOR THE FIRST TIME something was different.

Once again, he threw a perfect spiral which morphed into a slowly revolving key. Once again, Michael caught it and ran into the end zone for a touchdown. Once again, Ryan ran down the field, his arms raised in victory, only to run into the hospital room where he saw himself lying in bed. Once again, Dad and Michael stood behind the doctor who spoke to him. "You're going to make a full recovery," the doctor said, just like he had a hundred times before. Except this time, a pair of lights appeared behind Michael and Dad. The lights got larger and brighter with shocking speed. Ryan blinked and the lights became impossibly large and blindingly bright. They were going to engulf him! He couldn't breathe! He couldn't breathe!

Ryan awoke drenched in sweat. Shaken, he sat up and turned on the lamp that sat on his nightstand.

What the hell!

He had had that dream a hundred times and it was always the same. Until now.

What did it mean?

Did it mean anything?

It didn't help his memory. He still couldn't remember anything about the accident.

Ryan got out of bed and went into the bathroom and washed his face. He returned to his room, stripped off his tee shirt and shorts, and put on fresh ones. He got back into bed, turned his pillow to the dry side, and lay back. He left the light on.

He lay there for what seemed like a long time, thinking about the lights. Did they mean something or was it just an aberration? He didn't know.

Eventually, his mind stop churning and he felt his body relax. His thoughts drifted to his date with Maggie. After the movie they had stopped to grab a light bite. They started talking and didn't stop until the place closed. Then they talked for another hour in his car, parked outside her house. They talked about all sorts of things, including some details he hadn't even shared with Caitlin. Amazing!

They spent the last fifteen minutes in the car making out. That was amazing, too.

He felt an ache in his heart. This one was very different than the one that had been there for so long. He couldn't wait to see her again.

Ryan turned the light off. With his thoughts on Maggie and their second date, he drifted off to sleep.

CHAPTER 26

Sᴀᴍ ᴋɴᴇᴡ ᴡʜɪᴄʜ ᴀᴜᴄᴛɪᴏɴ ʜᴏᴜsᴇ ʜᴇ ᴡᴀɴᴛᴇᴅ ᴛᴏ ᴜsᴇ. Iɴ ʙᴜsɪɴᴇss ғᴏʀ over one hundred years, Standish Auctions Inc. had been conducting a sports memorabilia sale at World Series time for the last ten years. The World Series Auction had grown in popularity each year because of the quality and rarity of the items offered and the serious buyers it attracted. Standish printed a four color, glossy catalogue for its annual big event and it was a seller's dream to have his consigned goods make the cover because it was a guarantee of record prices.

Sam picked up the phone and placed a call to James Dent, Standish's president, a man he knew only by name. It turned out that Dent knew him by name, too. They got right down to business.

The Ruth pieces got Dent's serious attention, the cap in particular. Dent asked lots of questions about each item, mostly technical—how each was graded, their authentication, and the companies that had performed these functions. Sam shared with him the grades the cards received and the status of the other items.

Dent asked how the items came into his possession and Sam explained how Susan came to own them. When he mentioned the diary and Zel having been the Babe's barber during spring training 1926, James Dent didn't equivocate.

"Sam, your Ruth material will be amongst our featured items in our next World Series auction. They are going to command a great deal of interest."

"Think they're cover worthy?"

Dent chuckled.

"Everyone wants their material on the cover of our catalogue. To be perfectly frank, at this point, no. We've already received some amazing material."

"Care to share any specifics."

"Can't. Company policy. The cover stays secret until the catalogues are printed and mailed. Adds to the suspense and anticipation surrounding the auction."

Then he asked Sam to send him a copy of Zel's diary as soon as possible.

"I'll need to read it before we go to press on the catalogue," he said.

"I understand."

Sam knew Dent would want to read the diary with his own eyes and confirm that it was genuine. Standish went to great lengths to insure that all items in their auctions were "as advertised."

But Sam was in no hurry to send Dent the diary. Susan had a decision to make. Besides, until they figured out what was going on between Zel and the Babe, no one else was going to read it. That brought up another relevant question.

What's your deadline for submissions for the World Series auction?" Sam asked.

"June 1st."

"So soon?" He was caught off-guard by how far in advance they required the material.

"June 1st gives us ninety days to do all the preliminary work before the auction can take place. We have to verify every item to our satisfaction. Then we have to prepare the catalogue, have it printed, mailed, and in the hands of our customers by September 1st, a month before the auction.

We'll have over six hundred items in the World Series auction so we're talking about a lot of work. Believe me when I tell you, Sam, that we earn our 20% commission."

Sam thanked James Dent for his time and said goodbye, but not before Dent reminded him that, at some point, he would need to read the diary.

June 1st was less than ninety days away and Sam needed to get the ball, bat, and cap authenticated and graded before then, not a quick process. Suddenly, time was tight.

Sam made a list of the grading and authentication companies, including their addresses and telephone numbers. He spent the rest of the day learning about DNA hair analysis.

CHAPTER 27

THE FOLLOWING TUESDAY, SAM WAS BACK IN JUPITER TO MEET WITH Susan, but not before he made a stop along the way. Susan had mentioned that Ryan had a late afternoon game that day. Curious about Ryan's ability, Sam decided to do one of his favorite things—watch a ballgame. His encounters with Ryan left him wary, though, so he found a seat off by himself where he was as inconspicuous as possible.

Sam enjoyed watching a baseball game at the micro level—where he tried to figure out what the next pitch would be before it was thrown. What would the pitcher throw to try to catch the hitter off guard? Would it be a fastball, slider, or changeup? Inside or outside? High or low? Likewise, what was the batter looking for? Was he sitting dead-red? Or looking for something off-speed? It was the chess match that went on between the pitcher, the catcher, and the batter that fascinated him.

The chess match was sloppy in today's game because the opposing pitcher was wild. The kid had a decent fastball but he was all over the place with it. He seemed reluctant to throw his curve ball. By the time Ryan, who was hitting fifth in the lineup, came to bat in the bottom of the first, there was one out and the bases were loaded. Given the pitcher's wildness, Ryan should have been sitting back waiting on a pitch over the plate. In this situation, a walk was as good as a hit since it would force in the first run of the game. Instead, he swung at the first pitch, which was in the dirt, far outside the strike zone. He did the same on the second pitch, which was high and away. Ryan stepped out of the batter's box, took a deep breath, took a few practice swings and stepped back in. The next pitch was right over the heart of the plate, a perfect pitch to hit. But Ryan froze as the ball smacked into the catcher's mitt. Strike three. Ryan dropped his head and walked back to the dugout.

Ryan was up next in the third inning and had another poor at bat as he continued to swing at pitches outside the strike zone. He wound up dribbling a grounder to second base and was an easy out.

He was up again in the fifth and this time the pitcher inexplicably threw a fastball over the plate on the first pitch. It was a mistake. With Ryan swinging at pitches that were all over the place, there was no reason to throw one that was hittable. Ryan jumped on the pitch, his compact swing rifling through the strike zone. Bat made solid contact with ball and the leather-stitched sphere went rocketing between the outfielders in center and right.

Sam shook his head as Ryan loped into second base with a stand-up double. He looked like a completely different hitter than in his first two at bats.

In the seventh inning, with the game on the line, Ryan reverted to prior form and made himself an easy out by once again swinging at bad pitches, putting himself behind in the count, and grounding out ineffectually to the pitcher.

Ryan's play in the field was solid. He caught all the fly balls hit to him and he nailed a runner at second base trying to stretch a single into a double. He had a cannon for an arm.

His team lost the game 6–4.

Sam was confused about Ryan and his baseball ability. His desire, too. In the first game, Ryan showed a glimpse of talent that was special. His offense and defense were exceptional. He had a good-looking, left-handed swing that generated tremendous bat speed and power. But in his next game, he looked miserable at the plate. There didn't seem to be any in-between. He thought about what Susan had said about Ryan in passing...that he played baseball but she wasn't sure his heart was in it. He didn't seem to be invested in his performance. He didn't seem to care.

Sam had a feeling that Ryan could excel. After all, it just might be in the kid's genes. But he wasn't sure if that's what Ryan wanted.

Afterwards, Sam met up with Susan and updated her on the progress he had made with the Ruth items.

"I've identified the companies to send the bat, ball, and cap. It could take a couple of months or more to complete the process, so the sooner we get going on this, the better."

He then told her about Standish and their World Series auction, their deadline for receiving consignments, and his conversation with James Dent.

"He wants to read Zel's diary."

Susan shuddered. It fell on her shoulders to protect Zel's honor or so she thought. In her heart she knew that, when push came to shove, she would let whoever needed to read the diary do so—there was just too much money at stake—but, nonetheless, she hesitated.

"I'm not ready to let anyone else read it yet."

"Neither am I," Sam said.

She looked at Sam with surprise.

"We don't want anyone reading the diary until we figure out if Zel's envelope with the Babe's hair still exists," he explained. "Any luck finding the box?"

Susan grimaced.

"I haven't had a spare minute to even think about it. Been wrapped up with work." She smiled. "I placed my first sales rep with that new client yesterday. Getting that first one is the big challenge." Her eyes sparkled and there was pride in her voice. "This client has the potential to be big."

"I'm happy for you. But let's get back to the box," he said, abruptly. He had important information to share with her. "After what I've learned about DNA hair analysis, you really want to find it."

She tilted her head.

"Explain."

"At first, it didn't seem possible but then I found a company named DeNuAc, a forensic DNA laboratory. They have new technology that allows them to compare hair samples from clippings, without the hair root intact. That's what we have in Horace's and Annie's envelopes and presumably what's in the envelope with Ruth's clippings. I called DeNuAc and spoke with their hair specialist and gave her an overview of the situation, without mentioning any names. She told me that their analysis gets less reliable the greater the difference in generations. Comparing hair from today to the 1920's wouldn't be all that definitive. But..."

Susan interrupted. "But with hair samples from Annie, Horace, and Babe Ruth, we're only talking about one generation."

"Bingo! When I explained that we had samples within one generation of each other, she told me we should be able to get a conclusive answer as to who Annie's real father is. Can you believe it!"

Susan's face flushed with excitement.

Sam continued. "The DNA tests take forty days or so to complete so you need to find the box. We've gotta send a copy of the diary to James Dent by June 1st but we can't until we know what we're dealing with."

Susan thought for a minute.

"There are only two places it could be," she said. "In our attic or somewhere in my parent's house in Ocala. I've got a crazy week but I'll do my best to check out the attic," Susan said. "Promise!"

They agreed to meet the following week to review everything.

CHAPTER 28

SAM MET UP WITH SUSAN AT RYAN'S BALLGAME THE FOLLOWING TUESDAY.

"We have about eleven weeks to have everything in place to meet Standish's deadline for their World Series auction," he said. "The ball, bat, and cap are in the hands of the authentication and grading companies. Everything is on track. Anything with the box?"

Susan shook her head and exhaled. "I've set aside a couple of hours tomorrow afternoon to spend in the attic," she said. "Promise."

"You sound really pressed for time. Want some help searching for it?"

"Aren't you busy?"

"My meeting with the Secretary of State has been postponed, so I'm free. I'm retired. I've got nuthin to do that can't wait."

"You sure you want to spend a couple of hours rummaging around a hot attic?"

"When you put it that way, no. But I do want you to find the box." He shrugged. "Four eyes are better than two."

"Okay. Tomorrow afternoon. 3 PM. Don't wear anything good."

—

Ryan's coach had him batting fifth and playing right field. As Sam watched the other team's hurler warm-up, it only took a couple of throws to see that this kid was a lot more skillful than the pitcher Ryan faced the prior Tuesday. This pitcher had a lively fastball and a changeup decent enough to fool a lot of the batters he would be facing. But the kid didn't need to use his changeup in the first inning. Throwing only fastballs, he struck out the side.

He struck out the first batter in the bottom of the second, too. Four batters, four strikeouts. Pretty impressive. Ryan stepped into the batter's box and worked the count to two balls and two strikes, all fastballs. He showed some discipline, laying off the pitches outside the strike zone. The next pitch was a blazer, over the inside of the plate. Ryan pulled his hands in slightly as he swung, his bat slicing through the strike zone. Bat made solid contact as the ball soared out to right center field. It was a high drive that cleared the fence with room to spare. As fast as the pitch had been thrown, it flew off Ryan's bat even faster. The pitcher stared at Ryan as he rounded the bases.

Susan jumped up and cheered wildly.

Sam found himself nodding his head. Ryan could hit. He had used his powerful, compact swing to get around on a respectable fastball that was on the inside of the plate. *Not many ballplayers can do that,* he thought.

"Ryan's got talent," Sam said, after Susan sat down.

"He's always been a fantastic athlete," Susan said. "He was the starting quarterback as a sophomore." She looked toward the field. "It's really good that he's playing ball again."

Ryan's next at bat was another good one. He lined a double to left center field, timing a changeup that was on the outside edge of the plate and going with it. After that, he had two poor at-bats, swinging at bad pitches, falling behind in the count, striking out and grounding out weakly to the second baseman. Ryan's team lost the game 3-2 and headed to the locker room.

"He's so inconsistent," Sam observed, as they rose from their seats. "Sometimes he looks miserable out there." He shook his head. "I wonder what his coach thinks."

Susan looked towards the dugout where a solitary figure remained.

"Why don't we ask him? Come on, I'll introduce you to Coach Carruther."

They walked down to the dugout where the coach was seated on the bench, drinking a Gatorade while looking at a page in a beat up binder.

"Excuse me, coach," Susan said. "Mind if we talk a minute?"

Ryan's coach stood up. "Hello. Mrs. Buck." *Who is this funny looking dude beside her?*

"I'd like you to meet a friend of mine, Sam Frank. He's a real baseball nut."

They shook hands.

Ryan's coach looked to be in his mid-forties. He stood around six feet and was solidly built while showing too much stomach. He was in full uniform. Gray hair peeked out the sides of his baseball cap.

"Mind if I ask you a question about Ryan, Coach?" Sam said

"Name's Pete. You the baseball card expert?"

Sam smiled. "Ryan told you about me?"

The coach chuckled. He had heard Ryan talking about some kind of baseball card expert his mom was working with. But this fellow? Not what he was expecting.

"Nah. That's nothing he would talk to me about. Hell, he hardly talks to me at all. I overheard him talking to one of his teammates about it. Said Mrs. Buck here," he said, nodding at Susan, "brought in some kind of expert who knew about old baseball cards. Heard him say you know your stuff."

That was unexpected but Sam didn't dwell on it. Right now, while he had him, he wanted to hear what Pete Carruther had to say about Ryan the baseball player.

"Can I ask you a baseball question?"

"Sure."

"Ryan and his baseball ability. How good is he?"

"You know a lot about baseball. What do you think?"

Sam shrugged.

"I know baseball memorabilia but I'm no talent evaluator, Pete. How long you coaching baseball?"

"Twenty-one years," he answered.

Sam gestured with both hands towards him.

"I defer to you."

"No, no. I've seen you in the stands the last couple of games. You've seen Ryan a few times. Tell me what you think."

Exasperated, Sam gave Carruther an answer.

"Well Coach, I can't figure him out. On the one hand, he's got a beautiful swing. Great balance. The ball flies off his bat, so he must be generating tremendous bat speed. On the other hand, he shows his hitting ability only on occasion. He's incredibly inconsistent. His bad at-bats are really bad. And," he added, "he's a great defender with a golden arm."

Pete Carruther scratched his jaw, pulled his baseball cap from his head, and ran a hand through his thick, silver hair.

"Yeah," he said slowly, "that's Ryan. The kid with the million-dollar swing and the two-dollar attention span. You got him pegged perfect."

Carruther leaned back on the bench, and directed his comments to Susan.

"Twenty-one years I've been coaching baseball, Mrs. Buck; sixteen of them here. Never in all that time have I had a kid who I thought was good enough to have a shot at the big leagues. Twenty-one years. That's a lot of kids, a lot of practices, and a lot of ballgames. Then along comes your son with a swing that's as sweet as a summer peach. The kind of swing that can wait on a pitch and still drive it with power, just like the home run he hit today. Finally, a kid with the potential to make it big. Possibly my major leaguer, at last."

He paused and reflected for a moment.

"But Ryan's a special case. After all your family's been through..." He nodded at Susan. "He lugs a lot more out there," he said, pointing to home plate, "than a bat and a helmet. There's a lot going through his head when he's in the batter's box. I've talked about it with him but he doesn't have any answers." He paused. "He tells me he's happy playing at the level he's at. That it's all he wants and needs from playing ball."

"Even when you told him about his potential?" Sam said.

"Especially when I told him about his potential." Carruther scratched his head. "He wanted no part of it." He turned to Susan. "Mrs. Buck, I'm no shrink but he seems reluctant to let himself go, to commit. It's gotta be because of the accident; losing his dad and all. It's like he's afraid to care too much." He shook his head. "I'd push him if I thought it might do some good. But I think it would just drive him away."

"You've got a good handle on Ryan," Susan said. She gave Carruther a whisper of a smile. "You sure you're not a shrink?"

Sam was focused on something else Carruther had said. "You think he's good enough to make it to the majors?"

Carruther shrugged. "Who knows," he said. "It's a million to one shot. Then again, he has that million-dollar swing. And he's got great instincts for the game. You can see that by the way he plays the field. He's a natural right fielder with that arm of his. He always knows what to do when the ball is hit his way. And he's got that swing and the wrists to go with it." He took another slug of Gatorade. "Unfortunately, Ryan hasn't played that much. And he doesn't want it bad enough."

Susan looked at him questioningly.

"You really got to want to play this game to make it big," Coach explained. "Ryan doesn't feel that way and I understand why." Carruther stood up and then bent down to pick up a batters helmet that lay on the dugout floor. "Strange, isn't it? I finally get a kid who was born to play this game...and he doesn't want it." He shrugged again. "What you gonna do?"

Susan thanked Coach Carruther for taking the time to talk.

She and Sam headed for their respective cars. She drove directly home. Sam stopped for gas along the way.

The ten-minute drive to Susan's house wasn't long enough for Sam to fully digest Carruther's words. There was the part about the Coach overhearing Ryan talking to a friend about him, and the favorable review he apparently had received. Nice to hear, but not what he dwelled on. No, his thoughts were squarely focused on Carruther's analysis of Ryan and his baseball prowess. The Coach had confirmed Sam's own impression that Ryan had exceptional talent and he couldn't disagree with Carruther's psychological analysis, either. So why did he find what Pete said so unsettling?

He pulled up to Susan's house, parked his car, and gave the front door a couple of raps.

Michael called from inside, "Who's there?"

"It's me, Sam."

"Come on in."

Sam opened the door and walked in just as Michael came hobbling across the room on crutches. The crutches were for balance as his weight was borne by his right leg. He was wearing shorts so that what remained of his left leg was in clear view. It was the first time Sam had seen Michael without his prosthesis. He stopped dead in his tracks. Whatever preoccupation he had about Ryan disappeared instantaneously as he tried not to stare at Michael or the stump that protruded from the left leg of his shorts.

"You okay, Holmes?" Michael said.

"Sorry, Mike. I was caught off guard. Yeah, I'm okay," he stammered.

"Come on then." He gestured towards the dining room. "Dinner's ready and I'm starving."

"Okay. Let me go wash up."

Shakily, he headed for the bathroom as Michael continued towards the dining room.

Once there, he ran cold water and splashed it on his face. He did it again and then a third time.

There was a soft knock on the bathroom door.

"Sam, you all right?" It was Susan, and he heard concern in her voice. "Open the door. Please."

He opened it and stared at her. His face must have had a stricken look on it because she immediately embraced him.

"It's okay, Sam. It's hard to see Michael like this. Especially the first time."

"It hit me hard," he said.

He pulled away and looked her in the face. He could feel a tear slowly roll down his cheek.

"I didn't realize how much I care about Michael."

"Sam." She put one hand on his shoulder. "Michael doesn't wear his prosthesis all the time. Sometimes his stump gets sore and he has to give it a rest."

Sam had always thought of himself as a tough guy; a guy who always kept his emotions in check. But seeing Michael so vulnerable...it was painful.

"I'm okay, now," he said, sheepishly. "Phew. Sorry about that. Not very manly of me." He smiled weakly at her.

She gave him a warm smile and put her arm around his shoulder.

"Let's go inside. Dinner is on the table and I have a very hungry son waiting on us."

"I'm feeling embarrassed," he said. "I'm not sure I'll be able to look Michael in the eye."

"He sent me in here to check on you. He saw the look on your face when you walked in. You're not the first person to have that reaction, you know. Don't worry about Michael. Come on, let's eat."

"Ryan joining us?" Sam asked, as they walked towards the dining room.

"No, he's meeting up with this girl he went out with. They're grabbing a bite and then doing homework together. So, it's just the three of us."

"You all right, Sam?" Michael asked, as they entered the room.

"Yes, I'm fine now, Mike. Sorry for my reaction."

"It's okay, Sam. I get that from people who care about me. That's not bad if you think about it."

"No, not bad at all," he replied. Michael seemed to take it all in stride.

Sam searched for something to say that would lighten the mood.

"Hey, you know where your brother is tonight?"

"No idea."

"Having dinner with a certain someone named Maggie... and then they're doing homework together. Aren't you the little matchmaker!"

"No kidding! I've got to call Katie. I knew those two would be perfect for each other!"

Susan interrupted.

"Excuse me. Mind filling me in on what you two know and I don't?"

Michael proceeded to tell his mother about his dating Katie, Maggie's younger sister, and their plot to get their older siblings to go out with each other.

"You better not let your brother find out if you know what's good for you," Susan advised.

He smiled triumphantly.

"I won't tell if you guys don't."

CHAPTER 29

THEY DIDN'T GET VERY MUCH HOMEWORK DONE. NO SURPRISE THERE.

Instead, Ryan and Maggie talked and laughed. About college, music, Facebook, how annoying their younger siblings could be at times, their favorite foods, best friends, the beach. Everything under the sun.

Ryan found himself transported when he was with Maggie. He couldn't stop himself from babbling and making silly jokes, each of which she found funny. Not that all they talked about was light and airy. She was a good listener and he found himself opening up to her about the things that troubled him, too. How he had always wanted to become a professional football player, a quarterback. How that became unthinkable after the accident. His surprise that he enjoyed playing baseball but his frustration with his inconsistent performance, his inability to concentrate when he was up at bat. He told her about the recurring nightmare and how it had haunted him; how Caitlin had helped him to keep it under control; the mysterious key and the dream's new incarnation. He asked what she thought it might mean.

Maggie ran a hand through his dark, wavy hair. Gently, she kissed the bridge of his nose, then his lips.

"I don't know," she said, softly. "I think you're very brave, though. Being able to talk about it." She touched her forehead to his. "Be patient and positive." She gave him a lingering kiss. "If you enjoy baseball, give it a chance." Then she hugged him. Tightly.

Ryan hugged her back and he could feel their bodies meld together. It was like he couldn't tell where he ended and she began and he knew she was feeling the same. They stayed that way for a minute that seemed to stretch longer.

They ended their embrace. Their faces were aglow.

They smiled at each other and embraced again.

This time, though, Ryan held on for dear life, as a cold shaft of fear coursed through his body.

CHAPTER 30

SAM HAD JUST BACKED OUT OF HIS DRIVEWAY WHEN HIS CELL PHONE buzzed. It was a text from Susan.

"change in plans. call me."

What now? he thought.

The day was sunny and mild so Sam was driving his '98 Porsche 911 Cabriolet, the one he reserved strictly for low humidity, top-down weather. He pulled to the side of the road and punched Susan's number. It was a good news/ bad news call.

"Sam, that new client of mine, the one I just placed my first candidate with, they're having a sales meeting at the Breakers Hotel in Palm Beach. They invited me to join them for a late lunch and stay through the afternoon training session. It's a terrific opportunity!"

"That's good news."

"But it means I have to leave now to get there in time. I'm afraid I'm going to have to cancel this afternoon's attic exploration."

"That's too bad. I'm already in my car on the way up." He sighed in frustration.

"I'm sorry to disappoint you, Sam."

"It's not that, Susan." With the deadline for Standish's auction fast approaching and with some key questions that needed resolving, he was feeling pressured for time. "How about tomorrow?"

She sighed.

"Won't work. I'm jammed up the rest of the week and I'm hoping I'll be even busier after my meeting today." She knew that finding Zel's journal box was important but she wasn't prepared to let the search for it upend a golden opportunity like this.

"I understand." Sam decided it was time to share the stress he was beginning to feel. "Susan, I firmly believe that Standish's World Series auction is where you're gonna get the best prices for the Ruth memorabilia. Figuring out what went on between Zel and Babe Ruth is gonna have a huge impact on those prices. We're talking about a *lot* of money, Susan. Game-changing amounts of money!" He paused to let what he had just said sink in. "There's not much more than ten weeks until the auction deadline. We don't want to miss it."

He's right, Susan thought. But she had worked so hard to get to this point with her client and, now, finally a breakthrough. Then she got an idea. It was hardly ideal but it would do.

"Sam, what if you meet Ryan here and check out the attic with him? He's finished with school in an hour. I can text him and the two of you can look for the box together. How does that sound?"

It didn't sound so good to Sam. He didn't think it would sound good to Ryan, either.

"Think he'll go for that?"

"I doubt it would be his first choice but it's only an hour or so. It's not too much to ask of him." She paused. "I haven't told him about the box or why we want to find it," she said, thinking out loud. "I'll let him know what we're looking for but I'm not going to tell him why. Don't want to get into that unless I have to."

This is getting complicated. "I don't know, Susan."

"At least we'll find out if the box is there or not," she rationalized.

Reluctantly, Sam agreed.

"Okay then. I'll text him to meet you in front of the house."

"Very well. Knock 'em dead at your meeting!"

"Thanks, Sam. I'm so excited!"

Sam turned into Susan's driveway just after 3 PM. A few minutes later, Ryan pulled in right behind him and pushed a button on his rearview mirror. The garage door slowly rose to greet them.

Ryan was angry. The last thing he wanted to be doing was spend a couple of hours scrounging around the attic with Yoda, the overage dwarf who had seemingly become a fixture in their lives. Not that Sam was a bad guy. He definitely knew his baseball but why had he latched onto the Buck family? It had to be more than what mom said—that he was lonely. Ryan exited his car determined to get the attic search over as quickly as possible. Maybe he'd have enough time afterwards to stop by Maggie's, the place he *really* wanted to be. He did take a moment, though, to stop and look at the gleaming silver Porsche.

He proceeded silently into the garage, past Yoda, and pulled on the rope dangling down from the attic entrance. It took a good tug to get it going. Once open, he reached up, grabbed the bottom of the attic stairs and unfolded them down to the floor. He checked their sturdiness and carefully climbed up into the attic. A couple of steps from the top, he was able to poke his head in and look around. He found a light switch, flipped it on, and a bulb lit up, providing enough light to see for ten feet or so. Beyond that, though, it was difficult to see clearly. He swiveled his head around and took stock. Then he climbed down the steps.

"Wait here."

He turned and walked through the door that connected the garage to the house.

Sam let out a sigh. No greeting or any form of recognition. He stood alone at the base of the stairs. *Why did I agree to do this?*

Ryan returned with a large spotlight, two towels, and a couple of bottles of water.

"It's hot up there. We'll need these," he said, handing Sam a towel and a bottle.

Sam followed Ryan up the steps.

From Sam's limited experience searching through attics, this one was pretty neat. Most everything was in cardboard cartons with the exception of a couple of lamps without shades and a metal case with swivel locks on either side. He counted fifteen cartons of various sizes, most of which were within the ten foot circle of light. It was hot, though... a good ten to fifteen degrees warmer than outside. That put the temperature above 90. It only took a couple of minutes for the sweat to start beading on his forehead.

"Glad you got the towels and water," he said. "Your mom told you what we're looking for?"

"Some kind of wooden box that belonged to her great grandmother. What's so important about it?" Ryan said, gruffly.

Following Susan's wishes not to tell the boys what could be inside the box if it turned up, Sam was vague.

"There might be something inside the box that will make the Ruth items more valuable."

"Like what?"

"Not exactly sure," he lied.

Ryan gave a shrug and grabbed a carton, opened it and started looking through it.

The metal case with the swivel locks got Sam's attention.

"Know what this is?" he said.

Ryan shook his head.

Sam bent down, flipped the locks and, with a bit of effort, pulled the case off its base. Inside was a sewing machine that looked like it dated from the nineteen-sixties. Sam replaced the cover and pushed it to the center of the attic, closer to the light. He decided it would serve well as a bench he could sit on as he examined the contents of the boxes that sat around him.

As he looked closer at the cartons, he could see that two of them were cardboard filing boxes, the kind people use to file away old tax returns, receipts, and papers too important to throw away but not important enough to take up active storage space downstairs. He decided to start with those, thinking he would be able to get through them quickly. He opened the first box and found tax returns that went back a couple of decades. One end of the box had a tax return filed by Susan under her maiden name, Coster, from 1990. The other side of the box ended with Form 1040 for 2010 for William and Susan Buck—their entire marriage's financial history in a file box three feet long. He resisted the temptation to pry and didn't look at any numbers. Instead, he flipped through the pages in the carton looking for anything that might resemble a box. Nothing but papers though, so he quickly moved onto the next carton which was filled with what looked like back-up financial information; receipts and bank statements for a half dozen years or so, each bundled together by a rubber band. There were other papers in the carton, too. But only papers. Sam moved the two cartons he had inspected off to the side, piling one on top of the other.

Meanwhile, Ryan finished looking through a carton without success. He repacked the contents, moved it next to the cartons Sam had examined, and turned on the spotlight, shining it into all the dark areas.

"I can't remember the last time I was up here." He said it in a low voice, like he was talking to himself.

Probably when your Dad was still alive, Sam thought. He wondered if Ryan was thinking the same thing.

"Shit!" Ryan mumbled, sullenly. *He didn't want to be here!*

They each opened several more cartons, working in silence. Complete silence. The tension level in the attic seemed to rise as rapidly as the temperature. Sam couldn't decide what made him more uncomfortable—the heat or the stifling silence. He started to sweat profusely.

Enough, he thought. "When's your next game?" he offered.

Miserable that he was stuck in the attic instead of being with Maggie, hot and uncomfortable himself, Ryan exploded, like a dam bursting.

"Never mind my next game. What are you doing here! What's in this for you?" he shouted, accusingly.

Surprised by Ryan's outburst, Sam protested.

"For me?"

But Ryan wasn't interested in any explanations.

"What's in this for you!" he repeated. He had been crouched as he rummaged through the cartons but now he stood tall as his anger poured out. "Why are you spending all this time in Jupiter when you live in Boca? Why are you in our attic? I don't get it! What do you want from us! Why don't you leave us alone! Why are you here!!" He threw down the towel he was holding, bulled his way to the attic entrance, and stomped down the stairs.

Sam heard a car door slam shut and a motor start. Shaken, he realized he had been holding his breath during Ryan's rant. He exhaled slowly. *Why am I here?* He thought about it. *That's an easy one, Ryan.* He grasped his towel, wiped the sweat from his face, opened his water bottle and took a long swig. He bent over and picked up the towel Ryan had thrown to the floor and placed it beside himself on the metal case. *Is that what's bothering him?* He sat still for a couple of minutes as he dissected Ryan's tirade. He realized Ryan had asked two questions and, as he thought about it, he knew he had answers to both. It was time to clear up a few things with Ryan the next time they were together. He was tired of walking on egg shells around him. After a while, he pulled another unopened carton in front of him and started looking through its contents.

After leaving the attic, Ryan got in his car, slammed the door shut, turned the key, backed out of the driveway, and headed to Maggie's. He drove halfway down the block, stopped, then pulled to the curb.

Do I really want Maggie to see me like this? His internal cup of anger, which had reached overflow levels, was now empty. It had begun to refill with remorse and guilt. *I just bullied an old man,* he thought. *Didn't even give him a chance to explain himself. And I left him alone in the attic.* He suddenly felt embarrassed and ashamed. *Not going to be able to explain this to Mom. Damn! This is not right. Gotta go back!*

His head buried in a carton, Sam didn't hear Ryan climb the stairs. Suddenly, there he was, back in the attic.

Ryan found himself unable to make eye contact with Sam. Instead, he mumbled, "I'm sorry. I was out of line." He walked over to the carton he had been examining, and continued where he had left off.

This couldn't have been easy for him, coming back like this. He's a mensch, Sam thought. He took a long minute to compose his thoughts.

"I understand the questions you asked. What you must be thinking. 'Who is this strange looking guy who showed up from out of nowhere? Why is he here? And what's in it for him?' If positions were reversed, I'd be thinking the same thing. Maybe you should have asked those questions sooner." He paused. "Well, I'm gonna give you the answers but

I want to make a deal with you." He didn't wait for Ryan to respond. "If you don't believe what I'm saying, if you think I'm bullshitting you, I'll walk down the steps, get in my car, and you'll never hear from Sam Frank again." He paused. "But if you do believe me, there's another subject I want to discuss with you. Is it a deal?"

After his blow-up, Ryan was willing to at least let Sam explain himself. He nodded his head.

"Okay. You're first question was, 'Why am I here?' The answer is simple. 'Because your mother asked me.' Why did she ask me? Because I saved her from making a big mistake. I happen to know enough about this memorabilia stuff that I'm not gonna screw it up. I will make sure your mom gets the maximum prices for the items she's gonna sell. And we're not talking chicken feed." Sam spoke matter-of-factly so what he said didn't come off like he was bragging. "Your second question, 'What's in it for me?' That's a little more complicated." He paused. "But not much." He lowered his voice a notch. "I turned seventy this year; it's a bigger deal than I ever imagined." He chuckled, mirth-lessly. "People say sixty is the new forty, or some crap like that. Well, there's no getting around the fact that seventy is old." He sighed and shifted his weight on the makeshift metal bench. "It caused me to take stock of my life and, to be perfectly honest, I've been struggling ever since." He shrugged. "It's ironic. I've got more money than I'll ever be able to spend; own a fancy house in Boca and a beautiful apartment in Manhattan; got two cars, one of them a cool looking Porsche. Not bad, huh?"

He looked at Ryan who seemed to be listening intently.

"Not bad."

"But *nuthin* I'm doing is of any consequence. I got *nobody* of importance in my life. Friends, a few; family, none; no one of significance. I'm a solitary man." He paused, folded shut the flaps of a carton, and moved it alongside the other cartons they had examined. "Don't get the impression I'm feeling sorry for myself because I'm not. I don't blame anyone. It's the choices I made that got me where I am. But for some time now I've been feeling rather useless. Then, completely by chance, I meet your mother and save her from making that big mistake. Over coffee, I learn what happened to your family and the reason why she's selling the Ruth items and suddenly I have a purpose, a connection. I meet you and your brother which gives me all the more reason to use what I know to help all of you get ahead. Why? Because the Buck family is worthy of whatever I can contribute." He rubbed his hands over his face and sighed again. "You ask, what's in it for me? Nuthin more than the satisfaction of lending a hand." Sam looked up at Ryan. "Can you accept that or is my explanation too bland for you?"

"You make it sound pretty simple," he said, skeptically.

"Simple?" He laughed, softly. "Maybe so." He slid over another carton. "Have you ever heard of Occam's Razor?"

Ryan shook his head.

Sam said, "I read about it somewhere. It's a principle that says the simplest explanation is usually the right one. Ryan, I can make up some convoluted plot if you'd like, but it wouldn't be true. You can buy what I say or not but that's my story and I'm not changing it. I guess the real question is: are you willing to accept it?"

Ryan didn't answer. Instead, he knelt down and opened another box.

Silence returned to the attic's confined space.

After a while, Ryan spoke.

"I've got a question."

Sam looked at him.

"You've got money, you're smart, and you're obviously successful. Mom says you've got character." He paused. "Why are you alone?"

Sam, who boxed as a kid, always could see a knockout punch coming long before it got there but Ryan had just landed a real haymaker with his simple question, "Why are you alone?"

That was a damn good question, one that Sam wasn't expecting nor had a ready answer for. As he thought about it, a gear shifted in his head and he experienced a moment of blinding clarity. Unexpectedly, a few things became well-defined and suddenly he understood why Coach Carruther's analysis of Ryan was so unsettling to him. Carruther thought Ryan was afraid to commit to baseball, because of the loss of his dad; Ryan was unable to allow himself to care too deeply, because it hurt so badly if you lost that thing you cared so much about. It hit Sam that Carruther's depiction of Ryan was also a description of him. With sudden lucidity he recognized why he had avoided serious relationships all the years since Frankie died. It was because he didn't want to expose himself to the type of pain and hurt he had endured when he lost his wife. That was the underlying reason, not the myriad excuses he made to himself over the years as he avoided getting too close to anyone. It was an epiphany.

A minute or so passed as Sam sat silently, deep in thought. He realized that the question Ryan had asked him was a bridge to the other subject he wanted to talk about with Ryan.

Ryan waited patiently for an answer.

Finally, Sam shook himself. Slowly and deliberately, he shared what he had just discovered.

"You know, you're never too old to learn something about yourself. Your question just now helped me get a better glimpse of myself." He looked off into space. "The reason I'm alone is that I've been afraid of finding someone I could love and then losing that someone. Like what happened when I lost Frankie. I've been afraid to get too close to anyone ever since; because I didn't want to feel that pain again." He looked at Ryan. "When your whole world gets turned upside down you get gun shy." He paused. "And I didn't understand why until just now, when you asked me that question." He turned back to Ryan. "That's it. Are you satisfied? Are we good so far?"

Sam's words were ringing in Ryan's head. "When your whole world gets turned upside down you get gun-shy." *My feelings exactly!*

Ryan gave a slight nod of his head.

Sam felt relief. *So far, so good. Now, the next part.*

"Okay then. Let's talk baseball. After your last game, your mom spoke with your coach. I tagged along. He's a pretty smart guy...when it comes to baseball and when it comes to people. He told your mom you've got the best swing of any ballplayer he's ever coached. He said you play defense instinctually and you have a cannon for an arm. That you are the most talented ballplayer he's ever worked with." Sam paused. He looked at Ryan and tried to gauge his reaction before he continued. Would he explode again? Was he interested in what he had to say? But all Ryan did was blink a few times. Sam couldn't tell what he was feeling. After a moment he continued. "He also told your mom what I just told you about myself. He thinks it's hard for you to commit to making the most of your talent. That it's difficult to care too much, just like me. Me, because of the loss of my wife; you because of the loss of your dad. What I know that he doesn't is the type of pain you feel when you lose someone you love more than life itself." He paused. "The kind of pain that will allow you to only go so far.

"Now, though, I look back over the last twenty years and I see that not allowing myself to care was no way to live my life. It might have been safe, but..." His voice trailed off and he looked away before turning back. "Ryan, we can't be afraid to have passion in our lives. We can't fear embracing the opportunities that come our way." He took a deep breath, and exhaled.

"Why am I telling you this? I know we're different people, you and I. We've had to deal with very different tragedies. I know we each have to find our own paths. But maybe this insight into me, which you helped me discover, can help you find your path a little faster and make it a little easier."

Ryan's mind was churning. When Sam spoke of a fear of commitment it rang true. His budding relationship with Maggie was exhilarating and scary; letting his feelings out, allowing himself to care was an excruciatingly difficult thing. It wasn't a matter of trust; he trusted her completely. It was about how it could all disappear in an instant; it was thinking that another tragedy could tear someone dear from him and turn his world upside down again. He didn't think he could go through that another time.

Ryan realized that six or twelve months ago he probably wouldn't have been able to acknowledge the accuracy of what Sam had just said. But he had made progress; he was mentally stronger and he was highly motivated: because of Maggie he desperately wanted to be able to let himself go, to care without fear. He didn't want to screw this up!

This funny looking little man who was old enough to be his grandfather had a more willing audience than he suspected. He had a lot to think about.

Sam continued. "Can an old guy, who's still learning things about himself, give you a piece of advice?"

Ryan nodded.

Sam leaned forward and looked directly in the eyes of the young man who might possibly be the great, great grandson of Babe Ruth.

"Ryan, you're a very talented ballplayer. I've watched you play and I think you might be able to do great things. More importantly, so does Coach Carruther. You've got a couple of months remaining to your baseball season. Give it a shot, a real shot. Challenge yourself and find out how good you are. Make the commitment and let yourself care. Treat each at-bat like it's the last one you'll ever have. Give it everything you've got!"

Ryan tried to digest what Sam had said. He was enjoying playing ball more and more. He had begun to wonder how good he could be. And treating each at-bat as if it was going to be his last was an idea that sat comfortably with him.

They got quiet, each lost in their own thoughts as they opened and scoured through the remaining cartons.

Sam wasn't sure if he had reached Ryan.

The wooden box remained elusive.

One unopened carton remained. It differed from the others in two ways. It looked newer and, unlike the other boxes with folded flaps, it was sealed with packing tape.

"This must have the family jewels in it," Ryan said. "Check out the extra security system in place."

Sam took a gulp of his almost empty water bottle, wiped the sweat off his face with the now grimy towel, and fished around in his pocket for his key ring. He used one of the keys on the ring to slice open the top and did the same for the tape that sealed the edges.

"Behold, your family fortune awaits you." He gestured to Ryan to open the box.

Ryan knelt down and pushed back the flaps to reveal a man's beige sweater, neatly folded. He removed it from the carton to find a blue striped shirt, also carefully folded, beneath it.

"What is this?" Ryan wondered aloud.

He took out a few more articles of clothing before he realized what he was looking at.

"Oh, God!" he said, softly. He looked up at Sam, his eyes wide and his full lips quivering. "These were my father's clothes."

Sam stood up, took the clothes from Ryan's hands, and gently laid them on the metal case.

Ryan continued removing clothes from the box. Half way down, he pulled out a dark green sweatshirt, one that by appearance had seen lots of use. Ryan put it to his face and breathed in deeply.

Tears came to Sam's eyes as he watched him because he knew what Ryan was doing. He had done the same thing when, a year after she died, he had finally got the courage to pack up Frankie's clothes. He remembered putting her favorite purple sweater, the one she wore most often, to his nose and breathing in her scent. He could still smell her.

"Can you smell him?" he asked, gently.

"I don't know. He wore this old sweatshirt a lot. I'm so glad Mom saved these things."

Ryan had a brave smile on his face as tears glistened in his eyes. Sam wanted to pull him close and hug him tightly, but he had already turned back to the box after carefully laying his dad's sweatshirt next to the other articles of clothing.

Ryan continued to remove his dad's clothes. Somewhere near the bottom he pulled out a neatly folded white tee shirt with a thin, blue neckline. As Ryan opened it, its back facing Sam, Sam could see something written on the front.

Ryan stared at it. Tears overflowed his eyes and ran down his cheeks. After a while, he sniffled and spoke as he continued to stare at the tee shirt he held in front of him.

"One year, when we were little, Michael and I got it in our heads to make Dad a special tee shirt for Father's Day. Mom helped us pick out the shirt and letters that could be ironed on. We were all excited about doing this. Mom showed us how to iron on the first letter, Michael did the second, and I put on the last letter. Only I had a problem. I ironed my letter on the wrong way, so instead of it reading D A D, it read D A ◖, with the second D backwards." Ryan turned the tee shirt to Sam, revealing what he had just explained. "I was so embarrassed, but Dad loved it. He wore it all the time. Mom had to fight with him to take it off so she could wash it. It was his favorite shirt and became his trademark. He wore it to all our games."

Ryan pulled the tee shirt to his face and breathed deeply. "I can smell him," he sobbed. "I can smell him."

Sam pulled him close. Ryan cried for a while as Sam silently held him.

Later, they carefully repacked the carton with his Dad's clothes. Ryan went down and got more packing tape and resealed it. He turned out the light in the attic and descended the steps, Sam following him down. Ryan closed up the stairs and they headed into the house to wash up, Ryan with his Dad's tee shirt in his hand.

They hadn't found the wooden box but maybe, Sam thought, Ryan had found something far more important.

CHAPTER 31

WHILE THEY WERE WASHING UP, RYAN RECEIVED A TEXT FROM HIS mother saying that her client had invited her to dinner, a positive sign. Michael was eating at Louie's so Sam invited him out for a burger and fries. They exited the house through the garage.

"Nice car," Ryan said. He ran his hand lightly over the ultra-smooth finish of the Porsche.

Sam tossed him the key.

"Wanna drive?"

Something jogged in Ryan's head as he caught it. A momentary flash. *The key!* A chill surged down his spine as he felt a sense of foreboding.

"No thanks," he said. He walked around the car and handed the key back to Sam. "Don't know how to drive a stick."

"Another time."

They got into the Porsche, both of them preoccupied with their thoughts.

Sam was thinking that maybe he and Ryan had connected. And here they were going out to eat together. But Ryan had yet to respond, positively or negatively, to the baseball appeal he had made. Had he reached him? Or, had he gone too far, maybe pushed him too hard? What was Ryan thinking? What was he feeling?

Ryan was trying to process a jumble of thoughts. What Sam had said to him in the attic, about overcoming his lingering commitment fears and how it related to his relationship with Maggie; Sam's challenge to give it all he had on the ball field; the concept of treating every at-bat like it was his last which struck a responsive chord within him; Dad's tee shirt and the emotions it stirred. And then that chill down his spine when Sam tossed him the car key. *A key floating through the air. What does it mean?*

Sam shifted into third gear and the Porsche surged forward as they left Ryan's community and turned onto a four lane road that would lead them to the burger joint. Sam pushed the radio's on-button and the sounds of the Who's "Who Are You" blanketed them.

"Classic rock okay?" Sam said.

"Sure," Ryan said, absentmindedly.

Ryan tried to push down all the thoughts that were jumping around in his head. He had never driven in a Porsche before and he wanted to concentrate on the experience.

They drove in silence.

"How do you feel about our conversation?" Sam asked, breaking the stillness which had started to become uncomfortable again. He needed some feedback from Ryan.

"Still processing it. It's a lot to think about."

"Sorry if I said too much."

"No. It was a good conversation. I'm glad we had it."

The Who ended and they were immediately followed by Jefferson Airplane. Grace Slick intoned, *One pill makes you larger, and one pill makes you small.*

Ryan felt another chill run down his spine. He shook his head. *What the hell is going on?*

Out of the corner of his eye, Sam saw Ryan shake his head. "You alright?" he asked.

"Yeah," Ryan said, without conviction. "I guess I'm a little tired."

Sam drove on hoping that he hadn't overwhelmed Ryan. Ryan remained silent.

They were less than a mile from the restaurant. Sam kept the Porsche in third.

More silence, other than Grace starting to build to the song's crescendo.

"I'm going to get me a mushroom burger with cheese," Sam said. Something to break the tension that seemed to have enveloped them. "How about you?"

"Not sure," Ryan said. The last thing on his mind was food. He felt his throat tighten and it became hard to swallow.

The dream popped into his head. *What the fuck! This only happens when I'm sleeping!*

Feed your head, feed your heaaaaaaad!

Suddenly, it all came back to him in a cascading flood of memory...

Sam saw Ryan start to shake. He immediately slowed the car, and turned off the radio.

"Ryan, what's the matter! Are you all right?"

"No," Ryan said, in a strangled voice. He raised his hands and covered his face. "I need to be alone. I need to think."

Panic rose within Ryan as his throat tightened further. He started breathing rapidly. Sweat poured down his face. He needed to escape the car. He felt nauseous.

"Stop the car, Sam. I'm gonna puke!"

Sam pulled off the road.

Ryan opened the door before the car came to a complete stop and exited. He took a couple of steps, leaned over, put his hands on his knees and began retching.

Sam sat in the car, nervous and agitated. What was happening to Ryan? Was he the cause of this? What should he do? Paralyzed by doubt, he finally pushed the button for his emergency flashers and sat there feeling helpless.

Ryan felt calmer after he threw up. He took a few deep breaths. He decided to stop fighting the images that were surging through his head and go with the feeling and when he did, the panic subsided; enough that he could think. After a minute, he got back in the Porsche.

"Take me to the ball field, Sam. Drop me off."

"Ryan, I can't leave you alone like..."

"Do it, Sam! I just remembered something that I haven't been able to remember. I need to think about it. Please! Take me to the field!"

Sam recalled what Susan had told him about Ryan.

"The accident? You remember the accident?"

Ryan's eyes widened but he didn't say a word.

They drove to the field in silence as Ryan pieced it all together.

CHAPTER 32

THE PASS WAS THROWN WITH A PRECISION TOUCH.

As the ball spiraled towards the corner of the end zone and softly settled into his fleet receiver's hands, sixteen-year-old Ryan threw his arms in the air victoriously. With no time outs and less than two minutes remaining in the game, he had engineered a seventy-two yard touchdown drive to propel his team to a breathtaking, come-from-behind victory. His teammates mobbed their star quarterback and pounded him on his shoulder pads and helmet until he fell to the ground and then they piled all over him. What a win!

Afterwards, he met up with Dad and Michael. As they walked along the sidelines towards the parking lot, Michael tossed a football to him and scampered onto the empty playing field.

"Post pattern," he called back, and took off in a sprint.

Laughing, Ryan dropped his gear, positioned the football in his left hand as he made his four step drop, and, as his brother cut for the right goal post, winged the ball. The pass was a yard too long but Michael seemed to kick his stride into another gear. He stretched out as the ball reached him, corralled it with his fingertips, and charged into the end zone.

"Touchdown!" Michael called out. "Buck to Buck for six points!"

"He's going to be better than you in another year or so," their father said, low enough that Michael wouldn't hear. His youngest son's ego definitely did not need any feeding.

Michael met back up with them and they walked to the car three abreast, William Buck in the middle, his arms around each of his sons.

"Pretty soon, you boys will have a couple of years together to perfect your pass routes. I'm looking forward to that."

Ryan was a sophomore and had already earned the starting quarterback position; Michael, fourteen, would become a freshman next season. While Ryan was a gifted athlete, Bill Buck knew that his youngest son was the more talented of the two. He thought about those moments-to-be as he double-clicked the electronic key that unlocked the doors to their SUV.

Ryan opened the hatchback, heaved his equipment into the cargo space, and slammed it shut.

"Want to drive?" His father tossed him the car key.

Ryan caught it but tossed it back. "No thanks. I'm dog tired." That last touchdown drive was a huge adrenaline rush. In its wake, he was feeling weary.

"I'll drive!" Michael piped up. But his driving days were a couple of years away.

"Don't think so," said his dad, as he opened the rear seat driver's side door. "Difficult to drive from back here." Michael slid in.

The sounds of Credence Clearwater's Bad Moon Rising filled the air as Bill Buck, a Classic Vinyl fan, pulled out of the near empty lot. He hit a few buttons on the console and soon the ringing of a phone could be heard inside the car. "Calling Mom," he said, before the boys could ask.

"Tell her I'm starving," Michael called out from behind him.

Bill glanced in his rearview mirror, caught Michael's eye, and gave him a sarcastic look.

"Think she doesn't know?"

When Susan answered the phone, Michael was the first to speak. "We're on our way home, Mom. What's for dinner?"

"Chicken Mama." One of their favorites.

"Great! I'm starving!" Michael crowed.

"Shocking!" Susan said, and then changed the subject. "How was the game?"

"We won," Ryan said.

"In dramatic fashion, I might add," said Bill.

"Can't wait to hear all about it. How far away are you?"

"Ten minutes," he said, as they rounded a curve in the road. Up ahead, the annoying traffic light, the one which took forever to change, blinked from red to green. "Maybe less."

"Okay," she said, then added for Michael's benefit, "Food will be on the table."

"Thank you, Chef Susan," Michael quipped.

"See you soon," said Bill, and ended the call.

The radio returned and Jefferson Airplane's "White Rabbit" pulsed through the confined space of the car. For the moment, Michael sat quietly in the back seat.

"When's your next game?" Bill asked, glancing towards Ryan.

"Next Friday," Ryan answered, as he turned to his father.

As they crossed the intersection, the song reached its crescendo and Grace Slick cried out commandingly, *Feed your heaaaaad!*.

From seemingly out of nowhere, Ryan saw headlights, impossibly close, through his father's side window. His eyes widened and he felt a huge adrenaline pulse as he cried out, "Da..."

And then everything exploded.

The speeding car hit them square on, front of center, with a force that drove their mortally wounded SUV dead right, halting their momentum far too suddenly. The crash unleashed forces that strained the safety features of their car to the limit...and beyond. Ryan felt himself thrown violently to the right as everything telescoped in on him. His head smashed into a side strut and he felt an unbearable pain in his left leg. The car seemed to slide in slow motion, as if it would slide forever. Strangely, he seemed to hear a melody from far off, *Feed your heaaaaaaaaaad...*

Then everything went black.

CHAPTER 33

JUPITER, FLORIDA
MARCH, 2013

Ryan sat in the bleachers for over an hour without moving. Then, he reached in his pocket, pulled out his phone, and dialed a number.

Sam, who had been sitting silently in his car, never taking his eyes off of Ryan, pushed a button that lowered his window. He heard Ryan say, "I remember. I need to see you." Ryan listened for a moment and then said, "I'll be there as soon as I can."

He got up and started walking towards the roadway.

Sam tapped on the horn twice and turned on the headlights. Slowly, he drove up to Ryan. "Ryan, let me give you a ride."

A calm and controlled Ryan nodded his head and got into the Porsche.

Sam dropped Ryan off and watched as he knocked on the door of his therapist's office. A woman answered and let him in.

Sam exhaled slowly, then took out his phone and dialed Susan.

She answered on the first ring.

"I was just getting ready to call you!" She sounded cheerful. "I had a great meeting and dinner. They've given me five sales positions to fill, Sam. This could be my big break!"

The excitement in her voice made what he was about to tell her all the more difficult.

"That's good news." He cleared his throat. "Susan, something happened." He tried to keep his tone calm but didn't succeed.

"What?" There was sudden panic in her voice as she flashed back to the accident.

"I'm parked outside Ryan's therapist's office."

"Is Ryan all right? What happened?"

"He's inside talking with her. He remembered the accident."

"Oh my God! How is he?"

"He seems to be under control. Maybe you should…"

"I'm on my way. Call me if anything changes."

A half hour later, Susan's car pulled alongside the Porsche. She jumped out and joined Sam in his car. He explained what had transpired: their attic discussion, their decision to go out for dinner, Ryan's strange behavior in the car, his hour of solitude in the bleachers, his phone call to his therapist, and their ride here. Sam gave her as much detail as he could recall, right down to the song that was playing when Ryan freaked out.

"It was Jefferson Airplane, 'White Rabbit,'" Sam said. "I hope I didn't do anything wrong, Susan. I feel terrible. I wasn't sure whether I should call you from the field or what."

"You did good, Sam," Susan said, reassuringly. She shared with him what Caitlin had told her; that repressed memories can come flooding back as a result of being triggered by an event.

"Caitlin also told me that the mind will allow repressed memories to surface when the person is strong enough to handle them. I don't think that what happened is a setback."

Susan wasn't sure if she was saying that for Sam's benefit or her own. Her heart was in her mouth since Sam told her what occurred. She turned to him.

"I'm going to wait inside. I want to talk with Caitlin myself. You go home." Her distinctive blue eyes pooled with liquid. "Thanks for watching after Ryan. I'm glad you were there for him."

She reached across the stick shift, gave him a hug, and exited the car.

CHAPTER 34

RYAN STOOD IN FRONT OF HIS BATHROOM MIRROR ABSENTMINDEDLY brushing his teeth as he tried to process his day. Between his recall of the crash and the ensuing discussion with Caitlin and Mom, his attic conversation with Sam, and the unearthing of his Dad's special tee shirt, his mind was bursting. It wasn't until his gums started hurting that he realized he must have been brushing for a good ten minutes. He put his toothbrush away, rinsed his mouth, and stared into the mirror. The image staring back at him was the same person who had brushed his teeth that morning but now he saw himself differently.

He no longer had to contend with the black emptiness of not knowing what had happened. It was as if a giant weight had been removed from his shoulders. He felt lighter, relieved.

But his relief was tinged with the guilt he had been feeling all along. Only now he thought he knew why he felt guilty. The key. If he hadn't tossed it back, things would have been different. But, Caitlin and Mom convinced him it would not have been better. After all, it was Dad who taught him to drive and he drove just like Dad. So it could very well have been him who died in the crash. A shiver ran through his body as he stared into the mirror. He was glad he was alive and he didn't feel the need to apologize about that.

Ryan walked into his room and picked up the D A ᑕ tee shirt that lay on the bed. He slipped it on. A perfect fit. It made him feel closer to Dad than at any time since the crash and he wanted to wear it to bed. But he had other plans for the shirt so he took it off, folded it neatly, and placed it on top of his dresser.

He got into bed and, after a while, fell into a deep, dreamless sleep.

CHAPTER 35

IT WAS EARLY THE NEXT MORNING, EARLY ENOUGH THAT SUSAN HESITATed before picking up the phone to call Sam, but then she figured he was probably up.

"Did I wake you?" she asked, when he answered.

"Wake me? I didn't sleep more than ten minutes last night. How's Ryan?"

"He's good, Sam. He spent a couple of hours with Caitlin and then I joined them for a while. When we got home we talked until midnight. Then we both collapsed."

Sam exhaled.

"That's a relief. What happened?"

Susan explained the sequence of events that led to Ryan's sudden recall: the tossing of the car key and the significance of the song, the fact that Ryan's recurring dream had recently changed with the addition of the glaring headlights, an indication that his memory was returning.

"Caitlin talked him through it and helped him make sense of it all. The car key, that's what bothers him the most."

"What do you mean?"

"Apparently, Bill tossed him the car key and offered to let Ryan drive. But Ryan tossed it back to him saying he was too tired. Ryan talked about how things might have been different if he hadn't tossed the key back and, instead, got behind the wheel himself and driven home. Caitlin made the point that, if that were the case, it might have been him who was killed. He said he realized that but it also meant that his father would be alive today and that maybe our family would be better off. Caitlin told him that the most painful and hardest to bear of all losses is a parent losing a child. Later, when I joined the discussion, he posed the question to me."

"What did you say?"

"I didn't say anything. I just shook my head and cried and cried and cried. He got the message."

"So, you think he's all right?"

"Actually, I think he's relieved. When we got home he said 'knowing is a lot better than not knowing."

Sam sighed in relief.

"Sounds pretty positive."

"Before he went to bed, he showed me the famous D A D tee shirt you guys found in the attic. Oh Sam, we both had a good cry when I saw it. I remember when the boys made it for Bill and how upset Ryan was when he ironed the letter on backwards. And his reaction when Bill saw it and loved it. He told Ryan and Michael the tee shirt made him feel special. That no one else in the whole world had a D A D tee shirt like his, which made him feel like he was a one-of-a-kind dad. Ryan went from embarrassed to beaming in a heartbeat. It's a memory I'll always cherish."

"When Ryan found the tee shirt, he put it to his face and said he could smell his dad."

"He told me that and asked me to do it, too."

"Could you smell him?"

"I don't know. Maybe. I told Ryan I could. It made him happy. Then he said something strange. He asked me if it was okay if he wore the tee shirt."

Sounds morbid. "How do you feel about that?"

"I thought it was weird. Until he explained what he meant."

"What was that?"

"He wants to wear the tee shirt under his baseball uniform when he's playing ball. Only then."

Sam took a breath and sat up in his chair.

"What was your answer?" he asked.

"I told him I thought it was a fine idea. Michael laughed and said why not. Superman had his cape, why shouldn't Ryan have his special tee shirt? Maybe it will imbue him with super powers."

Not so crazy, Sam thought.

"When's his next game?"

"Tomorrow night."

"How about we watch him play?"

"Sure." Then Susan shifted gears.

"With everything going on I forgot to ask Ryan about the box. Any sign of it?"

"None."

"Too bad." She sighed. "It must be in my parents' house. We're going to have to go to Ocala and search for it."

"We'll get it, don't worry."

"Maybe," she said, wearily, "but it won't be easy. It's a big old house filled with a lot of stuff that's accumulated over the years."

CHAPTER 36

THE NEXT MORNING SAM RECEIVED A CALL FROM JAMES DENT, THE president of Standish Auctions. In his no-nonsense manner, Dent got right to the point.

"Sam. When are you going to send that diary for me to read?"

"Soon," Sam said. "I've been busy arranging for everything to be graded and authenticated. You'll have the diary in plenty of time to verify its authenticity."

The truth was he wanted to delay sending him the diary until they knew about the hair clippings.

"It's situations like this, that pop up out of the blue, that's the fun part of what we do," Dent philosophized. "Bringing newly discovered material to light. I look forward to representing you. Please call me if I can be of assistance."

That afternoon, Sam picked up Susan and drove to the ballpark. They were both excited about Ryan's game and how he would play. Would they see a noticeable difference? Sam told Susan the key for him would be Ryan's discipline when it came to not swinging at pitches outside the strike zone. Susan wanted to see him hit a few home runs.

There was the usual sparse crowd in attendance: a few parents, some students, and a small group of neighborhood people. Sam and Susan saw Michael and two girls enter the stands from an entrance on the first base side. They sat chatting idly as the players finished their pre-game warm-ups. Ryan was down the first base line, tossing a ball to a teammate. He didn't acknowledge their presence.

From their right, Susan heard a cry.

"Yo, Mom!"

It was Michael bellowing to them. Susan waved. He said something to the girls, got up from his seat, and started threading his way through the rows of aluminum benches.

"Hi kids," Michael said, jauntily. "Come to see Ryan play with his Jedi warrior shield in place underneath his uniform?"

"Michael, please," Susan said. "I hope you're not making fun of your brother about this. I think he's taking it seriously."

"I know he is. But I was kidding him about it, too, before he went out on the field. I think he needed it. He's very intense." Michael turned to Sam. "Hey, Holmes."

"Is that Katie over there?" Susan asked, before Sam could answer.

"Yeah. And that's her sister Maggie, next to her."

Susan waved and they waved back.

"Why don't you bring them over to sit with us?" Susan suggested.

"That's all right, Mom. We'll sit over there. We haven't prepared them enough to meet you."

"Okay, be like that." She pretended not to care.

"See you later, Holmes." Michael gave Sam a smile and extended his hand to slap five, which they did.

As Michael headed back, Susan pretended to watch him but she was really checking out the girls.

"They look cute," she said. "Clean-cut, too." The girls were far enough away that they looked the same age. Katie was fair, with light brown, almost blonde, hair. Maggie was a brunette. "I like the look of them," Susan decided.

"So do the boys."

Just then Ryan's team took the field. Coach Carruther stepped out of the dugout, stretched, and took a glance at the stands. When he looked their way, he gave Sam a nod of his head. Ryan made his way to right field.

The top of the first inning went uneventfully. Three up, three down.

In the bottom of the first, it was clear by the time the third batter came to the plate, that the other team's pitcher was going to have a rough outing. He walked the first two batters and the third batter smacked a double down the left field line, scoring one run and putting runners on second and third. He then proceeded to walk the next batter. This brought Ryan, hitting fifth, to the plate with the bases loaded and no one out.

Susan and Sam sat forward as they watched him step into the batter's box. Before assuming his batting stance, Ryan tapped his chest twice with his right fist, right where the letters would be on the D A C tee shirt he was wearing under his uniform. He swung his bat easily a couple of times and then set himself, waiting for the pitch. Ball one, outside. He set himself again. Ball two, low. *This is good*, Sam thought. While both pitches were outside the strike zone, they weren't off by much. He had watched Ryan swing at similar pitches and miss. By not swinging, Ryan was forcing the pitcher to put the ball somewhere over the plate.

Before the hurler could throw his next pitch, the other team's coach called time and walked out to the mound. A brief discussion ensued.

As the coach returned to the dugout, Ryan stepped back into the box. The pitcher stared in at his catcher. As the pitcher went into his windup, Sam quietly said to Susan, "Ryan should get a good pitch to hit here."

The pitcher threw and Ryan swung. Bat connected with ball and they immediately knew it was a home run. It was a no-doubter that soared over the right field fence. Ryan had himself a grand slam.

Susan and Sam leaped from their seats, cheering lustily and high-fiving each other. Across the way, Michael and the girls did the same. Sam watched Ryan as he rounded the bases, all business. *What a start!*

As the game went on, Ryan continued to have success at the plate, going four for five, with two doubles and a single to go with his grand slam. He drove in six runs and scored three. They won the game eleven to two and Ryan was the star.

After the game, as Ryan was in the locker room changing, Michael and the girls joined Susan and Sam.

Michael did the honors, introducing everyone to each other, identifying Sam as a friend of the family. The girls were personable, friendly, and at ease. Susan helped make them feel comfortable as she went out of her way to be nice and ask questions about them. They all marveled at the game Ryan had. Maggie beamed when she talked about him.

Before they ran out of things to talk about, Ryan emerged from the locker room. He tried to play it cool, especially with the girls there, but even he had to acknowledge he had a great game.

"We weren't exactly hitting against the toughest pitchers today," he added, just to keep everyone's feet on the ground.

"Who do you play next?" Sam asked.

"A tougher team...from Stuart. And the game's at their field."

"How's their pitching?"

"They've got a couple of guys with live arms. Should be a good test."

Sam got the sense that Ryan was looking forward to the challenge. Perhaps it was wishful thinking on his part, but he thought he could see an intensity that he hadn't seen before. But it was one game, against mediocre pitching, as Ryan had pointed out. They would just have to wait and see what transpired.

"Maggie and I are gonna grab something to eat," Ryan said to his mom.

"Sure," Susan said. "You two have a good time."

"You need a ride home, Katie?" Ryan asked.

"That would be great, Ryan." She smiled up at him. Katie was a shade over five feet, her sister a few inches taller. "Michael, you want to come over?" Katie asked.

"I'm in," he said.

With that, they were gone, laughing amongst themselves, as they headed to Ryan's car.

"How nice is that?" Sam said.

Susan watched the four of them, Ryan with his arm around Maggie, Michael and Katie holding hands, walk to the parking lot.

"Very nice," Susan said. "Very nice, indeed."

Susan and Sam headed to a local Italian place. The topic of discussion was the elusive journal box. Susan shared her thoughts.

"I'm going to need you with me when I go there," she said, referring to her parents' home. "It's a three-and-a-half hour ride from here to Ocala and it could take all day trying to find it." She explained. "I tried to get my father to clean the place up after mom died but he'd never do it. Then the dementia set in and that ended that. Mom's gone almost ten years; a long time for stuff to accumulate."

"Any idea where it might be?"

"I've thought about that. I think Mom would most likely have stored it away safely somewhere. The first place we should look is the attic; after that, the library. If it's not in

either of those places, we'll have to search room by room."
She sighed. "This could be a big job, Sam. You up for this?"

"It's gotta be done, Susan," Sam said, without hesitation.
"If the box still exists, we need to find it."

"Okay then. What are you doing Saturday?"

Sam grimaced. "Sorry. I've got a meeting with the Joint
Chiefs of Staff."

"Very funny."

He smiled. "Saturday, I think I'm going to Ocala. Would
that be correct?"

"That would be correct. And we're leaving early. My house,
5 AM."

"Jeez! What are we doing? Going fishing?"

"We're going to need all day." Susan laughed, mirthlessly.
"And we *are* going fishing. Let's just hope we catch something."

CHAPTER 37

Sam was the only member of Ryan's rooting section at his next game. Stuart was twenty-five miles north of Jupiter and a forty-five minute ride to the high school field where they were playing. Far enough away that Susan, who was busy unearthing candidates for the positions she had to fill, couldn't be there, while Michael had classes that ran through the start of the game.

It was too bad they weren't able to see Ryan's performance, Sam thought. Against much better pitching, Ryan excelled again. He went three for three with a walk, smacking two doubles and a triple. He was locked in. With his newly found focus his command of the strike zone improved dramatically. He laid off a number of close pitches that were called balls. When pitches were in the strike zone, he was exceptionally efficient. By Sam's unofficial count, he swung and missed at only one pitch in his four at bats. Remarkable hitting.

His team won the game, 7–3.

Ryan approached Sam before boarding the team bus back to Jupiter. He appreciated Sam coming to an away game to watch him play. He had yet to say anything further about their attic discussion.

"How's my focus, Sam?" he asked. There was a sparkle in his eye.

"Lookin' sharp, Ryan. How you feel?"

Ryan thought for a second.

"Passionate."

He gave Sam a nod of his head and stepped onto the bus.

Because of a rainout earlier in the season, Ryan had a game the next day, too. With the hot streak he was on, he wasn't complaining. With Susan, Michael, Maggie, and Sam in attendance, Ryan made a running catch in the top of the first to take away a sure double that saved a couple of runs.

Coach Carruther had moved him up to the cleanup hitter's slot in the batting order, the spot usually reserved for the team's top power hitter. Ryan didn't disappoint, as he went three for four that included a homer, a double, three runs batted in, and three runs scored. His home run was a monster drive down the right field line that went far over the fence. Susan and Maggie cheered as Michael excitedly thumped Sam on the shoulder and yelled, "What a shot! Did you see that shot!!" It was a major league blast.

Since Ryan had donned his dad's special tee shirt, he had played three games, getting ten hits in twelve at bats, including four doubles, a triple, and two home runs. It was an amazing hot streak. Sam wondered how much of it was related to the talisman Ryan wore underneath his uniform shirt, how much was a result of their discussion in the attic, and how much was Ryan coming to terms with the accident. What he really wondered was how long it would last.

CHAPTER 38

THEY WERE AN HOUR INTO THEIR RIDE TO OCALA WITH SAM BEHIND THE wheel, something he insisted on. He had always been a better driver than passenger. The sun was just beginning to lighten the eastern sky and the road was practically empty.

"How'd your family come to live in Ocala?" he asked.

"We moved there from outside Tampa when I was three. My father got a job teaching American history in the high school."

"Must have been tough, having him as a teacher in your school."

"By the time I got there, he wasn't teaching anymore. He had opened a bookstore in town. It was a dream of his. I guess it went along with his love of reading. But the business always seemed to struggle. Then, when one of the chain stores came to town, it put him under. He had to shut his doors after six years."

"Bet it didn't help his disposition any."

"No it didn't," she replied. They drove silently for a while, Susan lost in her thoughts. "I think that was the happiest I ever saw him...when he first opened the store. I remember him being excited." She paused. "Most emotion he ever showed."

"You don't like your dad very much, do you."

Susan shrugged. "There never was very much to like. He was a cold fish. Very self-centered." Susan had a comfort zone with Sam that allowed her to open up and share her feelings about her father. "He looked down on my mother's family and would always make disparaging remarks whenever she'd bring up Zel or Annie. It caused hard feelings between them. Mom told me that when Zel was an old woman my father mocked her in front of the rest of the family. Zel walked out of the room seething while Grandma Annie burst into tears. That was before I was born. He never stopped, though. I remember him picking fights with my mom about the family," she said, thinking in particular about that one quarrel she had overheard when she was twelve, the one where he had called Zel a whore. "It was a recurring theme. It hurt my mom and colored their relationship." She went silent for a minute as she pondered her thoughts. "And the irony is he had no family at all. I think he was jealous. I know he could be nasty."

Unhappy emotions stirred up, Susan retreated into silence.

They arrived at the house in Ocala at 8:30. Susan had called the previous day and spoken to Isabel, her father's housekeeper and aide, and said she would be visiting and bringing a friend. Susan liked Isabel and was thankful she was there to care for her father. In turn, Isabel enjoyed Susan's occasional visits that were a pleasant break from her monotonous routine.

Isabel greeted them at the door. Susan introduced Sam.

"How is my father?" Susan asked. She thought it best to get the visit with him over first. Then they could concentrate on the search for the box.

Isabel sighed. "About the same. Maybe a little worse. You know how it goes Miss Susan.

Susan nodded. "Can I see him?"

"He's still sleeping." She grimaced. "A bad night last night. I found him wandering around the hallway. He was agitated. I gave him medicine to calm him. I'm afraid he might be sleeping for a while longer." Isabel took Susan's hand in hers. "I'm sorry, Miss Susan. I didn't want to give him the medicine because I knew he would sleep late and you would be here to visit. But he was getting in a bad way."

Susan was silently relieved. She found her infrequent visits to her father painful. Not because of his deterioration, which she could view clinically, with a coldness that surprised and disturbed her, but because she had no loving feelings for him. The only feelings he engendered in her were anger and, since his illness, resentment that she had to expend valuable resources on his care. She didn't like him and, in the aftermath of a visit, she didn't like herself either.

"Isabel, you did the right thing. Don't be upset. Watching after him is your first priority. Besides, Sam and I expect to be here a while." She segued to the box. "Isabel, I'm looking for something that belonged to my mother. Actually, it was my great grandmother's. It's an old wooden box, about this long, this wide, and this high." Susan motioned with her hands. "It's recognizable because it has an ornate Z carved in the top. Do you remember ever seeing a box like that?"

Isabel gazed off into space as she thought. After a minute, she shook her head.

"No, Miss Susan. I don't think I've ever seen such a box. I'm sorry."

"That's okay, Isabel. I didn't expect you had. Sam and I are going to look around the house for it. We'll start in the attic."

"Okay, Miss Susan. You will want to use the ladder from the garage to get up there."

"Not a problem," she said. "I know my way around. I'll take it from here. You go care to my father." She took Isabel's hand and squeezed it. "And thank you for looking after him. He couldn't have better care anywhere else."

Susan led Sam through the house and towards the garage. As she passed the library she stopped and flipped on the lights. They found themselves surrounded by books. Everywhere. The room looked to be fifteen feet square with a ten foot ceiling with bookcases that were wall-to-wall, top-to-bottom. There wasn't an empty space on any of them.

"The library," she said, needlessly.

Sam contemplated the task ahead of them. "That's a lot of books! Maybe we won't have to go through this room. Let's get up in the attic."

She continued down the main hallway to a cutout in the ceiling. It was the entrance to the attic. Next, she led him to the garage where they found a ladder neatly hung on hooks that were fastened to an old fashioned pegboard. Sam noticed lots of tools and gardening equipment, all of which rested tidily in their designated places.

Returning down the main hallway, he opened the ladder and carefully placed it beneath the opening. He climbed up and pushed the cutout up into the attic. Susan handed him a flashligh which he shined into the dark space. It looked forbidding and it smelled stale. Sam got the sense that no one had been up there in a long time.

He saw a string hanging motionless and shined the light upwards. It revealed a light fixture that was nothing more than a bare bulb in a socket. He stepped up into the attic and gave the string a yank. The bulb lit up and, to his pleasant surprise, threw off a nice amount of light.

"I'm coming," he heard Susan call.

"Okay."

He knelt down and extended his hand to her, as she ascended the ladder.

They stood and surveyed the attic. What they saw was disheartening. It was large, with floorboards that extended to the rafters and it was filled with all sorts of stuff—cartons, shopping bags, trunks, luggage, old furniture, mirrors.

There seemed to be no organization to what they saw around them. It looked like everything had been put in its place haphazardly. Forty years of detritus...and, perhaps, one small wooden box that they badly wanted to find. There was a pervading sense of stillness.

"Let's get to work," Sam said.

"Okay, how do you want to do this?"

"You take this side, I'll take that side." He bisected the attic in half by drawing an imaginary line in the air.

They started with the cartons.

The attic was warm, but because it was morning, not unbearably so. It was dry and it felt decayed, more from disuse than any physical deterioration that could be seen. As they moved around they kicked up a thin layer of long undisturbed dust that had settled over everything. This wasn't going to be fun.

They worked as fast as they could, balancing speed versus thoroughness. There were over thirty cartons and shopping bags to go through. They hoped to spend no more than two hours in the attic but it took them two and a half hours before they were finished and satisfied that Zel's diary box wasn't up there. Sweaty and dirty they climbed down and carefully replaced the ceiling cutout.

Sam lugged the ladder into the library while Susan took paper towels from the kitchen and cleaned up the dust that had drifted down from the attic onto the hallway floor. They headed for the bathroom where they washed their hands and faces of the grime that had adhered to them, and then proceeded to the library.

Once again, they divided the room. This time Sam took the top half while Susan concentrated on the lower five feet of shelving. Sam moved the ladder midway between four bookshelves, climbed up a few steps and ran his eyes across each shelf, scanning the various volumes that stood like pickets in a fence. The problem, he quickly surmised, was that, unlike a picket fence, the books were of different size and width and, more significantly, many were unmarked on their binding, leaving their identity a mystery. They were packed together tightly and he couldn't really tell if one of them might have been a box, instead of a book. This was a problem. Given the number of books, it would take more hours than they had to take each unidentified volume from its shelf and check it. He shared the problem with Susan.

"I have the same issue," she said.

He heard frustration in her voice.

"We'll just have to use our judgment," he said. "Do the best we can."

"As I recall, the box wasn't very thick. Not much more than an inch," Susan said, helpfully.

The scanning went much quicker once they decided to eyeball the unidentified volumes, taking a close look at only those that were plus/minus an inch in width. A couple of hours later, Sam finished the last bookshelf.

"No box," he said. His face was covered in sweat.

Susan, who had finished a few moments before him, stood in the middle of the library, scratching her head.

"Where do we look next?" Sam asked.

"I'm thinking," she said.

"Well, while you're thinking, I'm gonna put the ladder back in the garage. Unless we still need it."

"Uh-uh. You can put it away," she said, absentmindedly. "Maybe my parents' bedroom?" she wondered.

Sam headed for the garage. As he returned the ladder to its spot on the pegboard, he glanced around. It was the neatest, most organized garage he had ever seen. Everything had its place. Shovels, rakes, a pitchfork, a couple of hammers, screwdrivers, a variety of wrenches, saws. The garage was pristine. As he headed back into the house, he walked past Susan's father's workbench which had a vise and an assortment of containers for screws, nails, and the like.

Suddenly, he stopped in midstride. Something caught his eye. He turned back and moved an old coffee can that held an assortment of picture frame hangers. Next to it was a wooden box. It had an ornate Z carved into the top. *I'll be a son of a bitch!* He opened it and found it full of metal washers of various sizes. Sam grabbed the box and headed back into the house.

He found Susan, her arms folded, deep in thought, standing in the hallway at the base of the stairs that led to the bedrooms on the second floor.

"Sam, the next place we should look is my parents' bedroom. But I think my father's still sleeping. So..."

"Susan, look what I found."

"Zel's box! Where was it?"

"In the garage. He opened the cover. "Look, it's full of washers."

"No envelope?"

He poked around.

"Only washers," he said, disappointed.

Susan's shoulders sagged. "Now what?"

They had found what they had come for. But without the hair clippings, it was just an old box that wouldn't take them anywhere.

"We're at a dead end," he said. "I'm afraid the identity of Annie's father is going to remain a mystery."

Susan let out a sigh. She took the box from Sam. "Let's get out of here."

"Do you want to see if your father's up before we go?"

Susan thought about it. "No," she said, firmly. "Let's let sleeping dogs lie."

CHAPTER 39

SAM HAD ONE HAND ON THE STEERING WHEEL, THE OTHER ON THE TURN signal as he moved into the left lane to pass a slower moving car. Susan examined the box.

"This is magnificent," she said. "Horace must have put a lot of time into it. The carving of the Z is so intricate."

Sam stole a glance.

The box was stained a dark brown and was raised in the center, where the Z, encircled in a delicate filigree pattern, was carved. Brass hinges and a clasp anchored the top to the bottom. Susan opened the box and began removing the metal washers, placing them in an empty coffee cup.

"Look at the detail inside, Sam. Horace lined the box with a fancy paper. It's almost like linen."

He took a peek.

"It's beautiful," he said. "What a waste for it to wind up in a garage as a container for old washers."

With it now empty, Susan ran her fingers lightly over the bottom of the box. Out of the corner of his eye, Sam saw her suddenly peer closer.

"This is uneven," she said. "I feel an indentation." She ran her fingers the width of the box, along a straight line. "I think there's something underneath the lining!"

She dug a fingernail into a corner of the box and slowly peeled back the lining.

"There's something here!"

As she removed more of the lining, she was able to extract what lay underneath. She held up an envelope for Sam to see.

"Well, whadda ya know!" he said, wondrously.

Written on the front of the envelope, in handwriting that was the same as in Zel's diary, was the name Babe Ruth.

"I can't believe we found it!" she cried.

In her excitement, Susan grabbed Sam's arm, which made him steer left, almost into the next lane.

"Easy now," he said.

"It's sealed. Should we open it?"

Sam thought about it.

"No. We know what's inside. Let's leave the envelope as is for now."

With the lining half off, Susan continued peeling back the rest and didn't stop until it was completely removed. There appeared to be another lining that lay hidden beneath the first. She started to peel it back, just like the other one. Except it wasn't a lining at all. Instead, it was a thick piece of paper that had been carefully folded in half. She removed it and found another one below that. Susan opened them to reveal two 8 X 10 photographs.

One was a photo of a draped Babe Ruth sitting in a barber chair, his face lathered with shaving cream, a cigar in his mouth. Standing next to him, holding a straight edge razor, poised to begin shaving him, was a pretty girl. Susan recognized Zel, wearing what must have been a barber's smock. Both the Babe and Zel were looking at the camera, the Babe with a deadpan expression on his face while Zel had a slight smile.

The other photo showed Zel sitting in the barber chair as a clean-shaven Ruth, scissor in hand, stood solemnly poised to begin cutting her hair. Zel had an ear-to-ear grin on her face.

All the pieces had fallen into place. Everything Zel mentioned in her will was accounted for. They had accomplished their mission after all.

Sam felt a rush of adrenaline as he thought about what might unfold. The impossible was now possible.

He reached over and gently squeezed Susan's hand.

"Fasten your seatbelt tighter, kiddo. This adventure's just beginning!"

CHAPTER 40

By the time they reached Jupiter Susan was getting that overwhelmed feeling, once again.

Ryan was meeting up with Maggie and Michael was eating at a friend's house, so she and Sam headed straight to dinner. As they waited for their food, Susan asked the questions she had been afraid to ask, but that had been circling her mind since she first heard Sam's theory. Sam tried his best to answer them.

"Let's say we do the test and the results come back that Horace was Annie's father. What do I do with that information?"

"Nuthin'," Sam said. "It's a non-event."

"Okay. We do the test and it comes back that Babe Ruth is Annie's father. Do I tell the boys?"

"You would tell them first."

"Then what?"

Sam thought. "Don't know yet but, sooner or later, word's gonna get out. Then all hell's gonna break loose unless we plan very carefully." Sam paused. "For instance, suppose you held a press conference," he extemporized. "You make the announcement and have the evidence presented to back up your claim. The Buck family goes from leading a quiet, under-the-radar life to instant celebrity."

"You really think it would be that big a deal?"

"Susan, a couple of years ago someone's old home movies of Babe Ruth playing right field surfaced. The video was shot from the stands, wasn't very clear, and was maybe thirty seconds long. But it's the only moving picture footage of Ruth playing right field. The story made the front page of the *New York Times*. Babe Ruth was born over a hundred years ago, has been dead for over sixty years, and hasn't played a ballgame in over seventy-five years. Someone finds a few seconds of him in right field and it's on the front page of the *Times*. Not *Sports Illustrated* but the fuckin' *New York Times*! It's gonna be a very big deal!"

"That doesn't sound like a lot of fun to me." She cringed as she spoke.

"Either way, whether you control it or not, the media's gonna pick up on the story."

"What about the boys? How is it going to affect them?"

"Obviously, the biggest impact's gonna be on Ryan."

"What will people expect of him?"

Sam shook his head.

"Talk about having big shoes to fill! On the other hand, Michael would have it easier. Different expectations, obviously. No, the burden of this becoming public would fall on the shoulders of our young right fielder, which, by the way, is the same position the Babe played."

"Ryan's not ready for this, Sam," Susan said. She felt distressed.

"Don't be so sure. Your son is a very talented baseball player. He has the ability to make it big in baseball, whether or not Babe Ruth is his great, great grandfather. If the Babe is, though, it'll launch Ryan's career."

Susan took his hand and patted it.

"You are a dear man and I appreciate everything you are doing for us. I know that in a short period of time you have come to care for my boys. And I am totally impressed by your knowledge of baseball. But don't you think you might be a bit prejudiced about how good a ballplayer Ryan is?"

Sam protested. "It's not just my opinion. You heard what his coach said. Carruther said he thought Ryan had big league talent. What was missing was his ability to concentrate and commit. That was then. Now, look what Ryan's doing at the plate, Susan. He's killing the ball. The pitchers he's facing are overmatched. I know it hasn't been a long time but we're seeing your son's baseball ability blossom in front of our eyes."

"That's not exactly what I see," she said.

"You don't?"

"No. I see a kid who has struggled mightily trying to deal with his father's death, an accident he unreasonably blamed himself for. I see him finally making progress, getting to the point where there's a smile on his face and enjoyment in his life. To throw this at him? It's a bit much. Don't you think, Sam?"

"I don't know what to think," he said, feeling frustrated. "I can't disagree with a thing you just said. You know Ryan best. If you think it would be damaging to him, make him regress, or fall apart from the pressure and scrutiny, that's a real source of concern. On the other hand, it could be the greatest thing that ever happened to him. It could catapult him to the major leagues. If not, it could still provide him with celebrity, fame, and fortune. Not too shabby."

Sam continued. "I'll tell you what I do know. If it turns out to be true, your memorabilia will not only wind up on the cover of Standish's catalogue as the featured pieces in their World Series auction, but each item is gonna sell for record prices. Collectors will empty their wallets to own the bat, cap, ball, and cards that belonged to Zel Hitschnik. They'll go crazy over the photos. And her journal? That's priceless altogether." He paused. "Obviously, it's not a factor in deciding what to do..."

"It's a small factor," Susan said.

"It's a predicament," Sam said.

"Well, I don't like it. I wish it would go away."

"Aahhh, the genie's out of the bottle and it's not going back in."

"Oh, I can make the genie go back in," she said. "Maybe we should just leave things as they are, with Horace as Annie's father. Let's leave it alone. That would resolve the predicament, wouldn't it?"

"It wouldn't resolve it," Sam pondered. "Might make it go away for a while, but it would still be there." Sam couldn't imagine not finding out the truth. "Susan, the last thing I want is to see harm or unhappiness come to Ryan, Michael, or you. You've become important to me." He needed to say what he was feeling in the right way. "I don't have a crystal ball. I don't know what will happen. It's more than a little scary. But how can we not find out the truth? If it turns out that Babe Ruth really is your great grandfather, how can you not share that with Ryan and Michael? Then the three of you can decide what to do next. Don't put this all on yourself. Trust the boys enough to pull them into the discussion."

They sat silently after that, each lost in their thoughts. There were no easy answers.

After a while, Susan spoke.

"We need to sleep on it, Sam. My inclination is to play this safe, which means leave things as they are. But your points are well taken. I can't deny there is potential magic in all this. However, I won't consider it unless there's some way for us to control it, some way to avoid Ryan getting swept away by the tornado that could be unleashed by all this. Understand what I'm saying?"

"I do, Susan. Let's see what we can come up with."

Later that evening, back home in Boca, Sam tried to get his arms around what he now thought of as "their predicament."

If it was true, there would be a lot of ripples in the pond once this pebble hit the water. However, there wasn't much to do if Susan chose not to go forward. He was having trouble with that possibility. But the potential for damaging outcomes, from unrelenting pressure and scrutiny, was a definite concern. As he sat struggling with the dilemma that confronted them, the phone rang. It was Susan.

"Sam, I need to talk to you. I spent the evening with Michael and Ryan. It felt weird. I'm not going to be able to keep this from them."

After thinking things through, Susan realized she couldn't bear keeping the possibility of DNA testing from her boys. It would just be another family secret to go along the others—Zel's diary, the suspicions it raised, and the problems it had caused. It was all too much. With the unearthing of the journal box and the Ruth hair cuttings, she grasped that it was possible to resolve all the old doubts and question marks once and for all. The subject was no longer what Zel did or didn't do. It now had become putting it all to rest, even if the truth raised other issues, some of them astonishing, that she and her boys would have to contend with. It was an opportunity to bring four generations of family turmoil to an end and, as long as the boys were willing, she wasn't going to pass it up.

"Did you say anything to the boys?" Sam asked.

"No, not yet. But you're right. I'm going to have to trust them. I don't like secrets. They divide families. I can't imagine spending the next forty days with them and not being able to talk about this. Besides, if we tell the boys now and the tests do confirm that Babe Ruth is Annie's father, it won't come as such a shock."

"So, you've decided to move forward with the testing?"

"We're going to discuss it. I want us to read Zel's diary, together. And then talk about it. I think they're mature enough to handle it."

"When are you gonna do this?"

"Tomorrow night."

Susan sounded downright chipper, as if a burden had been lifted from her shoulders.

"You sound a lot better than a couple of hours ago," he commented.

"I'm feeling better. Pulling the boys into this is the right move. Thanks, Sam. I have confidence we'll figure this thing out."

"I have to say, the possibility of not finding out is a hard one."

"I know. You're hoping to see Babe Ruth reincarnated."

"That's not it," he protested. "All I'm saying is..."

"Imagine if it is true, Sam," Susan interrupted. There was a tone of wonder in her voice as, for the moment, she cast caution to the wind and got caught up in the possibilities. "I can't wait to see the boys' reaction if it is."

He chuckled.

"The mystique of Babe Ruth lives on. 'It ain't over 'til it's over', as Yogi would say."

"Who?"

"Ah, that's another story."

CHAPTER 41

RYAN AND MICHAEL DIDN'T LIKE THE IDEA OF THEIR FRIDAY NIGHT'S plans being disrupted. In fact, they were downright pissy, so Susan got right down to business.

"You know that Sam and I have been looking for a very special box that once held your great, great grandmother's diary. We needed to find it because it contained more than Zel's journal." Susan took Zel's diary box from her lap and carefully placed it on the table. "Well, we found the box and what was inside it, which creates an interesting situation. That's what we need to discuss."

"Where was it?" Michael asked.

"In your grandfather's house."

"He gave it to you?" Michael knew his mom and her father weren't on the best of terms.

"Let's just say we rescued it. The important thing is we have it."

"What was in it?" he asked.

"Hair clippings of Babe Ruth. Zel was his barber."

Michael looked at his brother and rolled his eyes.

"That's fascinating!" he said, with mock seriousness. "But, what does that have to do with us?"

"Maybe nothing," Susan said. "But it could also be very important."

"Would you mind explaining, Mom?" Michael was losing patience.

"In her diary, Zel writes about her life as a barber in St. Petersburg, Florida and what happens to her, including meeting Babe Ruth. There are a few mysteries along the way and I need you both to hear what she wrote and share with me what you think might have happened."

"What kind of mysteries?" Michael asked.

So far, Ryan hadn't said a word.

"It's best if you hear it in Zel's own words. What we're going to do is take turns reading her diary aloud. When we're finished, we'll talk about it."

Her idea went over like a lead balloon.

"Can't you just tell us what these mysteries are?" Michael complained.

"It's not that simple," Susan explained. "You really have to hear it as Zel wrote it."

Michael started to protest further but Ryan stopped him.

"Let's just do this and get it over with," he said. "How long do you think it will take?"

"I'd guess about two hours," Susan answered. "But we're going to want to talk afterwards. I can't tell you how long that will take."

"Not long," Michael volunteered.

Susan opened the diary and handed it to Michael.

"You start," she said.

Michael began reading Zel's first entry on Sunday, August 1st, 1925. When he finished, he passed the book to Susan who sat to his left. She read the next passage and then passed the journal to Ryan on her left. Between bathroom and drink breaks, and the discussion specific entries elicited, it took over three hours to get through Zel's last entry on January 30, 1927. But the boys stopped complaining shortly after they began reading.

"Well, what do you think?" Susan asked when they finished. She returned Zel's diary to the box. "About Great Grandma Zel and Babe Ruth?"

Unabashed, Michael spoke right up.

"I think old Zel did the nasty with the Babe."

Susan's natural reaction was denial, to defend Zel. She tried not to come off defensive. "Why do you say that?"

"Come on, Ma. She partied with him in his suite. They were all alone. He was Babe Ruth. What do you think happened?"

Was it that clear? She looked at Ryan.

He shrugged. "The way Zel writes it, you don't know for sure. But I think Michael's right."

Susan nodded. "Sam thinks so, too." She paused. "What about her marrying Great Grandpa Horace and then having Grandma Annie nine months later?"

"Yeah, I was thinking about that," Michael said. "Now don't go crazy on me, Mom, but if Zel did sleep with the Babe, he could be the father of Annie."

"If you're right, do you know what it means?"

"What?"

"It means Babe Ruth could be our great, great grandfather," Ryan answered.

Michael looked at Ryan, stunned.

"Holy shit! You're right. I didn't think of that. Holy shit!!"

Everyone sat quietly for a minute, letting it sink in.

Susan broke the silence.

"But it's only a possibility. It is just as likely that Horace was Annie's father. We can't be sure from just reading Zel's diary." She paused. "There's more. But first, tell me how you feel about playing baseball, Ryan."

This was a subject that was very much on Susan's mind. Based on her discussion with Sam it seemed likely that the Buck family could be thrust into the media spotlight if the DNA tests confirmed they were direct descendants of the

Yankee icon. It would bring attention to each of them, especially Ryan and the fact that he was playing baseball and, apparently, improving rapidly. But was baseball nothing more than a leisure activity that he wasn't really invested in? Or had it become more than that? She needed to know how he felt because there would undoubtedly be pressure for him to play ball if Babe Ruth's DNA was in his veins.

Ryan thought a moment before he answered. "I like playing ball. I like it a lot." He paused. "That wasn't the case until just recently." After a moment he looked at his mother. "I think I could be a good ballplayer. I've decided to find out how good."

"You're really hitting the ball lately," Susan said.

"I'm able to concentrate better in the batter's box. Being able to remember the accident has really helped."

"What about Dad's tee shirt?" Michael offered.

Ryan looked at his brother and nodded his head.

"It helps me to focus more."

Susan stared at her oldest son. He sounded serious about baseball. This was an important point. She didn't want him pressured into doing something he didn't care about. With that in mind, she shifted back to the question at hand.

"Back to Zel, Babe Ruth and hair clippings," she said.

The boys looked at her questioningly.

Susan explained the existence of hair snippets of Ruth, Horace, and Annie, the DNA tests that could be run, and the likelihood that they would provide a definitive answer to the question of who was Annie's father.

"This is what we need to talk about," she said. "Do we go ahead with the tests?"

"Why wouldn't we?" Michael asked.

Susan replayed her discussion with Sam from the day before. She talked about the positives and the negatives that would result from the discovery that Babe Ruth was the boys' great, great grandfather. She zeroed in on the pressures it could put on Ryan, in particular. When she finished, she looked at Ryan expectantly, waiting to hear his reaction.

He took his time responding.

He ran his fingers through his thick brown hair, slid his chair back a few feet, and sat back with one leg partially extended. He stared at his hands, which lay on his lap, his fingertips touching each other, making a steeple.

"I understand you being concerned with the pressure that might be put on me to fill Babe Ruth's shoes," he said. "But that's a pipe dream, Mom. I'm not a major leaguer."

"Coach Carruther told me you're very talented. Look how you're hitting the ball the past few games."

Ryan laughed. "That doesn't mean I'm good enough to play in the majors. Come on, Ma. What you been drinking?" He paused and looked off into space as if a vision had come to him. "But if I was good enough, and it turned out I was related to Babe Ruth? That would be pretty cool!"

Susan sat quietly, absorbing what her oldest son had said. She looked at Michael.

"You?"

He shrugged his shoulders.

"We've got to know the truth." It was that simple.

Susan took a moment to compose herself.

"Very well. We'll move forward with the tests. They take about forty days to complete so we are going to have to keep this to ourselves until then." She looked at Ryan and then Michael. "This is private family business. I don't want us discussing this with *anyone*. Only the three of us and Sam until we know what the truth is. No exceptions. That includes girlfriends. Understood?"

Both boys answered together.

"Yes, Mom."

"Okay, then." Susan looked at her watch. It was almost midnight. "It's late. Let's go to bed."

Before she went to sleep, Susan called Sam, as she promised she would, and told him the DNA test was a go.

CHAPTER 42

I<small>T WASN'T</small> S<small>AM'S TYPICAL</small> S<small>ATURDAY AT THE BEACH.</small> T<small>ODAY HE HAD ONE</small> and only one thing on his mind—how the Buck family could best deal with upcoming events.

He placed a telephone call to a top-notch attorney for one of Florida's largest law firms, Donald Kurtz, who had handled the sale of *Everything Baseball*.

He wanted a second opinion on how they went about conducting the DNA hair test. If it turned out the Babe was Annie's father Sam imagined everything they did would undergo intense scrutiny. They needed to eliminate, or at least minimize, any second-guessing of the test results. There would be plenty of skeptics looking to prove fraud and fakery.

Sam got Donald Kurtz on the phone and, after a few minutes of bantering, he got down to business. He represented the situation as one involving an estate settlement but included all the relevant facts including the question of parentage, the generational time span, the hair samples, including one of the hair samples being in a sealed envelope, the DNA testing they planned, and the name of the lab they wanted to use. Don listened without interrupting until Sam finished.

"It's good you called now, Sam. Usually, my clients call after they've already fucked things up. You want to do a forensic DNA test, which means you will be able to show chain of custody of the material being tested for every step in the process. This is important because it eliminates the opportunity for tampering and second-guessing. The lab you've chosen has an excellent reputation so you're in good hands with them. But, to make it as airtight as possible, you need to start before the hair samples ever get to DeNuAc."

"How's that?"

"The hair in the sealed envelope. You said the envelope dates back over eighty years?"

"That's correct."

"That's powerful evidence that the material is genuine and comes from the person identified. If I were you, I'd have the right people open that envelope; people who can attest to its age and the fact that it was sealed. It becomes a building block in constructing an airtight case."

Sam said a silent blessing that they hadn't opened the envelope with the Babe's name on it.

"Can I ask you a question, Sam?" Kurtz continued. "With so much money at stake, why doesn't your friend have legal representation? Someone who can make sure everything is done correctly?

"It's a situation that just came up. We're developing our plan. That's why the phone call to you."

"I'm here if you need me." He changed the subject. "Isn't Saturday a beach day for you?"

"Not today. Today, I'm doing something important."

Sam thought about what Kurtz said and how lucky they were not to have opened that envelope. Don's advice made him realize that they were flying blind. Susan was relying on him to provide guidance and he wasn't sure what he was doing. They were way beyond memorabilia. He had learned an invaluable life lesson when he started his business: know what you don't know; then surround yourself with people who do. They were in unfamiliar territory and were in need of experienced guides to help them avoid making any serious mistakes. It was time to call in the experts.

Saturday nights were the toughest for Susan. For the better part of two-and-a-half years she hadn't known what to do with herself when that weekend evening arrived. For a while after the accident, her friends, all married, made sure she was busy but eventually they had resumed their regular social lives. Susan had gotten used to being home alone on Saturdays, especially with the boys so busy now. So when Sam called she didn't hesitate when he asked if she was free for dinner.

"How are the boys after last night?" he asked, as they clicked wine glasses. They had decided on a return engagement at Susan's favorite Italian restaurant.

"They were fine. Normal. I reminded them about keeping our discussion last night confidential. Michael asked me, what conversation? His way of saying he understood. Ryan was quiet, nothing unusual for him."

Sam told Susan about his discussion with Don Kurtz and his comments regarding the sealed envelope. They didn't want to screw things up before getting to first base. He lobbied her to hire Gershon, Trask & Associates, the firm Kurtz worked for, to guide them through the DNA testing process.

"I've known Don a long time," Sam said. "He's first rate and I trust him completely. Gershon, Trask is one of the largest law firms in Florida with the resources to support us, whichever direction this thing goes."

Susan was in agreement but she asked how much it would cost to get Kurtz and his firm involved. Cost and her ability to pay for the steady stream of expenses that kept popping up were becoming a concern to her. Sam offered to front all the expenses but she made it clear that taking money from him was out of the question, nor was she interested in a loan.

"I don't know what it might cost," he admitted. "But I'm thinking if the Babe is Annie's father, the Buck family is going to need a lawyer."

Susan looked at him questioningly.

"To make sure everything is done correctly, like the DNA test. I can see interviews, appearances, and maybe even product endorsements." He paused. "Suppose you meet with Don, tell him the whole story, and see what he thinks. At least find out what the cost would be for them to help us with the DNA test. You can trust him to keep things confidential."

"All right," Susan said. "I wonder how he'll react to hearing the details."

Sam shook his head.

"He's a thick-skinned lawyer. It'll just be another case to him."

"Is he a baseball fan? Like you?"

"He's a fan. But not like me."

Over dinner they talked about Ryan and the passion he was developing for playing the game of baseball. It seemed as if a confluence of forces—his new found focus, the historical connection to the Babe, his recall of the crash, and the emotional springboard of his Dad's special tee shirt—had come together to propel Ryan to a level of excellence that was startling.

Susan talked about college and the possibility of a professional baseball career. Her expectation was that Ryan would continue his education after he graduated. She acknowledged, though, that the possibility, however slight, of being drafted by a major league organization was a viable alternative. She decided to meet with Coach Carruther to get his opinion on Ryan's chances.

Susan's major concern was the potential crush of publicity. She shared her anxiety with Sam. "My biggest worry is that we don't get swept away by all the exposure this might cause. I don't want Ryan or Michael overwhelmed. Is there any way this can be controlled?"

"I know that's a big concern and it's been on my mind since you decided to go forward with the DNA tests." He paused. "I've got an idea, Susan. Call it a contingency plan if the tests come back positive. I think it could give you the kind of control you're talking about." He shared his thoughts with her.

"But there are no guarantees," he concluded. "With this big a story, things could go wrong."

Susan had listened intently as Sam talked. She thought about what Ryan had said, *But if I was good enough, and it turned out I was related to Babe Ruth? That would be pretty cool!* She nodded her head. "I like it, Sam. But it's up to Ryan."

"I understand." He opened his phone calendar. They were now in the last few days of March. Realistically, they would not get the DNA test results back until mid-May. "Talk to him about it and if it's a go we should get the DNA tests started as soon as possible."

"I'll speak with him tonight."

As they lingered over their cappuccinos, Susan noticed that the tee shirt Sam was wearing accentuated his muscular forearms. *Unusual for someone his age,* she thought.

"How did you get those muscles, Sam? From lifting weights?"

"Never lifted a weight in my life," he said. "I boxed."

"You were a fighter?"

"Not really. Only had one fight. But I boxed a lot."

She tilted her head. "Explain"

Sam took a sip of his cappuccino and then looked off into space as an old but familiar memory resurfaced.

"I was thirteen years old and the runt of the litter—the shortest boy in the eighth grade at PS 197. One day, I accidentally bumped into Tony Muccio, the toughest kid in school.

Muccio was always looking for an excuse to fight and that was all he needed. He kicked my ass but good. I wound up with a bloody nose, a swollen lip, and a black eye. That night, when my father got home from the store, he made me tell him what happened. I think he was more upset than I was. 'Tomorrow, we'll take care of this,' he said.

"I remember being nervous because I had no idea what he was gonna do. Next day, I'm working the back counter when Sallie Coconuts walks into the store."

"Who?"

Sam explained. "My father loved to bet on baseball games. This guy Sal was the neighborhood bookie. Everyone called him Sallie Coconuts. I don't know why. So, Sallie walks into the store and I see my father talking all private to him. Then he hands Sallie a piece of paper and a pencil and Sal writes something on it. After Sal left, my father did something I had never seen him do before. He tells me to watch the front of the store and then goes into one of the pay phone booths in the back, closes the door, and makes a call. My father *always* used the phone behind the counter in the front to make his calls. For him to use a dime to make a call? That was the only time he ever did that.

"Anyway, when he finished the call he comes over and hands me a piece of paper which says Nicholls on it with an address in Bay Ridge, a different section of Brooklyn. He says to me, 'you go to this place Saturday morning'. Then he looks at me and says, 'The luck of the draw made you short. Nothing you or I can do about that. But this is gonna be your equalizer. Every Saturday and Sunday you go there. Pay attention and do what Nicholls says and no one will ever push you around again.'"

I said, "But who's gonna work the back counter?"

He said, "Don't think about it. This is more important."

"So, I take two buses and travel an hour to get there. Who is Nicholls? A trainer. He ran a gym in Bay Ridge and taught boxing. He worked me like a dog. A hundred pushups and sit-ups. Not just on the two days I was there. Every day of the week. And he taught me how to box. He told me it didn't matter that I was short. I had quick hands."

Sam sat contemplatively.

"Changed my life."

"How come only one fight?"

"Didn't need any more than that. One day my sopho-more year in high school, I'm walking in the hallway be-tween classes and I see this girl being picked on by some big fella. When I got closer I realized I knew her from the neighborhood and she was in a few of my classes. She was a nice kid, shy, and quiet. She was one of those girls who was just coming into her own. The braces had come off her teeth a year or so earlier, she began dressing cooler, and she started to show a figure. You could tell she was gonna be a knockout. Maybe that was why the guy was picking on her. Anyway, turns out the big fella was my old buddy Tony Muccio. I don't know what possessed me but I walked up and told him to leave her alone. Muccio looked at me and laughed. So did a bunch of his friends who were with him. I understood them laughing; he was a foot taller than me and must have outweighed me by fifty pounds. No con-test. I remember him saying, 'Frank, you're a dumb son of a bitch. I guess I gotta teach you another lesson about fuckin' with me.' As we squared off, a crowd gathered to watch the slaughter that was gonna take place. After all, Muccio was an experienced brawler and I was still pretty much the runt of the litter, although the runt had devel-oped some muscles by then. Nobody knew I had a couple of years of Nicholls and close to a hundred thousand push-ups and sit-ups behind me. Turned out it *was* no contest. I kicked his ass all over the place. He didn't know what hit him." Sam paused. "That was my one and only fight. Never had to do it again."

"That's a great story," Susan said, smiling.

"It's better than you think. The girl who I had the fight over? Her name was Frances. But I called her Frankie.

"Your wife?"

"That's right. The next day she came into the store and ordered an egg cream. I wouldn't let her pay. From then on we were together until the day she died."

Susan sighed.

"Sam, that's a sweet story." She reached across the table and squeezed his hand,

He shrugged. "Anyway, that's how I got the muscles."

Later that evening, Susan called Sam.

"I talked with Ryan about your idea. His first reaction was to laugh. I think his exact words were, *You guys are nuts!* He said there's no way a major league team is going to be interested in him. But then he thought about it more and said he liked it. I could see he was intrigued by the prospect of it."

"Okay, I'll set up a meeting with Don Kurtz for Monday."

CHAPTER 43

DON KURTZ ESCORTED THEM DOWN A PLUSH CARPETED CORRIDOR INTO his paneled office. There was expensive looking wood all over the place as befitted a prestigious law firm with a Palm Beach address. *Susan was right to ask the cost question,* Sam thought.

Susan placed Zel's wooden box on a table around which the three of them sat.

Kurtz looked at it curiously.

"Don," Sam began, "What I discussed with you on Saturday were not the actual facts we're dealing with. Susan is going to tell you what this is really about but first I have to ask that you keep everything confidential."

"Of course," he said, without hesitation.

Over the next half hour Susan and Sam took turns giving him the abbreviated version of the Ruth memorabilia, Zel and Horace, the diary, Zel's encounters with Babe Ruth, the birth of Annie, the hair cuttings, and their suspicions. Susan opened the box, removed the diary, and turned to the first of five entries they had bookmarked and asked Don to read them. The first entry told of Zel getting the barber's job at Spud's. The second entry was her initial encounter with Babe Ruth when she first cut his hair. The third was the night she met the Babe in his hotel suite. The next bookmarked entry covered Horace's marriage proposal and her acceptance. The final entry was the birth of Annie, some nine months later.

Silently, Kurtz read. When he finished, Susan handed him the two photographs of the Babe and Zel in the barber shop.

Kurtz smiled at the photos. Then he asked, "What about the hair samples?"

Before coming to the law offices, Susan had replaced the inner liner of the box. Once again, she peeled it back, and showed Kurtz the envelope that lay snuggly underneath. She lifted it out, and handed it to him. He peered at Babe Ruth's name written on its front, then turned the envelope over and ran a finger over the seal.

Then Susan took her family album from a bag, and opened it. From the pouch in the back she pulled out three more envelopes that had the names Horace, Zel, and Annie on them. She explained their significance.

Don Kurtz sat there, his left hand on his chin, a contemplative look on his face. He sat that way for a full minute, not saying a thing.

Susan and Sam looked at each other. He gave her a slight shrug. Finally, he couldn't stand it any longer.

"So whadda ya think?"

Kurtz began to rub his chin but continued to look off into space. He started to chuckle and then spoke.

"I love what I do. I tell you, I love it! Rarely is there a dull day. Today looked like it might be dull, but not anymore! As a matter of fact, I know I'll remember this day for a long time. Mrs. Buck, your story has an undeniable ring of authenticity to it. Babe Ruth could *really* be your great grandfather!"

"I think it's a possibility," Susan said. "We need to find out."

"I'll be damned!" Don Kurtz said, as he slapped the table, emphatically. "How can I help?"

Sam jumped in.

"We want your assistance with the DNA test. We need to be sure we do things right, every step of the way."

"We can help you there," said Kurtz.

"I'm concerned about the cost, though," Susan blurted out. She explained her financial situation.

"I understand. Let me see what I can do. I'm sure we can come up with something that you will be comfortable with."

Sam let Kurtz know they had serious time constraints they were working under. When he asked why, Sam told him it had to do with the upcoming auction of the memorabilia and left it at that.

"I think I understand what needs to be done," Kurtz said. "Let me discuss this with a few of my partners, of course in complete confidence," he emphasized, "and I will be back with you very quickly. Would you mind if I made a photocopy of the diary entries you had me read? Just in case any of my partners are skeptical," he added.

Susan looked at Sam. They hadn't anticipated the request.

"I guess so," she agreed.

"Great. I'll let you know soon enough," he concluded.

It didn't take long for them to hear back from Kurtz.

As they sat in Starbucks, nursing a couple of cappuccinos, reviewing their just concluded meeting, Sam's phone rang.

"It's Don Kurtz. He wants to speak with you."

Susan took the phone.

"Susan, my partners were astonished by your story. We would like to be part of this and here's what we're prepared to do. Gershon, Trask and Associates will oversee each step of the DNA testing at no charge. If it turns out that Horace was the father of the baby girl, there's not much to be done and we'll all go our separate ways. If Babe Ruth proves to be Annie's father, we want to represent the Buck family going forward."

"Would you mind repeating what you just said to Sam?" She handed him back his phone.

Kurtz reviewed the offer he had made to Susan and added, "We don't do things like this, Sam. But we really want to be a part of this story if it plays out." He laughed. "You should have seen my partners. They were astounded! Sam, this is a great offer. We've got top-flight people who will work on it. And please! Make sure she understands that we know how to keep a secret."

"Hold on." He looked at Susan. "This is a good deal. Take it."

She nodded her head.

"It's a go, Donald," Sam said. "And thanks!"

"No, thank you." He got right down to business. "We'll need Susan and Ryan at our offices as early tomorrow as they can make it."

"For what?"

"DNA. We'll need samples from both of them."

"Is that going to double the cost of the tests?" Sam knew Susan would ask him about it.

"We're one of DeNuAc's best customers. You'd be surprised how many DNA cases come our way. We've got special pricing with them. It won't cost you any more than you anticipated."

As he hung up with Kurtz, Sam felt they had the right guys on their team. This was going to work out well.

The next afternoon, Sam received a call from Susan. She and Ryan were done having their cheeks swabbed. She had given Don and his team three envelopes that contained hair samples—the sealed Ruth envelope and the two that held Horace and Annie's hair.

The samples would be delivered to DeNuAc the next day, which happened to be April first. The forty-day countdown would begin on April Fools' Day. Sam hoped it wasn't a bad sign.

CHAPTER 44

O<small>N</small> T<small>HURSDAY</small>, S<small>AM</small> <small>RECEIVED A PHONE CALL FROM A JUNIOR ASSOCIATE</small> at Gershon, Trask who informed him all was in order. The proper handling of the hair samples and communication with DeNuAc had disappeared from his To-Do list and the peace of mind he felt was tangible

They were now in a holding pattern and would be until the test results came back. That didn't mean there weren't things to do, though. He shifted his focus back to the valuable items they were preparing to send to auction and got progress reports on each piece, making sure everything was moving forward.

None of this weighed on Ryan as he shagged balls in right field before the start of his game. It was a night game and the Ryan rooting section was there in full attendance. Ryan had another strong outing, going two for four, including a double that drove in two runs. He made a nice running catch in right center and threw a runner out at home. An all-around solid performance that, nonetheless, didn't help his team win the game. But given his recent hot streak, Michael and Katie expressed disappointment that he hadn't hit a home run. Expectations were on the rise and it was tough pleasing everyone.

After the game, Susan and Sam got to talk.

"Things should calm down now, at least for a while. Might just be the calm before the storm." Sam chuckled, thinking about what could be. "When are you going to talk with Ryan's coach?"

"Next week, before his game on Thursday. That's his last one before Spring Break. He doesn't play again until April 19th. I thought I'd give Coach Carruther time to think about Ryan over the break. Can you be there when I talk with him?"

"Count on it. I wanna hear Carruther's take on Ryan's recent performance."

Susan found Sam's presence invaluable. She had come to rely on his opinions and recommendations. What started out as selling one baseball card had expanded exponentially into something complex and potentially momentous. She couldn't imagine being able to manage all the issues that had begun to pop up by herself. Sam had started this journey with her and he had been right by her side throughout, never faltering, and giving of himself unselfishly.

Later that evening, sitting in front of his computer, the Miami Marlins schedule in front of him, Sam called Susan.

"When exactly is Spring Break?"

Susan gave him the dates.

"The Marlins are playing the Phillies the afternoon of April 13th. Think your boys would like to see a ballgame? Gershon, Trask has fantastic seats and I think I can pry them away from them with a little help from Don Kurtz. Interested?"

"Sounds great but it seems that girlfriends rule these days so let me check with the boys."

The following Monday, Sam received a phone call that he was expecting but not looking forward to. It was James Dent, the President of Standish Auctions, following up on the status of Zel's diary. Dent wanted to know why Sam had yet to send it to him.

"We're not ready to do that yet. There are items of a personal nature that the family is not comfortable revealing at this time," Sam explained.

He and Susan had discussed the likelihood of Dent calling about the status of the diary. They had decided they weren't going to let him read it until the test results were in.

"I assure you, Sam, that we maintain complete confidentiality in situations like this."

"Understood. Mrs. Buck is not ready for other people to read it as yet."

"I can arrange that only I read the diary, if that would be helpful," Dent pressed. "I will even go so far as to sign a confidentiality agreement. But I will have to read the diary if we are going to use it as a source that provides provenance for your material."

"I do understand," Sam reiterated. "And I do believe you will maintain confidentiality. Give us time. Let me assure you that the diary provides irrefutable documentation that the items were given to Susan Buck's great grandmother by Babe Ruth."

There was a pause before James Dent spoke.

"I confess that I'm intrigued, Sam. A question: in your estimation, does the diary improve the likelihood of your material becoming the cover items in our World Series auction?"

Sam laughed.

"You are intrigued! But I can't give you an answer at this time. Please be patient." Until the test results were in, there was nothing they could do.

Later, he joined Susan for her meeting with Ryan's coach. As the assistant coaches ran the team through fielding practice, Pete Carruther sauntered off to the side and spoke with them.

"What did you say to Ryan?" Carruther looked at Susan as he leaned on a bat. "Since we had that chat, there's been a huge turnaround in his intensity level, his concentration, and his discipline. He's really showing that potential we talked about."

"I think Ryan has a lot less on his mind these days when he's up at the plate," Susan said. "That conversation we had was very helpful, Coach. Thanks."

Carruther beamed.

"Glad to be of help. Mrs. Buck, your son has been murdering the ball. His game on Tuesday, three for five, four rbi's. He's got a fourteen game hitting streak and he's hitting almost .500 over those games. He's not giving up any at-bats, battling every time he's up, and showing real intensity. The other kids on the team think it's that tee shirt he started wearing. I think he just started caring. Like we talked about."

"That's what we wanted to talk with you about, Coach," Susan said. "Ryan has shown tremendous growth the past few months as he's come to terms with a number of things. He realizes baseball is important to him and that he may be a pretty good ballplayer. He's challenged himself to see just how good he is and he's very serious about it. As you said, the results have been startling. I wanted to get your opinion on what his chances of being drafted might be, or maybe a college scholarship. His top two schools are UF and Miami. What do you think?"

The look on Carruther's face was a cross between surprise and disbelief. It was disconcerting to see. Susan could tell she wasn't going to hear good news.

Carruther took the bat he had been leaning on, gripped it with both hands and idly broke his wrists back and forth, as he thought about what he would say.

"Ryan has a lot of talent," he said. "Maybe even major league ability. But it's shown up awful late. We're not more than a month from the end of Ryan's high school career.

Mrs. Buck, I'm sorry to tell you this but those schools have picked their ballplayers and allocated their scholarships months ago. They're two of the top programs in the country. Their new recruits are high school All-Americans and Florida All-State caliber ballplayers. They've been scouting some of these kids since middle school. Most of the Division One teams do it that way. Honestly, I don't think Ryan would qualify for a Division One scholarship at this late date. He just hasn't shown enough. He might make a team as a walk-on, but that wouldn't get him a scholarship." He paused for a minute, took his cap off, ran his hand through his hair, and continued. "But I do have contacts with some scouts and a few minor league and semi-pro teams." Something caught his attention on the field and he yelled to one of the coaches to repeat an infield drill. He turned back to Susan. "I really didn't know Ryan wanted this. He never said anything to me about it." He paused at this point. "Let me talk with a few people I know. Send them some video of Ryan."

"Video?" Susan said.

"Yes. We videotape our games. If you look, you'll see a kid doing that at the back of the stands every game. Maybe I can get a coach or two to come down and see him in person." He thought another moment. "Let me see what I can do," he said. "Call in a few favors."

"Thanks," Susan said.

"No, it's nothing. Your son's a terrific kid. Modest. Mature. I'd love to help him. Just wish he had shown what he can do sooner. I'll be back to you after Spring Break."

"That was disappointing," Susan sighed, as they left Coach Carruther and walked up to the stands.

"He doesn't know what we know," Sam said, frustrated by the discussion that had just ensued. "The Ruth connection can overcome Ryan's short track record and be the thing that gets him noticed."

Ryan's performance in the game made their conversation with Carruther all the more infuriating. He continued to pound the ball, hitting two doubles and a triple in four at-bats.

Then Susan got a scary thought. What if the Babe is not the father of Annie? How would they get teams to see Ryan's potential in that case? Ryan had finally reached the point of being able to fully commit to something and it had begun to illuminate his life. He was flourishing. What if it turned out that nobody was interested in him? How would he handle that? There had to be a school with a baseball program that would take him in. All Susan knew was they would find a way. They had to. She let out a long sigh.

CHAPTER 45

APRIL 13TH WAS SUNNY AND THE TEMPERATURE WAS FORECAST TO REACH the nineties. The sky was bright blue and cloudless. Great baseball weather if you didn't mind the heat. But that didn't matter because the Marlins' new stadium was domed. The roof would be closed and the fans and ballplayers, too, would enjoy the game in air-conditioned comfort. Sam reminded Susan to tell the boys to bring their gloves. Their seats were practically on the field and the chance of a foul ball coming their way was better than average.

The Marlins, relative newcomers to the major leagues, played their inaugural season in 1993. Although a brief period of time by baseball standards, Marlins fans had known more than their share of excitement. The team had a perfect record in post-season play, having gone two for two in World Series appearances. Nonetheless, they often played in front of a sea of empty seats that, here and there, were occupied by paying fans. They were a small market team in a large market. Perennially at or near the bottom of the league in attendance, there were two underlying factors that were the cause: hot and humid weather combined with late afternoon thunderstorms kept fans from coming to see them play in their old ball park and lack of an historical fan base (most everyone originated from somewhere else where they had a team they rooted for). Nonetheless, with one of the smallest payrolls in baseball, the Marlins almost always fielded a competitive team. Now, with a new, retractable roof stadium in hand, perhaps their fortunes would change.

Gershon Trask had first row seats just above the Marlins dugout. Sam hadn't told the boys and Susan where they were sitting and, as they walked down the long aisle to their section, balancing trays of hotdogs, nachos, peanuts, drinks, and Cracker Jack, Sam could see them wondering when he was going to say stop. When they got to the end of the aisle, where the top of the dugout began, he shouted, "Left turn and take a seat."

Michael was the first to speak.

"These are our seats?"

"Close enough?"

"Cool!"

"Look how close the players are!" Susan exclaimed.

They were less than ten feet away.

"They're so young," she added. "Ryan, you could be playing for this team."

With his newfound intensity and love for the game, Ryan didn't blow his mom off. Instead he looked intently at the ballplayers.

The emerald green diamond, bordered with neatly limed foul lines and offset by clay-dirt symmetrical base paths, was a thing of beauty.

"I'd love to be out on that field someday," Ryan said.

Just then, one of the Marlins returned to the dugout after warming up. As he got close, Michael stood up, waved, and yelled to him, "Hey Bobby, kick some butt today!"

Bobby Janrow, the Marlins second baseman, smiled up at Michael and, in one motion, took a ball from his glove and tossed it to him. Michael caught it and displayed it proudly, an ear-to-ear grin on his face.

"Great seats, Sam!" he shouted.

"First ball?"

"Yep." He gripped it tightly in his hand.

"Nice catch, bro," Ryan called out to him.

"Not too difficult," Michael said.

"My advice would be to use your glove if a pop foul comes in our direction." Sam suggested. "Much less painful than trying to make a bare-handed catch."

None came their way, but the four of them had a great time. Susan decided to adopt two of the youngest looking Marlins and rooted extra hard for them. Michael cheered every time one of the Marlins stuck their nose out of the dugout. He waved to them all and most acknowledged him in some way. Ryan was mostly quiet and watched the action intently, soaking it all in.

In the middle of the seventh inning, the Marlin cheerleaders, gorgeous girls in their early twenties, came streaming down the aisle, hopped onto the roof of the dugout and, in their scanty outfits, danced to music booming from the stadium loudspeakers. Sam nudged Susan and chuckled. They turned to look at Michael who sat in his seat clapping and moving to the rhythm of the music.

"Really great seats, Sam!" he cried out, not taking his eyes off the girls.

Ryan sat back with a big smile on his face as he eyeballed each of the cheerleaders. One of them, a raven-haired Latino-looking girl couldn't keep her eyes off him as she danced. He made eye contact with her midway through the girls' routine and they stayed locked on each other. When they were finished, he extended his hand to her as she stepped down from the dugout roof and back into the aisle. She blushed as she said thank you to him.

"I think that one likes him," Susan whispered to Sam.

"Ya think?" he said.

It was a fun ballgame with lots of offense. The Marlins won 7–6 when their closer worked his way out of a bases loaded situation in the bottom of the ninth. Maybe this would be the Marlins' year.

Afterwards, they headed to South Beach where the plan was to meander around and then have dinner, not that Sam could imagine the boys would be hungry based on what they consumed at the ballpark. But, Susan reminded him, these two were eating machines.

It was a long game and traffic was a mess so they didn't get there until 7 PM. The area was as deserted as the beach on a rainy day. South Beach wouldn't come alive until they were finished with dinner and on their way home. Nonetheless, they walked and explored for an hour. The boys got to see a few long-legged beauties and Susan got to shop. They decided to eat at one of the restaurants on Ocean Drive, outside, where they could people watch. As the traffic picked up they had fun checking out the crowd. There was enough bizarre to keep them entertained.

Eventually, they headed back to Boca. Sans traffic, it took them a little over an hour.

As they pulled into Sam's driveway, they were beat from the sun, the food, the walking, and the cheerleaders. The boys piled into their car and Susan got behind the wheel but not before they thanked Sam for a fun day. Susan gave him a hug and the boys high-fived with him.

Sam lingered as their car drove away. He felt better than he had in a very long time.

CHAPTER 46

SUSAN AND SAM MADE A POINT OF GETTING TO RYAN'S NEXT GAME EARLY so that they had a chance to talk with Coach Carruther.

"You kept me busy over Spring Break, Mrs. Buck," Pete Carruther said. Susan got a pained look and started to apologize but he stopped her. "Quite all right. It's part of the job. Besides, now that I know Ryan's desires, I'll do whatever I can for him."

He got down to specifics.

"I called a friend of mine who coaches at a junior college in Georgia. He asked for video and said he'd give Ryan a close look. He doesn't have any scholarships to offer but I'm thinking Ryan might have a decent chance of making the squad. That's one you should definitely explore."

Susan's shoulders sagged. *That's the best he could come up with?*

Sam could see the disappointment on her face as she turned to him. He pursed his lips and tried not to show any emotion, although he was sure his face mirrored Susan's.

But Carruther wasn't finished.

"I also contacted a good buddy who's a scout. He's going to be in our area in a couple of weeks. I asked him to watch Ryan play. I sent him video."

"Who does he scout for?" Sam asked.

"The Boston Red Sox."

"You're kidding."

"I've got another friend who scouts for the Cubs. I also sent him video. He'll be in town in a few weeks, too."

Susan's heartbeat quickened on Carruther's news. Her boy playing in front of major league scouts! Talk about pressure! But was this realistic? Ryan himself didn't think so. Susan spoke what was on her mind.

"Coach Carruther, are you telling me a major league scout would be interested in Ryan when the best college program he can get into is a junior college somewhere in Georgia?"

"You never know, Mrs. Buck. If Ryan keeps hitting the ball the way he has, he might impress a scout and get himself recognized. The Amateur Entry Draft is in June and a lot of young kids are going to get drafted by one big league team or another. The best I can do at this point is get Ryan looked at. Maybe he'll shine and get noticed. Stranger things have happened," he concluded.

Susan looked at Sam. Part of his contingency plan involved the June Amateur Draft. In fact, it was the upcoming Amateur Draft, rather than the auction, that was the reason for quickly moving forward with the DNA tests.

Ryan had an uneventful game. A single in three at-bats. It was his quietest performance at the plate in the past three weeks.

But it was a momentary pause, as he blistered the ball in his next game. The other team could not get him out. He went four for four, including a home run and two doubles. His teammates joined in and they whipped the other team 14-6.

It was exciting to watch Ryan at the plate. His now established routine of tapping his chest twice with his right hand as he stepped in the batter's box, his deliberate couple of practice swings as he got himself set, his smooth, deceptively powerful swing as he made contact with the ball. And he wasn't striking out very much, unusual for a hitter with his power.

Over the next week, Ryan continued his errorless ways in the field while extending his torrid hitting. The level of excellence he was playing at had gone on too long to be called a hot streak. Ryan had taken his game to another level. He had become a man amongst boys.

It was an eventful week in other respects, too, as Michael and Katie broke up when they decided they didn't want to be tied down. But they were both affable about it and they continued their friendship. Their decision had no impact on Ryan and Maggie, who seemed to be completely enchanted with each other. Meanwhile, Susan's client hired four of the five candidates she recommended, which was a feather in her cap as well as handsome commissions. It seemed the Buck family was on a roll.

To celebrate her success, Susan invited Sam to a fancy steak place. With a silky smooth Cabernet as accompaniment, they dug into their steaks. As they ate, Sam expressed his wonder over Ryan's performance. He had trouble containing his enthusiasm because he had received a phone call earlier in the day from Don Kurtz informing him that the testing at DeNuAc was ahead of schedule. Gershon Trask now expected the results the first week in May, less than two weeks away.

Susan's eyes widened and she inhaled at the news. It wouldn't be long before they knew what they were dealing with. Ryan's growing baseball prowess combined with the possibility that he was a direct descendant of Babe Ruth was a heady mixture. She allowed herself the luxury of drinking from that cup for a few minutes but then steered the conversation in a different direction.

"I called Coach Carruther today to get information on the junior college program in Georgia. He told me why the scouts for the Red Sox and Cubs are coming to town. On May 14th, Cardinal Newman is playing Ryan's team. They have a ballplayer who is considered one of the top baseball prospects in the country. He'll be pitching against them that night in Jupiter. Carruther's buddies will be there scouting him but now they're going to check out Ryan as well." Susan leaned forward. "Sam, he told me there will be scouts from other major league teams, too. I'm nervous just thinking about it."

"Did he give you the pitcher's name?"

"I think he said it was Peters, or something like that."

Sam took out his phone and googled the hotshot that Ryan would be facing. He was surprised to see how many listings there were for him. As he jumped back and forth reading various articles, it became apparent that the kid was the real deal. Peters had lost only one game in his high school career, had an ERA of less than two, and averaged twelve strikeouts a game. He was projected as a first round draft choice in next month's Major League Amateur Entry Draft. Some websites projected him in the top ten picks. Physically, the kid, if one could call him that, was a mountain at 6'6" and 230 pounds. He featured a blazing fastball, a devastating change-up, and an above average slider. To top it off, he was supposed to have a mean streak. His name was Turnbull Peters but everyone, it seemed, called him Bull.

"He sounds scary," Susan said.

"He probably is. This will be one hell of a test for Ryan. Not only facing Bull Peters but with all those scouts watching."

Susan worried how Ryan would handle the situation.

"I'm feeling nauseous, Sam. The pressure. I hope Ryan will be okay."

"Ryan is ready for this. He'll rise to the challenge. In fact, Big Bull better pitch him carefully," he blustered, "or else

Ryan might just turn him into Bull Shit, if you know what I mean."

Susan frowned.

"You boys, you're all alike," she sighed, hopelessly.

The prospect of Ryan facing Bull Peters led to another discussion. They now anticipated getting the test results the first week in May. Susan's natural inclination was to tell the boys as soon as she knew. But with the big game coming up on May 14th, should she wait until after it was over to tell Ryan? They kicked the question back and forth for a while and eventually Susan decided she would tell the boys right away if it turned out the Babe was Annie's father. If that wasn't the case, she would wait until after the big game to let Ryan know. They didn't want anything negative before the biggest game of his life.

CHAPTER 47

THE FOLLOWING WEEK SAM CALLED THE COMPANIES DOING THE AUTHEN-
tication and grading of the Ruth memorabilia. Everything was
on track. Each of the items would be processed and shipped
to Susan prior to June 1st, sufficient time for her to get them
to Standish for inclusion in their World Series auction. Sam
didn't call James Dent of Standish to let him know because,
until the DNA test results were in, he wanted to avoid talking with him. He was feeling antsy so he called Susan.

She had a busy work day scheduled and didn't have a
lot of time to talk with him.

"There's one thing you need to do today, Susan," he said.

"What's that?"

"Call Coach Carruther and ask him to bring you a copy
of the video he's compiled of Ryan. We need to have a copy
for ourselves."

"When do you want it?"

"Before tomorrow's game, if possible. I don't know when
we're going to get the test results but we don't want to have
to sit around waiting on the video once we get them."

"Okay. I'll call him now. Gotta go."

The next day he got to the ball field before Susan and early enough for a brief visit with Ryan before his pre-game

warm-up. Sam watched Ryan as he walked towards him, his glove tucked under his arm. Ryan seemed to have filled out since Sam had first met him a few months earlier. Dressed in his uniform with the blue and yellow trim of his team, he looked like a ballplayer. Not your average high school ballplayer, though. He was taller and more solid than any of his teammates. And, he carried himself in a manner that silently screamed "athlete." Sam wondered why he hadn't noticed this before. Maybe it was because he usually watched him from the stands but now he was seeing him at field level. Maybe he simply hadn't paid attention. Either way, he had the sense that Ryan had grown in stature. And not just in a physical sense.

"Ryan, ready for today's game?" he asked.

"You bet. What a groove I'm in, Sam. I'm seeing the ball real well. Just hope it continues." He spoke with quiet intensity.

Sam put his hand on Ryan's shoulder.

"Just stay focused, kid, and it will continue. You're playing great ball. Go have a good game."

"I'll give it my best."

Glove in hand he jogged out to right field.

"Go get 'em!" Sam yelled.

Susan and Sam sat ten rows up from the field as they watched Ryan draw a walk in the first inning. Word was getting around about his hitting ability and pitchers were starting to throw more cautiously to him. This would test Ryan's patience. With fewer pitches being thrown over the plate, it would require discipline on his part to resist swinging at pitches outside the strike zone. Sometimes he would have to settle for a walk.

His team got a rally going in the third. As Ryan came up to bat with men on first and second, Sam's cell phone rang.

Annoyed by the distraction, he pulled out the phone and checked the caller ID. It was Don Kurtz calling.

"Sam. Don here."

Out of the corner of his eye, Sam saw Ryan tap his chest twice as he stepped into the batter's box.

"Don, any news?"

"DeNuAc called a few minutes ago. Can I speak with Susan"

His heart took a leap. But there was enough noise that he was having trouble hearing Kurtz clearly.

"Hold on a second, Don."

Sam put his hand over the speaker.

"This could be it," he said to Susan.

They got up and moved to the top of the stands where it was quieter. Sam handed his phone to her.

"Don, it's Susan."

Silently, she listened to what Kurtz had to say.

"I understand," she said. "Yes, I will. Thanks." She closed the phone and handed it back to Sam.

"What?" Sam asked, anxiously. "What did he say?"

Susan looked towards home plate just as Ryan swung and hit a shot into the gap between left and center field. She watched him round first base and, as Ryan raced for second, she answered Sam's question.

"He said the test results were definitive. The young man sliding into second base is the great, great grandson of Babe Ruth."

Sam gasped and threw his arms around her.

"Did you get the video?" he asked, breathing hard.

"Yes," Susan said, breathlessly.

"Good. We're gonna need it!"

CHAPTER 48

SUDDENLY, THERE WAS A LOT TO DO.

First, Susan had to give the boys the news and reconfirm Ryan's concurrence with what they had already discussed. Sam had to make a critical phone call that hopefully led to several key meetings. They had to talk further with their attorneys. Before Susan hung up, Don Kurtz said he wanted to have a meeting in his office as soon as possible.

Susan and Sam stayed seated in the last row of the stands so they could talk without being overheard. She elaborated on what Kurtz said about the DNA test results. There was no doubt the great Yankee slugger was the father of Annie and the correlation between Ruth's DNA and Ryan's was high for a five-generation span.

As preoccupied as they were, the game went by without them seeing much of it at all, except when Ryan came to bat a few innings later. With it now established that he was a direct descendant of Babe Ruth, they found themselves watching his every move. The feeling was magical. Ryan, unaware of what they knew, nonetheless obliged their attention by rapping another solid hit.

Later, back home at the Buck house, the four of them dug into chicken and ribs. Susan shared the big news with the boys and let it sink in. After a while, she asked them how they felt.

"Wait until everyone hears about this!" Michael trumpeted. His face was flushed with excitement. "I feel a little badly for Horace but having Babe Ruth as a relative? I can't wait to tell everybody!"

"We need to talk about that," Susan said. "We're not quite ready to go public with the news right now."

"What do you mean?" Michael asked.

She reviewed the plan that she had previously discussed with Ryan.

"So it involves us keeping this quiet for another couple of weeks," she said.

This didn't make Michael very happy but he understood.

Susan turned her attention to her other child.

"Ryan, tell us how you're feeling."

He spoke without hesitation.

"I'm excited, but not surprised. I've had it in my head ever since reading Zel's diary that I've got Babe Ruth's DNA in me." Ryan seemed to be taking in stride the news that had the rest of them jumping out of their skin.

He's committed, Susan thought. "All right. Let's move ahead." She turned to Sam. "Ready to make that phone call tomorrow?"

Before Sam could respond, Ryan spoke.

"There are a few things I'd like to talk about, just you and me, Mom." His face was suddenly a mask of concentration.

"Okay," she said. She looked at Sam.

"No problem," he said, trying to sound nonchalant. "I'll be at home all morning and I'll wait to hear from you."

After Sam left, she and Ryan talked for a while but quickly succumbed to fatigue. It had been an eventful day. They decided to continue their discussion in the morning.

Before they went to sleep, Susan turned to Ryan.

"Ry, time for a reality check. If this plan works out, you may find yourself right in the middle of a giant cyclone of attention. It could get crazy. You sure you want this?"

"What I want is to play ball, Mom." He looked his mother in the eye. "After everything we've been through...to wind up where I am. I can't believe it's all by chance." He paused. "I've begun to think it's what I was meant to be, a ballplayer."

"You're much more than a ballplayer, Ry," Susan smiled. "But what a ballplayer you are!" She shook her head. "When you step on that field...the transformation, Ryan, it's been simply amazing. Can you explain what's going on?"

Ryan stared off into space. His eyes began to well up as he struggled with what he had to say.

"I decided that I would never waste an at-bat. That I would treat each at-bat as if it were the last one I would ever have." He looked at his mom. "You never know."

Susan gave him a sad smile.

"I understand." She tousled his hair. "Think you're ready for what may transpire?"

Ryan gave the question some thought before answering.

"I do. I think I'm in the best shape I've ever been. I mean up here," he said, pointing his finger at his temple. "What's that expression? Older but wiser? That's me."

Susan smiled sadly. *I wish you hadn't had to grow up so suddenly.*

She embraced her son.

"Very well, old man. Let's both get some sleep. We've got more talking to do tomorrow."

CHAPTER 49

THE MORNING CAME AND WENT WITHOUT A CALL FROM SUSAN OR RYAN.

Sam had always thought of himself as a fairly secure guy. But by noon a bunch of "what ifs" were starting to pop up in his head. What if Ryan didn't want him to be involved? What if he had become tired of his presence? What if he felt Sam didn't know what he was talking about? Sam checked his watch for the umpteenth time and then he checked it again.

Finally, just after 2 PM, Susan called.

"Everything all right?" he asked.

"Come on up"

"Ryan okay?"

"He's fine. Get your butt up here!"

"I'm on my way!"

Keys in hand, he headed for the door.

Ryan and Susan sat him at the dining room table, where they had talked the night before.

"Sam, I've got something to say," Ryan began. "I didn't sleep much last night, thinking about everything we talked about but, after a while, I was able to focus in on what is important to me and how to go about achieving it. I talked it through with Mom all morning and I need to tell you about it because it involves all of us.

"This may sound weird but I believe it is my destiny to be a professional baseball player. There's no other way to explain the things that have happened. While I can't know for sure how helpful his genes are, I'm positive that being related to Babe Ruth will help get me there. I'm ready to take the next step and I need the help of both of you.

"Mom, college won't be a problem if I don't get drafted. But if I do, I may need your help in figuring that out.

"Sam, I'm on board with the plan. Start making your phone calls. Beyond that though, Mom and I talked. We want you to handle all business aspects of whatever comes up. That means dealing with lawyers, agents, contracts, and whatever else is needed. We have complete trust in you.

"For my part, I need to stay focused on playing baseball the best I possibly can, starting Tuesday night when I face Bull Peters. I know things will be getting much tougher but I'm psyched to take it on. Sound good?"

Very good! Sam thought. He was officially part of Ryan Buck's brain trust and he was charged with the responsibility of getting him drafted by a major league team in the upcoming Amateur Entry Draft, which was going to take place in a little over a month.

Sam excused himself from the group and found a quiet place where he took the first critical step of the plan they had agreed on. He reached in his wallet and pulled out a business card he had been carrying around for the past few months. The card belonged to Chuck Bernard, General Manager of the New York Yankees. Bernard had given it to him at the National Sports Memorabilia Show in Orlando, the day he first met Susan. It seemed like eons ago. At the time, Bernard told Sam to call him on his cell phone if he wanted to sell the Honus Wagner card he had outbid him on, but to call him on his office phone if Sam discovered the next Mickey Mantle. Sam dialed his office number and wondered if Bernard would remember him and their conversation.

He was nervous as the phone rang. The next few minutes would be crucial.

After three rings, a receptionist answered.

"Chuck Bernard's office."

"Mr. Bernard, please. This is Sam Frank calling."

"In reference to what, Mr. Frank?"

"He gave me a job to do and I'm reporting back to him. You should also mention Honus Wagner, 1915 Cracker Jack."

"Excuse me?"

He repeated the part about Honus Wagner.

"Hold on," she said, dubiously.

Sam waited almost a minute before he heard the booming voice of Chuck Bernard over his speaker phone.

"Sam," he cackled. "Calling about the Wagner? I thought I told you to call me on my cell phone."

Sam laughed. He remembered.

"I know you did, Chuck. You also told me to call you on your office phone if I found the next Mickey Mantle."

Bernard was quiet for a moment.

"That's right, my unofficial scout."

"Correct. I just wanted you to know I've been doing my job. I found someone you have to see."

He started to laugh.

"Another Mantle?"

"Maybe better."

He laughed harder.

"Okay, I'll bite. What's the kid's name?"

"Ryan Buck and..."

"Hold on."

Sam could faintly hear the clicking of a mouse followed by the sound of tapping on a keyboard.

"Ryan Buck," Bernard said. "Not much on Buck here. Other than a strong arm, I don't have anything on him."

Sam was amazed with the information Bernard had at his disposal.

"When was the last time you scouted him?" he asked.

"We haven't directly. This info comes from a scouting service we use. The report date is March 8th."

Ryan was just getting going around then.

He knew his phone time with Bernard wouldn't last long.

"Since then, the kid's hitting over five hundred," he said. "His on-base percentage is off the charts. He's killing the ball on a consistent basis and..."

Chuck Bernard was quickly losing patience with him and he interrupted again.

"Sam, let's talk baseball cards. You've got a good eye for them. Let's leave the scouting to the people who have a good eye for prospects. Professionals, with years of experience, who know what to look for, not just a kid on a hot streak."

Sam didn't want to push his luck. It was time to put his cards—actually card—on the table and, in the process, make an offer he didn't think Bernard could refuse.

"There's more to it than just a hot streak," he said. "Chuck, I know your time is valuable but I need fifteen more minutes of it." He heard him groan. "I'm willing to make a deal for your time and it involves the Wagner card that you want." Sam shut up at that point.

There was a moment of silence.

"Go on. I'm listening."

"Listen to my story about Ryan Buck for fifteen minutes and, if you want to end the conversation at that point, I'll sell you the card for half price, $12,000."

"Interesting."

"There's more. If, after listening to the story and you come to Florida to see him play in person, and you decide not to sign him, I'll sell you the card for a hundred bucks."

"Are you crazy?"

"No. You're gonna want to sign Ryan Buck."

Bernard was no one's fool.

"Okay," he said. "You've got a deal. What do you know that I don't?"

Forty-five minutes later, a stunned Chuck Bernard was still on the phone with Sam. He agreed to fly to Florida on May 14th to catch Ryan's game against Bull Peters. In addition, he decided to fly in his top scout for the Southeast United States to see Ryan play on May 13th.

Bernard was enthralled by the story of Zel and Babe Ruth and asked that Sam have her diary available for him to read and a copy of it to bring back to New York. He also wanted copies of the DNA test results. Sam told him he would have them for him but Bernard would have to sign confidentiality agreements for both. Bernard grilled Sam over Ryan's performance the past six weeks and listened quietly as he gave him an abbreviated account of Ryan's family tragedy and physical and psychological rebound.

"Quite a story, Sam," he exhaled.

"And you are the only one who knows it, for now."

"For now?"

Sam prepared to deliver the ultimatum he had held back until this point.

"Ryan's preference is to sign with the Yankees. Our top priority though, is for him to get drafted next month by a major league team. If the Yankees are willing to make a commitment, so is Ryan. But he'll need that commitment ahead of the draft. If that's not possible, we'll have to go public with the news prior to the draft, to increase Ryan's chances."

"I see," he said, slowly.

"We're telling you ahead of time because we prefer to avoid a three ring circus, even though it would likely mean a higher draft position and more money. That's the caliber of people you're dealing with, Chuck. It's not just about the money with the Buck family. That's why we approached you in this manner."

"Who is his agent?"

"Deal with me for now. We'll bring our legal team into the picture in the next few days to make sure we've covered all the bases."

"I understand. My assistant will get my travel particulars to you and I will see you next Tuesday. You'll FedEx the video to me today?"

"I will." Sam paused. "So, was it worth the time to talk?"

"There's only one thing that's bothering me."

"What's that?"

"The damn Wagner card. For a minute there, I thought it was mine."

Sam laughed.

"Not a chance. I had you all the way."

CHAPTER 50

COACH CARRUTHER CALLED A SPECIAL BATTING PRACTICE IN ADVANCE of Tuesday's game against Cardinal Newman and their sensational pitching talent, Turnbull Peters. He wanted to prepare his team the best he could for what they were about to face, not that hitting in a batting cage against a pitching machine would be the same as stepping in the box against Bull Peters who might throw one at their head or ruin their timing with a well-placed change-up. But there was only so much he could do. Then it was up to the players.

They had one more game, Monday afternoon, before they faced the Bull, so this was the last opportunity to get in some practice.

He cranked the pitching machine up to 100 mph, its highest setting, and called for his infielders to hit first. But he wasn't worried about them. Truth was he only had one player on his mind—Ryan Buck. This was the biggest game of Ryan's life; make or break time, what with all the major league scouts who would be in attendance. He wanted Ryan to get a taste of what he would be up against.

When his turn came, Ryan stepped into the cage and set himself for the pitch.

Whoosh!

He didn't move the bat off his shoulder, just trying to get a sense of the 100 mile fastball that had just whizzed by him. *I've hit 95 mile fastballs*, he thought. *But that extra 5 miles per hour...what a difference!*

He took a few more pitches, gauging the speed. Then he settled himself in earnest, waited, and swung at the next pitch. He fouled it off the side of the cage, barely getting a piece of it. He swung at another twenty pitches and, after the fifth or six pitch, his reflexes kicked in and he started to make solid contact. Tough!

After practice ended Coach Carruther called Ryan over.

"Want to spend another fifteen minutes or so hitting?" he said.

"Absolutely."

Ryan helped him load balls into the machine.

"I'm going to set the machine at 98. From what I've been able to gather, that's Peters' top speed," he explained. "The 100 mile setting was just to get you thinking fast."

Ryan walked back to home plate and set himself.

"Ready?" Carruther called.

"Fire away."

Twenty minutes later and drenched in sweat, Ryan was tired, but he knew he could hit a 98 mile per hour fastball.

As they walked back to the locker room, Coach Carruther talked to him.

"You can hit his fastball so don't be over anxious. Staying relaxed will help you with that change-up he throws. He doesn't tip his pitches so you'll need to concentrate when you're in there. You've been doing a great job of that; just keep it up."

Carruther stopped, turned to Ryan, and looked him in the face.

"And remember..."

Ryan stopped him. "I know," he smiled. "See the ball, hit the ball."

Coach smiled. "You got it!" He patted Ryan on the shoulder.

As they started to go their separate ways, Carruther stopped and turned back towards Ryan.

"One more thing. This Peters, he's a head hunter. He might want to distract you with a fastball at your ear. Don't let him!"

"Got it, Coach."

Ryan let out a long, slow breath as he opened his locker. *Jeez, this is gonna be a big game!*

As he drove home, Ryan thought about the importance of Tuesday's game and took stock of his feelings. He felt strong and quietly confident. Not cocky; just comfortable. He knew everyone was in his corner and rooting their hearts out for him and it made him feel good. Mom, Michael, Sam, and, of course, Maggie! She fell into a special category. He wanted to please them all.

But there was one person above everyone else he wanted to make proud. Dad.

He hadn't told a soul but ever since he put that tee shirt on, it was as if Dad was in the batter's box with him. He knew it was a key part of the dramatic improvement in his performance because it kicked his motivation and desire to succeed to another level. Well, on Tuesday, he and Dad would get to face Bull Peters. He hoped the two of them would be good enough.

CHAPTER 51

THE FOLLOWING MONDAY, SUSAN, MICHAEL, AND SAM LOOKED OVER the crowd that was gathering for Ryan's game, trying to pick out the scouts. Prior to the start of the game, Coach Carruther confirmed that scouts for the Red Sox and Cubs were in attendance. They didn't tell him about the Yankees' scout being there, too. They were keeping that information to themselves. Ryan was aware of the scouts which, Sam thought, was a good thing. He would be feeling some nervousness, good preparation for tomorrow when he would face Turnbull Peters in front of a crowd of more people, more scouts, and Chuck Bernard, General Manager of the New York Yankees.

The pressure didn't seem to bother Ryan. He had another solid game, coming up a home run shy of hitting for the cycle as he rapped out three hits including a double and a triple. But he was hitting against average high school pitching so it was hard to tell how much of an impact his performance had on the scouts.

The next afternoon, while Ryan got ready for the big game, Susan and Sam met up with Chuck Bernard in his hotel suite. They brought Zel's diary, a photocopy of it, copies of the DNA test results, and confidentiality agreements covering both. Their legal team was not happy with them meeting Bernard on their own. In fact, they weren't happy with them meeting with him at all. Gershon, Trask had favored a press conference and the announcement of the link between Babe Ruth and the Buck family as a way to garner publicity and maximize the likelihood of a high draft position for Ryan with the concomitant dollars that would go with it—but that was just what they were trying to avoid. After their discussions of the past few days, Ryan decided he had no interest in extracting the last dollar possible by creating a bidding war for the right to draft him. He wanted no part of a publicity blitz and the media circus that would ensue. He cringed at the thought of brazenly exploiting his ties to Babe Ruth which he saw as an unearned gift that gave him an opportunity to earn his spot. When Sam had mentioned contacting Chuck Bernard and the New York Yankees, he felt intuitively it was the right way to go.

Bernard spent the next hour reading the diary. After he finished, Susan pulled out the two photos of Zel and the Babe in the barbershop some eighty-five years ago.

Chuck looked lovingly at the photos.

"We might want to buy these from you."

"They're not for sale," Susan said.

"I understand." He shook his head in wonder. "Who would have thought something like this would turn up? Mrs. Buck, I hope your son has a hell of a game tonight and that he's a hell of a ballplayer." He patted Sam on the back and then looked at Susan. "Let's go see how he does against Bull Peters."

"Whadda you think of this kid Peters?" Sam asked, as they walked down the corridor of the hotel.

"Impressive. Probably go in the top five to ten picks in the draft next month."

"The Yankees interested in him?"

Chuck Bernard radiated energy as he walked and talked.

"Nah. We're looking to pick up position players in the first few rounds. Besides, we don't have a first round pick. Traded it away a couple of years ago. And we're not going to trade up high enough to get a crack at Bull Peters. He'll be long gone by the time we get to pick." Bernard got a gleam in his eye as he continued. "Although, when these other teams see me at the game tonight, they're going to think we might want to make a deal to get him. I love it!" he cackled.

They drove to the field in separate cars and didn't sit anywhere near Bernard when they arrived. He sat with his scout who Sam recognized from the previous game. The stands were already filling up and the game wasn't scheduled to start for another half hour. There was a cluster of spectators in the rows behind home plate. They were all male and most of them held radar guns. The scouting section.

Sam walked down to field level and called to Coach Carruther. He waved, walked over, and informed Sam there were scouts from more than half the major league teams in attendance.

"They're not here to see Ryan," he added. "But it's a hell of an opportunity for Ryan to introduce himself to them."

Just then, Turnbull Peters emerged from his dugout and headed down the leftfield line to the bullpen area to begin warming up. The ground didn't tremble as he walked by but, as Sam got a close look at him, he wondered why it hadn't. Peters was one of the biggest boys he had ever seen and there was no doubt that, once on the pitching mound, he would be an intimidating presence. It was hard to believe he was only eighteen.

Carruther and Sam stopped talking and stared at Bull Peters as he ambled by, oblivious to them.

"Bull Peters," Sam said, quietly.

"That's him."

"Pretty big guy," he observed.

"No shit," Carruther said, softly.

The stands were packed and there was an air of excitement as the game began. Bull Peters' pitching prowess had extended beyond the world of high school baseball and major league scouts. Everyday fans were curious enough to come out and see him pitch. In addition, a large contingent of Cardinal Newman fans had made the half hour ride to Jupiter.

The leadoff man for the Crusaders of Cardinal Newman managed to work out a walk before the next batter flied softly to left field. On a two and two count their number three hitter hit a sharp grounder between the first and second basemen into right field. Ryan charged the ball and came up throwing as the runner rounded second, digging for third. There was a cloud of dust as the runner slid just as the ball arrived, right on the mark. "Out!" the umpire signaled. It was a bullet of a throw by Ryan. Cheers of excitement and moans of disappointment blended together as the fans, evenly divided, let their feelings be known. Undivided, Susan, Michael, and Sam stood in unison and applauded Ryan's throw. Sam looked over to where Chuck Bernard was sitting and tried to gauge his reaction but he sat quietly talking with his scout.

After the next batter made out, all eyes were focused on Bull Peters as he ascended the mound and took his warm-up pitches. His fluid, relaxed motion made his pitches look even faster than they were. He seemed to throw effortlessly while the ball exploded out of his hand. Watching him, Sam realized that, if such an easy throwing style could produce 95+ mile an hour fastballs, a change-up, thrown at 80 miles per hour, would be devastating to a batter. Thrown with the same motion as the fastball, the change-up would play havoc with the timing of a hitter who was geared up and coiled to swing at his blazer. He glanced into Ryan's dugout and saw him quietly watching Peters throw. Sam's throat tightened as he wondered how Ryan would fare against this intimidating force.

"That's a very big boy out there," Susan remarked.

"No shit," Sam said.

Perhaps Bull Peters was feeling a bit of pressure himself because he walked the scrappy leadoff hitter on four straight pitches. This led to a quick consult between the catcher and his pitcher. Whatever they talked about seemed to help because Bull struck out the next two batters, throwing only blazing fastballs. That brought Ryan to the plate with the runner still on first base. Susan reached over and squeezed Sam's arm. With her other hand, she grasped Michael's arm but he shook her off.

"Not now, Mom. Let me watch. Let's go Ryan!" he shouted.

Ryan stepped into the batter's box and tapped his chest twice with his right hand. The blue trim of the DAD tee shirt peeked out from beneath his uniform shirt as he took his practice swings and got himself set.

Bull Peters went into his motion and unleashed a fastball that came in high and tight, sending Ryan sprawling backwards, away from the plate. The pitch missed hitting him by inches.

Susan gasped and squeezed Sam's arm so hard that it hurt. Michael stood and started yelling at the pitcher.

"It's okay," Sam said, trying to reassure her. "That's Bull Peters letting Ryan know that he's aware of his hitting ability. He's telling Ryan not to get too comfortable up there while he's pitching."

"Comfortable? I'd be scared to death!"

"Me, too. But that's why they wear helmets. Ryan better get used to it. You, too, because this won't be the last time he sees chin music."

"Chin music?"

"That's what it's called.... when a pitcher throws one up near the batter's chin."

As Ryan dusted himself off, he glanced into his dugout and saw Coach Carruther nod his head and give him a wink. He turned towards the mound and gave the mammoth pitcher a lingering stare. Bull Peters stared right back at him as they sized each other up.

"Is there going to be a fight?" Susan asked, anxiously.

Before Sam could respond, Peters turned towards the mound and Ryan stepped back into the batter's box.

Peters went into motion and threw to the plate. A fastball, on the outside corner, that Ryan swung at. But his swing was late and he missed. Peters came back with another fastball, on the inside corner, which Ryan took for another strike. The count was one ball, two strikes. Ryan stared out at Bull Peters as he calmly took a few practice swings. Peters peered in at his catcher, got the sign, nodded his head, and threw home. It was the first change-up he had thrown all game. It looked just like his fastball as he released it, except it took a second longer to cross the plate. Ryan swung at the fastball he was expecting and was well ahead of the ball as it landed in the catcher's mitt. Strike three. Ryan, badly fooled by Bull Peters' change-up, struck out.

That let some of the air out of Ryan's three person rooting section. *Round one to Bull.*

Sam glanced over at Chuck Bernard who, seemingly unfazed by the action on the field, continued his running conversation with the scout who sat alongside him.

Cardinal Newman scored a run on a couple of hits in the top of the second and, as Ryan's team came to bat, Sam asked Michael if he could wend his way over to where the scouts were sitting and find out how fast Bull Peters' pitches were showing on their radar guns.

Michael loved the assignment. He popped up out of his seat and inconspicuously worked his way to the scouts' section. Sam watched him squeeze into a space along the aisle, just above where several of the scouts were sitting, giving him a vantage point where he could see the numbers that flashed on their radar guns. The Bull retired the side in order, striking out two more batters. At the end of the inning, Michael made his way back.

"His fastball is right around 95," he reported. "He threw one that hit 98. He threw two change-ups, one at 78, the other at 80."

"Good going," Sam said. "Could you hear any of them talking?"

"Nah. They didn't say much. Just watched the Bull pitch."

Bull Peters was dominating. He retired the side in order in the third and got the first two batters in the fourth. As Ryan came to bat for the second time, Bull had yet to give up a hit, had walked one, and struck out seven batters.

Susan's stomach was in knots as Ryan stepped to the plate and unassumingly went through his routine. He stared out at the massive pitcher who must have looked closer than the sixty feet six inches in distance that he stood from Ryan. Peters, who had small eyes for such a big man, stared at his catcher's signals, went into his wind-up, and hurled a fastball at the inside part of the plate. Ryan pulled his hands in as he swung his beautiful compact swing, all in a fraction of a second. Susan and Sam leaped to their feet as the ball soared high and far to right center field and cleared the fence. They cheered lustily as Ryan rounded the bases and stepped on home plate. *Round two to Ryan!*

"I don't believe it!" Susan yelled, as she jumped up and down.

Michael double high-fived Sam as he tried to holler loud enough for Ryan to hear him.

Sam looked towards Chuck Bernard who was taking in the scene on the field.

The score was tied at one and it stayed that way through the sixth inning when Cardinal Newman scratched out another run on a walk, a single, an error, and a sacrifice fly.

Ryan's teammate, not at all the dominating presence that Bull Peters was, nonetheless was pitching effectively and kept it a close game.

Bull Peters continued his commanding performance. As he began the sixth inning, he had struck out ten, walked one, and had given up two hits, Ryan's homer in the fourth and a scratch single in the fifth. Bull retired the first batter in the sixth on a weak ground ball to the second baseman. He made the next batter his eleventh strikeout of the game. Ryan was on deck as their number three hitter battled the Bull. In a nine-pitch at-bat he drew the second walk of the game. Ryan stepped to the plate with two outs and a runner on first base. Everybody's attention ratcheted up a notch as the confrontation unfolded between the mighty Bull Peters and the batter who had hit a home run off him.

Ryan went through his ritual as Bull stared in for the sign. He shook the catcher off and then nodded his head. With a glance over his shoulder at the runner on first, he delivered the ball to the plate. It was a change-up that froze Ryan. He looked helpless as he watched the ball sail over the plate for strike one. With the next pitch, Peters tried to entice Ryan to swing at a slider that was a little low and a bit outside. Ryan, with his now entrenched plate discipline, laid off and took it for ball one. Bull came back with another fastball that was outside, too. It was obvious that he was wary of Ryan and was pitching him carefully. Now behind in the count, Sam thought Bull would come back with a fastball that Ryan should be expecting. It was a hitter's count and Sam's anticipation rose as Bull threw the ball. But he threw a beautiful pitch, a laser that caught the low outside corner of the plate, and evened the count at two and two. On the next pitch, Bull came inside with a slider that broke Ryan's bat in half as he managed to foul it off. Bull came back with a fastball, also inside, that Ryan swung at and almost missed, just getting enough to foul it at the catcher's feet. Bull Peters did not look the least bit tired on the mound. His fastball had as much zip on it as it did at the start of the game. Ryan was struggling to make contact with it. Peters, pitching from the set position because of the runner on first, unleashed another pitch. It was his devastating change-up, thrown at a point where Sam was sure Ryan was looking fastball. Or maybe he wasn't, because he managed to stay back on the pitch and make a hard, balanced swing on the ball. The leather sphere flew off his bat towards left center. The center fielder drifted back as far as he could go, jumped with his glove outstretched and watched as the ball fell out of his reach on the far side of the fence. Another home run for Ryan!

Susan, Michael, and Sam cheered mightily, once again. But this time instead of following Ryan, Sam looked to where Chuck Bernard was standing, watching Ryan intently as he rounded the bases. After Ryan crossed home plate, Bernard turned his gaze to Sam and nodded imperceptibly. It was enough of a gesture to know that he was impressed. *Round three to Ryan Buck.*

Ryan's team had a 3–2 lead as Coach Carruther went to his bullpen, which promptly surrendered two runs to Cardinal Newman. Trailing 4–3, they had one final inning to try to best Bull Peters, who took the mound in the seventh determined to finish what he had started. Ryan's home run the previous inning seemed to energize the Bull who stomped around the mound, exhorting his teammates to hang tough. Bull blew away the final three hitters with a combination of fastballs, sliders, and change-ups that left them helpless at the plate. The game ended with Bull Peters striking out the side, just as he did in the first inning, and letting loose with a loud bellow as the last out was made.

It was a magnificent pitching performance where he showed the heart and grit of a competitor. His final numbers were three runs allowed, three hits, two walks, and fourteen strikeouts. He showed why half the major league teams had scouts at the game watching him pitch.

Ryan had also distinguished himself, hitting the two home runs off the Bull. He was the only hitter who did any damage to Bull Peters all night, showing determination and toughness.

They lingered in the stands after the game. Maggie, who had been sitting with friends, came by and joined them. She was glowing over Ryan's play. Sam kept an eye on the dugout as several men, scouts he presumed, stopped to talk with Coach Carruther. At one point, the men looked their way as the Coach pointed in their direction. After they left, Carruther beckoned them over.

"Your son had quite a game for himself," a pumped up Coach Carruther said to Susan. "Those two fellas are scouts for the Red Sox and Cubs. You'll probably be getting a call from each of them, Mrs. Buck. They'll want to know Ryan's interest in playing professional ball. Sounds like they may factor him into their draft next month."

"Both of them?" Sam asked.

"They wouldn't say. Those guys are longtime friends, but they're also competitors. They're not going to reveal what they're really thinking. But I wouldn't be surprised if they both recommend Ryan to their people."

"That's fantastic!" Susan said.

"I'm pretty excited myself, Mrs. Buck," Coach Carruther said. He tried to be cool but he was beaming in spite of himself. "I may get my major leaguer yet!"

There was no waiting for a call from Chuck Bernard. It came before they got to the parking lot.

"Sam," he said. "Ryan had a terrific game. Impressive hitting and he's got a hell of an arm. I'd like to meet with him and his mother. How about tomorrow morning? Will that work?"

"Hold on."

He turned to Susan.

"It's Chuck Bernard. He wants to meet you and Ryan tomorrow morning. Can do?"

She gave him an enthusiastic nod.

"Tomorrow's good, Chuck. What time?"

"Early. Say 7 AM at their home. I've got a 9:30 plane back to New York out of West Palm. That will give us a half hour."

"Is that enough time?"

"Should be for now."

Thinking about Ryan's performance later that night, Susan knew she had witnessed a defining moment in her son's budding career. She got chills down her spine.

Ryan can go all the way!

CHAPTER 52

Susan had the dining room table set and the coffee waiting, along with an assortment of bagels, muffins, and fruit when Sam arrived at 6:30 AM. A few minutes later, Ryan stumbled into the kitchen, mumbled hello and then disappeared to get ready. A short time later a sleepy looking Michael came in on his crutches, which caught Sam off guard for a second, but he didn't lose his cool like the first time. Michael croaked a greeting and, like his brother, retreated to his room. The boys were in their last few days of the school year and Susan had given both of them the day off. Ryan would graduate in two days.

Susan looked as fresh as a newly picked flower as she flitted around preparing for the arrival of their special guest. She kept rearranging everything on the table, a sign of the nervousness she was feeling.

A few minutes later, they heard a car door close followed by the ringing of the doorbell.

"Mrs. Buck," Chuck Bernard said warmly, as he shook her hand. "Good to see you again." He looked around. "Nice house."

"Please come in. I have breakfast set out in the dining room." She ushered him through the living room towards the dining room.

Bernard stopped to stare at the framed yellow dress. "Is this the dress from Zel's journal?" he asked.

"It is," Susan said.

Bernard shook his head. "I'll be damned!" he said softly, as if he was talking to himself.

They continued into the dining room where Sam greeted him.

Bernard shook Sam's hand enthusiastically.

"So, it turns out that the baseball card expert has an eye for talent, too."

Sam shrugged. "It's just the way things worked out," he said, modestly.

"Maybe. But it's all pretty exciting and you're the one who brought us together. I owe you a big one."

Susan watched the two men interact. *They have an easy rapport,* she thought.

Just then, Ryan entered. Bernard extended his hand to Ryan and he shook it.

"Nice to meet you, Ryan. Congratulations on your performance, yesterday."

"Thanks," Ryan said. "It would have been better if we had won. I blew that first at-bat"

"One of the things we teach our young players is they can't do it all alone," Bernard said gently, already coaching. "Not to put so much pressure on themselves. You have to rely on your teammates to do their share, as well. Yesterday, against one heck of a pitcher, you hit two home runs, drove in all three of your team's runs, and threw a runner out at third. I call that a pretty good day at the office."

"Yes sir," he replied. This was the General Manager of the New York Yankees talking and Ryan soaked up everything Chuck Bernard was saying.

The GM continued in his relaxed, low-key tone.

"Looks like you've been having a lot of good days at the office of late."

"Yes sir," Ryan said.

"What do you attribute it to? Your recent success."

Ryan thought about what Bernard had just asked him.

"It's complicated." He looked questioningly at Bernard.

Chuck nodded. "Take your time."

Ryan paused and leaned back in his chair as he weighed what he would say. He seemed to make up his mind, leaned forward, and spoke from his heart to the Yankee GM.

"My Dad was killed in a car accident two and a half years ago. My brother was seriously injured. It was like the end of the world for me." He paused a moment before continuing. "In some way, I blamed myself for it even though everyone told me that wasn't the case. Much of the time I wasn't very happy with myself and found it hard to get excited about anything. I played ball, but without any passion. I was just going through the motions, in baseball and everything else." He looked Bernard in the eye. "It's hard to care very much about things when you're afraid you're going to lose them." Ryan stopped and took a drink from his glass of orange juice.

Bernard stared at him, listening attentively.

Ryan's voice got lighter. "Over time, though, I've been able to see things differently. I've been able to accept that the accident wasn't my fault. I've also been able to start caring about things again. Really caring. Along the way, I realized I have a tremendous passion for baseball. It kicked in a few months ago." Ryan leaned back in his chair and shrugged. "That's the only explanation I have."

Bernard refilled his coffee cup and added some cream.

"You have a girlfriend?" he asked, changing the subject.

Ryan's serious face lit up.

"I do," he smiled. "Maggie."

"That's nice."

Just then, Michael walked in, introduced himself, eyed the bagels, and took a seat at the table.

"So, you're the kid brother," Chuck said.

"That's me." Michael meticulously applied cream cheese to the onion bagel he had carefully selected. "I'm Ryan's agent-in-training. So I'll want to review the contract you offer him before he agrees to sign." He looked quite pleased with himself.

Susan rolled her eyes, Ryan got red in the face, Chuck Bernard laughed.

"I'll be sure to send you a copy," Chuck said.

He turned his attention back to Ryan.

"How does it feel to be Babe Ruth's great, great grandson?" he asked.

"It feels terrific! How do you feel about it?"

"Amazed! Frankly, I wouldn't be here if it weren't for that connection. Just as frankly, though, I wouldn't be meeting with you this morning if you didn't have major league ability and the maturity to handle it. You've got all three, son, so I'm here to tell you the New York Yankees are interested in drafting you at next month's Amateur Entry Draft."

Bernard surprised Sam with his "no beating around the bush" approach. Time for him to jump in.

"How interested?" Sam asked.

"Very. Let's leave it at that for now." Bernard looked at his watch. "I've got to be going but there are a few more points we need to cover. Ryan, is it my understanding that you are ready to commit to a professional baseball career?"

"Yes, absolutely."

"That means you are prepared to forego enrolling in college at this time?"

Ryan glanced at his mother who nodded.

"Yes," he said.

"Are we agreed that we all will keep your connection to Babe Ruth confidential until the draft?"

Susan looked at Sam.

"We'll need additional assurances regarding your intention to draft Ryan," he said, easily. "For now, though, we won't be saying anything about it to anyone else."

"Good, because if word does get out, you probably will wind up being drafted by another organization that picks ahead of us. I assure you, none of them will take as good care of you as the New York Yankees.

Chuck Bernard stood and shook hands with Ryan again.

"Ryan, it is a pleasure to meet you. You should feel very good about yourself. I have tremendous respect for what you and your family have had to deal with and how you all have come through it. Mrs. Buck," he said, turning to Susan, "you must be very proud. My hat's off to you. Michael, great meeting you, too. You're going to make a good agent someday, I'm sure."

Sam walked him to the door.

"Sam," he said, "give me a day and I'll call you so we can get the paperwork going."

"Looking forward to it."

And then he was gone, back to New York and, Sam imagined, further discussions about Ryan Buck, the great, great grandson of the Sultan of Swat.

As he walked back to the dining room, where the Buck family remained seated, playing it cool, Michael called out, "Is his car gone?"

Sam went to the front door and peeked out just as Bernard's car pulled away.

"Yes," he called, "he's gone."

With that, Michael hollered out, "I don't believe what I just heard! My brother is going to be a New York Yankee!! A Bronx Bomber!! Wooo, whooo!!" He started high fiving each of them as he walked around the table. "Unbelievable!!" he cried out, again and again.

Susan embraced her oldest son and started crying.

"Your Dad would be so proud of you, Ryan. Even prouder than me, if that's possible."

Ryan choked up and grabbed his mom tightly as the emotion he had been keeping inside released itself. Michael walked over, put his arms around the two of them, and held them tight.

Sam grabbed his coffee cup and headed for the family room, leaving the Buck family to share this emotional moment in private.

CHAPTER 53

A COUPLE OF DAYS LATER, SUSAN, WITH SAM NEXT TO HER, SAT WAITING for Ryan's graduation ceremony to begin. Michael and Maggie stood a few feet away, talking with friends.

Sam's mind was elsewhere, thinking about his latest conversations with Don Kurtz, Chuck Bernard, and the representatives from the Cubs, Red Sox, and several other major league teams who had called in the past two days.

Ryan's performance against Bull Peters had been noticed. The Yankees weren't the only ones interested in him and Susan referred all of those calls to Sam. Each team representative wanted to gauge Ryan's interest in entering the draft, sought clarification as to whether he wanted to sign or go to college, and asked to meet with Ryan and his mother in person. Sam had held them off by telling them Ryan was still considering college but leaning toward signing and asked them to give the family a few more days, which they reluctantly agreed to. Sam also heard from Chuck Bernard who told him he had a long discussion about Ryan with his senior team as well as Yankee ownership and they were in the process of preparing a formal offer. Susan, Ryan, and Sam had discussed all of this with their lawyers at a meeting in Don Kurtz's office. Gershon Trask had a sports management group that consisted of two attorneys, who specialized in that area, as well as a tax attorney. The lawyers wanted to establish guidelines for who would do what and how they would communicate going forward. Not surprisingly, they wanted to control all communication with the Yankees and any other teams that might enter the picture.

"I disagree," Susan said, quietly but forcefully. "I want all conversations with Chuck Bernard to go through Sam." She had tremendous confidence in Sam and was struck by the comfortable rapport he had with Bernard. "All the paperwork will go through you," she said, gesturing to the attorneys on the opposite side of the table.

The day before, Ryan played his final high school game. He ended the season with a flourish as he smacked three doubles. He was a hitting machine. After facing Bull Peters Tuesday night, he said it felt like he was batting in a slow pitch league. A number of scouts from Tuesday night's game, including the Yankee scout, were in attendance at Ryan's final game. This time they were there to watch him.

Lost in his own thoughts, Sam didn't hear what Susan was saying to him.

"Sorry," he said. "I was a million miles away."

"I said I feel like the luckiest parent at this graduation."

"I understand. You have much to be thankful for."

"I do...and you are a part of it."

Sam smiled. "Thanks for making me part of it."

Susan smiled and hugged his arm.

The band began to play and those standing scurried to their seats as the graduation processional commenced.

As Michael watched his big brother walk by dressed in graduation garb, he allowed his mind to drift to the World That Wasn't Possible, a special, private place he had created for himself after the accident. In the WTWP, Michael could run swiftly, jump high, and catch everything that came his way;

he was the premier athlete and star. WTWP was his escape valve and he only went there when he felt low in the world he lived in. Fortunately, he rarely had the need to visit his special place. He didn't feel sorry for himself and wasn't envious of others. It was a miracle he survived the crash and he was thankful to be alive. The same determination that might have made him an elite athlete, had given him the will to overcome his handicap. He was naturally upbeat and he was able to focus on the positives in his life the great majority of the time.

But with recent events—the connection to Babe Ruth and the opportunities it presented to Ryan—he found himself visiting WTWP more frequently. As he sat watching Ryan graduate a bunch of "what ifs" ran through his mind. He allowed himself a quick visit to WTWP. Then Ryan's name was called.

Susan craned her neck looking for Ryan. When his name was called and he accepted his diploma in his left hand as he shook the right hand of the Dean of Students, Susan, Michael, Maggie, and Sam cheered.

The roll call ended with Julie Zorn and, shortly thereafter, the recessional began. When it ended, they went looking for Ryan. There were pictures to be taken.

CHAPTER 54

MONDAY MORNING SAM CALLED BERNARD AND INFORMED HIM THEY HAD been contacted by eight other teams, including the Red Sox.

When Boston sold Ruth to New York after the 1919 season, it was arguably the worst transaction in the history of baseball. Prior to his sale, the Red Sox had won five of the first fifteen World Series while New York had never made it to the Fall Classic. After the Babe became a Yankee, Boston went 85 years before finally winning another one, while the Yankees became the most successful franchise in baseball, winning over twenty-five titles. They called it "The Curse of the Bambino" and Sam was sure the Yankees didn't want to chance allowing the Red Sox to get even.

Bernard seemed unfazed by what Sam had to say about Boston and the other teams but did tell him their discussions regarding Ryan were moving right along. In line with that, he requested that Ryan undergo a physical exam as soon as possible. Sam then gave Bernard their schedule as it related to the draft, which would take place on June 10th, three weeks away.

"Obviously, Ryan's preference is to sign with the Yankees," he said. "In essence, we've given you right of first refusal. But if we can't come to an agreement, we'll need time to meet with the other teams, all eight of them. While I'm not inclined to be giving the New York Yankee organization any ultimatums, I want you to know that your exclusivity period will end at 10 AM on Friday."

The Yankee GM didn't seem bothered by the deadline.

"Shouldn't be a problem," he said. Bernard gave him the name and address of a doctor. "Get Ryan over there; today, if possible."

The next couple of days went by with agonizing slowness as they waited to hear back from the Yankees.

Susan refocused herself on work, but with limited success.

Sam tried to keep himself busy but he couldn't seem to stop himself from checking his cell phone to see that it was working properly. A watched pot takes longer to boil.

By Thursday both of them were antsy and anxious. Sam hadn't heard from Chuck Bernard since their conversation regarding Ryan taking the physical. He worried that something bad had shown up or maybe the Yankees were having second thoughts. He started to think about speaking with the other teams.

Thursday afternoon his cell phone rang and the caller ID said it was Chuck Bernard. *Here we go.* He took a deep breath and answered the phone.

"Sam. Chuck Bernard here."

"Chuck, how did Ryan's physical go?"

"Perfect. He's as healthy as a horse. That broken leg of his from the accident has healed just fine. Sam, I'm going to need an extension on your deadline of 10 AM tomorrow."

Sam's heart sank as he heard this. He started to tell him no, when Bernard continued.

"I'm flying down tonight and would like to meet with Ryan and his mother tomorrow, say around 8, 8:30. I don't think we'll be done until 10:30 or 11. So I may need an hour's extension. That okay?"

Relieved, he played along.

"That depends. Are you gonna make us an offer we can't refuse?"

Bernard chuckled.

"No specifics over the phone. Suffice it to say, I'm confident Ryan, his mother, his agent-in-training, and even you, will be very pleased."

Really!

"Chuck, that's good enough for us to extend the deadline."

"Then I'll see you tomorrow."

As soon as he hung up, Sam called Susan and told her they would need more bagels and coffee.

Chuck Bernard stirred the cream he had just poured into his steaming cup of coffee as he made himself comfortable at the dining room table.

"How is the agent-in-training doing today?" Chuck asked Michael.

Michael took a bite out of an onion bagel covered with cream cheese and sliced tomato.

"Waiting to review your offer," he managed to mumble, as he chewed away. "Hope it's gonna knock my socks off."

"Our offer is going to blow your socks off, Michael. Let me get to the specifics." He pulled his chair closer to the table. "Ryan, you have been *the* topic of discussion around Yankee headquarters. It's a unique situation, to say the least. We've tracked some of the ballplayers in this upcoming draft since they were kids and you pop up ten minutes before final decision time. We've been watching you for all of two weeks. It's unprecedented.

"As I said last week, the reason we even took the time to look at you is your family connection to Babe Ruth. It's a compelling story that has captivated the Yankee brass. We carefully reviewed the DNA test results, read the copy of the diary, and we're convinced you are a direct descendant of Babe Ruth." Bernard paused and shook his head as if it was still hard to fathom. "You have his DNA in your veins—pretty exciting stuff for members of the Yankee family, not to mention how our fans will react. The past week, I've watched a few of our weathered, hard-bitten executives who are never fazed by anything walking around scratching their heads in wonder.

"It's a significant story that will play out soon enough. But what about your baseball ability? Did the Babe's genes translate into Ryan Buck having the ability to play ball at the major league level? That became the key question for us. We needed to satisfy ourselves that the likelihood was high that you could succeed in the big leagues. We did not want to engage in an exercise of futility that ultimately would be viewed as a publicity stunt. That wouldn't be good for you, the Yankees, or the legacy of Babe Ruth, an issue that became an increasingly substantive part of our discussions.

"Assessing young ballplayers is awfully tough," Chuck explained. "Our kids usually need a lot more learning and experience before they make it to the top, unlike other sports. Of course, there are always exceptions. Gehrig, Mantle, Griffey Jr., and your great, great granddaddy made it to the majors when they were nineteen. They hardly needed any time in the minors. Williams, Mays, Jeter, Mauer. They got to the Big Leagues at twenty. But, in general, it's a crapshoot. In your case, we didn't have a lot to go by in trying to assess your ability, just some video and a couple of games we saw in person, including the game against Bull Peters. The fact that you didn't play full-time until this year, and we understand why that was the case, kept you off the radar screen. But your performance against Peters got you noticed. It showed all those scouts an example of your ability. We all got to see Ryan Buck's bat speed and beautiful swing as well as an arm that's made for a right fielder.

"So what does all this mean?"

Bernard leaned forward and looked into Ryan's eyes.

"It means you are the stuff of dreams, Ryan. If you are successful you will be every kid's hero. And when it comes to this kind of thing, we're all kids."

They sat silently, caught up in Chuck Bernard's words, none of them wanting to say anything.

Bernard took a gulp of his coffee and continued.

"Ryan, we believe you have the ability to be successful. I'm betting you have the temperament, too. To withstand the pressure and the distractions that come with the territory. I'm confident you'll be able to weather it all. You've been through tougher." He shifted his gaze to Susan and then Michael. "You all have.

"We spent the past few days talking about how we could maximize the likelihood of your success and we've come up with a plan. Let me explain. The day after we draft you, we're going to hold a press conference where we introduce you to New York and the country. At the press conference, we'll inform the world of your connection to Babe Ruth. We'll also announce that you have been assigned to our team in the Florida State League and that you will immediately be reporting there. We expect all hell to break loose. There's going be an unprecedented amount of interest in our signing of you. You, your mom, and brother will be thrust into the spotlight." He paused and looked at them. "Not to worry. The New York Yankees will have your backs. We'll support you all the way. We'll assign a team of our best people, including a senior member of our public relations department and security personnel to assist you as long as needed. The entire Yankee organization will be behind you.

"I know I'm throwing a lot at you but there's a reason why we want to do it this way. We believe it is best to get the news out right up front. The quicker we get it out there, the quicker it will die down and fade into the background;

far enough that Ryan will have the opportunity to develop his baseball skills in something other than a media frenzy."

Susan chose to speak up at this point.

"I don't understand something, Chuck. Why hold the press conference so quickly? It seems to me the Yankees are looking to drag out Ryan and show him off as the great, great grandson of Babe Ruth. Is it necessary that it be done immediately? Can't he quietly go off and play ball without anyone knowing? Give him time to adjust?"

"I fully understand your point, Mrs. Buck," he said, unflustered.

"Please, call me Susan."

"Susan. I hear you. But realistically, I don't think it's going to be possible."

"Why not?"

"Because we plan on making Ryan our first draft pick and when we do there are going to be lots of questions from the press, not to mention clamoring by our fans, to know why. Your son is a complete unknown and there are people with the persistence, intelligence, and resources to figure it out on their own." Bernard paused as he leaned forward and rested his elbows on the table. "Susan, this is a story we want to be on top of and control. I don't deny that the publicity surrounding Ryan's signing is going to be good for the Yankees, but it's not the main driver. Our primary goal is to do what's best for Ryan and his development."

Number one draft pick! They were all speechless, except for Michael.

"What? Did you say you're making Ryan your first draft choice?"

"That's right," Bernard replied. "Of course, you need to realize that our first pick isn't until the second round. The fifty-fourth pick overall."

"Any chance Ryan could get picked before then?" Susan asked.

"Highly unlikely. As long as we keep The Secret to ourselves."

Acting as Ryan's de facto agent, Sam asked, "What does this mean in terms of money?"

Bernard responded without a trace of drama.

"We're prepared to give Ryan a signing bonus of $2.4 million."

Michael reacted immediately. "Two-point-four million..."

"Michael!" Susan admonished. "Sit down and be quiet, please." She was tense, as they all were.

Bernard laughed.

"That's okay, Susan. I wouldn't expect a future agent to react in any other way. Yes, $2.4 million." He turned his attention back to Ryan. "Ryan, the Yankees believe in you and we're not shy about putting our money where our mouth is. If you care to check, it's a very healthy bonus for a second round pick. As you can see, though, it's not just the money. We will throw the considerable resources of the Yankee organization behind you so that you have the very best chance to succeed. That means coaching, training, PR, security, the works. All we ask is a complete commitment from you to become the very best ballplayer you can be."

Ryan fidgeted in his seat before he spoke.

"I'm speechless, Mr. Bernard."

"Call me Chuck."

"When can we get started?"

"Slow down, Ryan. How do you feel about standing in front of a press conference?" Susan worried out loud.

"I don't know," Ryan replied. "I've never done it."

"Are you nervous?" asked Michael.

"No. I'm excited. I want to play ball." He started walking around the dining room, pacing off some nervous energy. "Playing for the Yankees." He paused to gather his thoughts. "Like my great, great grandfather did. That would be sweet."

Chuck Bernard ate it up. He rose from his chair and shook Ryan's hand, then got a hug from Susan, and a high five from Michael. Finally, he turned and handed Sam a folder as they walked to the front door.

"There's a contract in there, Sam. You and your lawyers look it over and get back to me with any questions. Let's get any issues nailed down by end of next week." He had a cocky grin on his face. "You satisfied?"

"Satisfied? That's quite a commitment you're making. I really don't know what to say."

"It's the way we do business. When we see something special we don't fool around trying to get it. We think Ryan's a special talent. Let's just make sure no one says anything before June 10th."

"Not a word."

"None of this would have happened without you, you know. What do you get out of it? Besides getting to keep the Wagner?"

"Don't worry about me."

"Just curious."

"What do I get out of it?" Sam thought about it for a few seconds. "I get the greatest adventure of my life. Not bad for a funny lookin old guy, huh?"

Bernard looked him up and down.

"You're not so old."

Sam grinned.

"No, Chuck. I guess I'm not."

CHAPTER 55

AFTERWARDS, RYAN AND MICHAEL ESCAPED TO MICHAEL'S ROOM AND talked alone.

"So how does it feel to be the number one draft pick of the New York Yankees? Not too shabby, Ry." Michael couldn't get the grin off his face. "How nervous are you? Really."

"Don't know. It hasn't sunk in yet."

"There's gonna be a press conference and everything."

He shook his head. "Hard to believe."

Ryan looked at his brother who was a picture of content-ment. He felt a pain in his heart as he thought about how much Michael loved to compete, how talented he was, and how, since the accident, traditional sports were cut off to him. But, wait. Why did it have to be just about Ryan Buck? Michael was a great, great grandson of Babe Ruth, too. Why couldn't he get a slice of the pie? An idea formulated in Ryan's head.

"Let's talk about you, Mike."

Michael looked up from the video game he had begun to play.

"Me? What do you mean?"

"I'm not the only great, great grandson of Babe Ruth."

"Yeah, but you run a lot faster than I do," he said, wryly.

"That hasn't stopped you before. Why should it stop you now?"

"What are you talking about? I doubt that I fit into the Yankees' draft plans." He turned his attention back to the video game.

"But you might fit into their organizational plans."

Michael turned off the game and looked at his brother.

"Have you forgotten, *I'm* still in high school. I'm not ready to start my business career just yet."

Ryan didn't respond. He just stared at him with a knowing smile on his face.

Michael stared back and then rolled his eyes.

"You want to tell me what you're thinking or are we going to play twenty questions?"

"There's no high school over the summer."

"So?"

"I read somewhere that a Yankee summer internship is a fantastic opportunity."

"Yeah?"

"How about we ask Chuck Bernard about an internship for you?"

Michael's face lit up.

"Cool!" He tossed the video game controller onto the couch, folded his arms, and nodded his head as he thought about it. *This could be as good as the WTWP.* "I could do that. I could definitely do that!" He looked at Ryan. "Think Mom will go for it?"

"That could be the tough part." He thought for a moment. "I think Sam will. That might help."

"Should I ask her?"

"No, leave it to me."

CHAPTER 56

THE BUCK FAMILY HAD TWO AND A HALF WEEKS OF ANONYMITY LEFT. Life would likely not be the same once The Secret was out.

Until then, they went about their business. Ryan, with guidance from Chuck Bernard, began working out and playing ball with an instructional school in the Ft. Lauderdale area. It was a school for elite athletes and they got him started on a conditioning program. Ryan thought he was in pretty good shape, until he started a brutal workout regimen with the coaches at the school. He came home dead tired every afternoon. When he wasn't training, he was with Maggie.

Ryan surprised his mom a few days after Chuck Bernard's visit. By then, their legal team had pored over the Yankees' contract and made their suggestions. It was Ryan who requested the biggest change when he asked that the Yankees agree to give Michael an internship for the summer. When questioned by his mother, Michael expressed great enthusiasm for the idea. If it came to pass, where he would live and how he would get by posed obstacles, until Sam came up with a brainstorm that involved Michael and Susan spending the summer together in New York.

"I own a condo in Manhattan," he said. "Nice building, down by Union Square. A very young area. Lots of NYU kids. There's a couple in the building with a nice two bedroom who always go to Aspen for the summer. They're always lookin' to sublet the place. But they're particular who they'll rent to. I could give 'em a call and see if it's available."

Susan got a pained look on her face. The possibility of spending the summer in New York was one more ripple in the pond; more change to deal with. Then again, as she thought about the idea of a summer internship for Michael, she realized it would be his way to participate in all that was going on. How could she deny him the opportunity if it materialized? But how would she pay for an apartment in New York? And was it too much for Michael?

"The idea of Michael getting around New York City frightens me," she said.

"Ever been to New York?" he asked.

Susan shook her head.

"It takes some getting used to. But Michael's got gumption and fire in his belly to take this internship with the Yankees." He paused. "My building is a two minute walk to the Union Square subway station where Michael can catch the number four train which is a straight shot to Yankee Stadium. It'll take him twenty minutes to get there." He looked at Susan. "It's not as difficult as you're thinking. Susan, I wouldn't suggest Michael go to New York on his own but he'll do fine with you there."

"I know it's the right thing to do for him." She addressed what else was on her mind. "Then there's the expense. How much is that apartment going to cost."

"Don't know. But Susan, your financial situation is going to take a dramatic change for the better. You're going to make a lot of money when you sell the memorabilia, not to mention Ryan's signing bonus."

"That money belongs to Ryan," she said, defensively. "I won't touch it."

Sam sighed. "Fine. You'll still be able to afford a few months in New York and have more than enough to get Michael the very best prosthesis and all that goes with it.

And," he added, "you can use your time in New York to meet with the top medical people about Michael."

Good point. She hadn't thought about that. But then there was Ryan and how would he get by if they were in New York?

All of these issues were coming fast and furious. She needed time to process it all.

After a few days of agonizing, she agreed to make the move to Manhattan for the summer on one condition: that Sam agreed to accompany them, so that she and Michael didn't have to navigate the Big City on their own. Her decision was made easier when Ryan pointed out that he would be getting his own place in Tampa, where the Yankees' Class A team played, and she wouldn't be seeing very much of him anyway. After further thought, she realized that he might be better off if his family were further away from him, so that they wouldn't be a distraction.

The next day Sam asked their lawyers about adding a clause to Ryan's contract that included an internship for Michael but they told him it should be a completely separate agreement and suggested he talk directly to Chuck Bernard about it. They were right. Bernard laughed when Sam told him what Ryan had requested and not only agreed to it but indicated he would have Michael assigned to his area.

From a business perspective, Susan's life began to change immediately. She decided to put account development on the back burner. Suddenly, she had too many distractions, all good, to be able to manage any additional business. Besides, her financial fortunes were about to change and the pressing need to make more money she had always felt was dissipating. Instead, she went into service mode, focusing on tending to her existing clients' immediate needs. Spending the summer in New York would have negligible impact on her existing business as long as she had access to her laptop and a phone.

That was the easy part for her, though. Coming to terms with the looming changes to the Buck family were far more challenging. Her first born was about to leave the nest and mama bird was pained over the prospect. She knew, of course, that Ryan's move to Tampa, where he would become a full time ballplayer and be on his own, was the right thing for him to do but, emotionally, it was difficult. She and her boys were a tightly bound unit. They had survived the terrible adversity of losing their husband and father by rallying around and relying on each other. But that chapter in their lives was coming to an end. Ryan's leaving was a triumph for all of them but it wasn't without sadness, wistfulness, and regret, too.

Between responding to questions from the attorneys, reading documents, and fending off other teams' inquiries, Sam stayed busy, too. He decided to tell the Red Sox, Cubs, and others that, for the time being, they should not consider Ryan in their plans and that he would let them know if the situation changed. It was a completely truthful statement that left them all unhappy. He received a phone call from Coach Carruther inquiring about what was going on with Ryan. Suspecting one of the coach's scout friends had called him to complain, Sam felt badly that he couldn't tell him the truth but Carruther would have to wait, too. Sam tried his best to explain that something was up with Ryan that he couldn't go into at this point, but as soon as he could, he would let him know. Pete Carruther wasn't too happy with him, either.

Ryan was soon to be an instant millionaire, without even buying a lottery ticket. He was cautious about his new financial status except when it came to getting a new car. He and Maggie spent a lot of time looking at a variety of sleek sports cars, including the newest Porsche models. For her part, Susan contacted her financial advisor, the one who was so helpful after Bill died, and developed a plan to invest

Ryan's money as well as the proceeds from the sale of the Ruth items.

Sam brought up the auction to Susan and whether or not she wanted to proceed, given Ryan's new economic status, as well as the potential for other sources of income that their unique situation might present. It was an opportunity to keep Zel and Horace's keepsakes in the family. But she remained intent on going forward with the sale. She felt strongly that Ryan's money belonged to him and was adamant about having the money available for Michael's needs without further delay.

With that in mind, Sam called James Dent, President of Standish Auctions, and informed him he would be FedExing him Zel's journal along with the results of several tests, but, prior to that, would require that he sign a confidentiality agreement prepared by their attorneys. Thinking ahead, their legal team recommended they copyright Zel's diary so that only the Buck family could publish it.

All of their thinking was geared towards the Draft on June 10th and the Yankees success in making Ryan their first pick. They had internalized Chuck Bernard's optimism that no other team would pick Ryan before the Yankees got their turn. Nonetheless, when the calendar finally reached the tenth of June, Susan, Michael, Ryan, Maggie, and Sam were very nervous as they gathered around the television in the family room to watch the draft on ESPN.

The Yankees had the fifty-fourth pick and it was akin to Chinese water torture as they watched the proceedings slowly move along, the talking experts giving so much information on each potential draft pick that Susan felt she knew more about these kids than their parents did. They cheered when the Red Sox, who had the seventh pick in the draft, selected Turnbull Peters. Sam looked at Ryan and offered that maybe he hadn't seen the last of the Bull, which elicited a grimace from him. When the Cubs announced their selection of Ryan Buccholz with the forty-fourth pick, Susan almost fainted. Ryan maintained a calm exterior while his heart beat like a bongo drum. After the Angels, with the fifty-third pick, selected a pitcher from California, it was finally the Yankees turn. They watched Chuck Bernard and his team huddle-up for a minute and held their breath as Bernard announced the Yankees' first pick of the Draft.

"With the fifty-fourth pick, the New York Yankees select Ryan Buck."

With that, everyone, except Ryan, jumped out of their seats cheering and hugging each other. Susan cried. Sam had tears in his eyes. Ryan finally stood and pumped his fist twice before accepting hugs from each of them.

Then they listened as the ESPN announcers, momentarily speechless, tried to make sense of the Yankees' pick. They didn't have anything on Ryan other than the most basic information: that he was eighteen, he hailed from Jupiter, Florida, and played right field for his high school team.

It was about then that the phone rang...and didn't stop ringing.

CHAPTER 57

BALTIMORE, MARYLAND
FOUR MONTHS LATER

SEE THE BALL, HIT THE BALL.

Back in January, a lifetime ago, it was the refrain he had used to help stop himself from looking back and getting lost in the mystery and heartache of the prior two years. After he was drafted by the Yankees it became his mantra, allowing him to concentrate and put aside the whirl of distractions when he stepped into the batter's box. It had worked extraordinarily well. So it was with reluctance that, a week earlier, Ryan felt the need to modify it. *See the ball, catch the ball.* But so far, so good.

The manager walked purposely to Ryan, who sat at the far end of the bench, and tapped him on the shoulder. "Go loosen up. You're in right in the bottom of the inning."

We plan. God laughs.

As he watched Ryan Buck jog out to right field for the bottom of the ninth, Chuck Bernard sat back in his seat, just to the side of the Yankee dugout, and thought about the small plaque that rested on his office desk. *We plan. God laughs.* His acknowledgment that it was wise to expect the unexpected. That certainly was the case this season.

After all the planning and calculating that he and his staff had done, the carefully crafted personnel decisions and trades they had skillfully pulled off, here was his team with the season hanging in the balance, and their only option in the bottom of the ninth was to bring in a nineteen year old rookie as their defensive replacement in right field. Definitely not the plan. In fact, he had done all he could to avoid putting the Yankees and Ryan Buck in that position. But that was the situation. He shrugged to himself. *Sometimes you get to where you are by design; sometimes you just get there.*

Today's game was the culmination of a breathtakingly close season during which three teams—the Yankees, Orioles, and Red Sox—had battled nose to nose for the American League East Division title. The winner would go onto the post-season. The losers would go home for the winter. Even on this final day of the regular season, anything was possible. If the Red Sox beat the Blue Jays, they were guaranteed at least a tie for first place. Same for the Yankees if they beat the Orioles. But, if the Orioles won the game, there would be either a two or three team tie. If that wasn't drama enough, both games hung in the balance as the ninth inning got under way. The Red Sox were up a run against the Blue Jays while the Yankees led the Orioles by two.

Susan, Michael, and Sam sat a few rows behind Bernard and they were feeling the pressure of the moment. Susan fidgeted nervously when she saw Ryan jog out to his position as the Orioles came to bat.

She looked around the jam packed-stadium and absorbed the sounds of the excited but tense crowd. "I can't believe this is all happening," she said, in amazement. Ryan had received the call to join the Yankees a week earlier and had seen action in four games as a ninth inning defensive replacement.

To say that it had been an event-filled summer did not do justice to the past few months.

It started with the press conference the day after Ryan was drafted, when the media first focused its glare on him. Chuck Bernard had carefully choreographed the press announcement, explaining the story behind the Yankees' mystery pick of Ryan Buck. Bernard began by saying that there were certain underlying factors, beyond Ryan's impressive baseball skills, that led to his selection as their first round pick. He asked everyone's indulgence "as I share an amazing story with you."

Twenty minutes later the place went wild. Ryan Buck was the great, great grandson of Babe Ruth!

The Yankee GM then introduced Ryan, Susan, and Michael. There was a barrage of questions that eventually pulled Sam into the story as the person who had contacted Chuck Bernard and revealed the connection, giving the Yankees the inside information that led to drafting Ryan.

The news was big enough that a few minutes after the announcement Susan's phone buzzed with a CNN News Update. "New York Yankees first draft pick, Ryan Buck, is great, great grandson of Babe Ruth." She showed it to Sam and whispered, "You were right. This is big!"

The next day, the news made the front page of the *New York Times* and virtually every other newspaper in the country. It made the morning and evening news on the major networks and ran all day on cable news stations. ESPN featured the story nonstop. Over the ensuing weeks a plethora of reports covered the story from every conceivable angle and perspective. It was startling news that stoked the imagination of the American public, sports fan or not. Ryan became an overnight sensation.

Chuck Bernard spent a good deal of time over the next week trying to manage expectations. He repeatedly warned the media and fans that, though a descendant of Babe Ruth,

Ryan Buck had yet to play a game as a professional ball-player. While Ryan's ability had a high enough ceiling to justify his second round pick, no one in the Yankee organization expected him to be the second coming of Babe Ruth. Reporters challenged him on whether the Yankees would have ever drafted Ryan without the Ruth connection, given his meager high school playing time. Bernard was honest with them and agreed that, but for the Ruth relationship, he might have slipped under their radar screen, although Ryan's performance against Bull Peters had opened the eyes of many.

The media scrutiny continued unabated throughout the summer, particularly as Ryan advanced up the minor league pyramid. Zel's diary was pored over by those who were allowed to read it. The DNA tests were carefully reviewed by experts. Naysayers made themselves known. But the vast majority of reporters and fans embraced the news and dreamed dreams of exactly what Chuck Bernard cautioned against: the second coming of Babe Ruth.

Once the press conference pandemonium died down, Ryan was whisked away to Tampa to begin his professional career in earnest. His performance from day one was nothing short of startling. After six weeks and thirty games in A-ball he was batting .380 and had an on-base percentage of .429, which included nine homers, and thirty-one runs driven in. Stellar offensive numbers. But what got him promoted to Triple-A was his defense. He was superb in the field, showing natural instincts combined with a Howitzer of a throwing arm and superior speed. Ryan's defensive prowess immediately got the attention of the Yankee brass because outfield defense was an organizational weakness, even at the major league level. As the season wore on, it became a vulnerability that opposing teams exploited. With few internal solutions available to him, Chuck Bernard traded for a defensive specialist at the July 31st trading deadline. It solved the problem until the new Yankee got hit by a pitch which broke his hand, sidelining him for the remainder of the season. Once again, the team had a gaping defensive hole in right field. The Yankees turned to their bench and gave the right field job to their top reserve player who did a credible job until he pulled a hamstring and came up lame. They put another reserve, for whom every fly ball was an adventure, but who was on the team because he could hit, in right field and kept their fingers crossed. By then, the Yankees had added Ryan, who had already been labeled the organization's top defensive outfielder in their minor league system, to their forty man roster, making him eligible to be called up to the big team in the final month of the season. They took this step with great reluctance but did it out of necessity. Even though Ryan was holding his own against the superior pitching talent at Triple-A and had exceeded their expectations at every level of play, Yankee management was deeply torn between the need for his defense at the major league level and the possibility of rushing him along too quickly and, in the process, damaging his long-term prospects. But by the end of September they felt compelled to turn to their insurance policy of last resort. They promoted him to the majors and informed him he would be used strictly as a late inning defensive replacement in right field. He wouldn't be getting any at-bats.

Susan knew all this because Michael told her. Michael had flourished in his internship with the Yankees. Chuck Bernard had become his mentor and had given him increasing responsibilities throughout the summer. This left Michael in a position to know about management's thoughts regarding Ryan, which he shared with his mother. The Yankee brass was high on Ryan but incredibly sensitive about exposing the great, great grandson of Babe Ruth to the type of pressure and scrutiny that would come with a promotion to the Bigs. But in the rare moments she got to speak to Ryan,

Susan could see he wasn't overwhelmed by all that was going on. As she watched Ryan take his place in right field as the Orioles came to bat, she thought he had handled his new found fame with grace and maturity.

The Orioles went down in order in the ninth inning with Ryan catching a lazy fly ball to end the game. The win guaranteed the Yankees at least a tie for first place.

As Susan, Michael and Sam left their seats and headed to the clubhouse to see Ryan, the scoreboard showed the Red Sox-Blue Jays game still in the ninth inning with the Red Sox leading 3-2. By the time they arrived they only got to see him for a minute because the team was leaving immediately for New York. The Red Sox had won and there would be a one game playoff the next night at Yankee Stadium.

It was a madhouse outside the locker room as reporters jostled each other to be the first inside when the locker room opened to them. Ryan hung back from the rest of the team so he could grab a moment with his family.

A reporter called out to him. "Ryan, how do you feel about playing the Red Sox for all the marbles tomorrow night?"

Ryan couldn't contain his elation. His eyes shined and his cheeks glowed.

"Pretty exciting!" It was all he could muster in the moment.

Then he spotted his mom, Michael, and Sam. He hugged each of them, added a kiss for his mom, and then said he'd see them in New York. Before they left, Chuck Bernard came over and invited the three of them to watch Monday night's game from his luxury box. With big smiles on their faces, they said yes.

CHAPTER 58

YANKEE STADIUM CRACKLED WITH ELECTRICITY AS THE FANS SETTLED IN for the first regular season playoff game between New York and Boston since 1978, when Bucky Dent broke Red Sox hearts with his seventh inning, three-run home run over the Green Monster in venerable Fenway Park. Though thirty-five years had passed since that black moment in Red Sox history, the Yankee shortstop, who hit all of five home runs that season, was still referred to as Bucky Fucking Dent by members of Red Sox nation. In a rivalry this heated, fans had long memories.

Tonight's game, whatever the outcome, would be another ride on the ongoing roller coaster that was a fitting metaphor for the contentious rivalry existing between the two teams. A history of gut wrenching wins and catastrophic losses stoked the passionate fires that burned deeply within the teams' respective fan bases.

Yankee fans, decked out in solid navy blue or all white, filled every seat in the Stadium. There was nothing random about the clothes they wore. A new tradition had begun mid-season when one of the more flamboyant New York radio sports personalities suggested that baseball fans wear their team colors during the annual interleague series that took place between the Yankees and Mets. This in itself wasn't unusual, except his bit of genius called for the fans sitting in odd numbered sections to wear one team color while the fans sitting in even numbered sections wore the other team color, thus creating a patchwork quilt of fan loyalty. The idea caught on. When the Yankees played the Mets at Citi Field, Met fans in the odd numbered sections wore royal blue while those in the even sections wore orange. When the Mets played at Yankee Stadium, odd section fans wore white; even section fans wore navy blue. The fans liked the idea so much that they kept it up for the rest of the season.

On this particular evening, with the season on the line and the detested Red Sox as the opponent, Yankee Stadium was a perfect checkerboard of navy blue and white, except for one section, behind the Red Sox dugout, that was solid red with Red Sox staff and family members.

Chuck Bernard's luxury suite was odd numbered, so everyone was wearing white. Sam took in the scene as he poured himself a cup of coffee. Susan chatted casually with Bernard's wife and other Yankee officials and their wives while Michael stood off in a corner listening intently as Bernard talked with two other Yankee executives.

The anticipation level reached a crescendo and a thousand camera flashes sparkled as the first pitch was thrown. Strike one! The ace of the Yankee pitching staff was on the mound and he looked to be throwing BBs to the Red Sox hitters, who failed to get the ball out of the infield in the first inning. The Stadium crowd gave their pitcher a standing ovation as he walked to the dugout. There wasn't much difference in the Yankee half of the inning. The Red Sox had their ace pitching, too, and he set the first three batters down in order, striking out two in the process. The crowd settled in for what looked like a tense, low scoring game.

Chuck Bernard sat with several of his assistants and seemed to watch the game through cool, analytical eyes. The wives left the men alone and, less intense and focused, talked amongst themselves. As a first timer to the suite, Susan wasn't sure of her place. After mingling a bit with the ladies, she joined Sam. There were enough distractions, including all sorts of tasty food, that she found it hard to concentrate on the game. Michael, who she would have expected to be rooting in his usual exuberant style, was in a different mode. He had adopted the same outward veneer of the Yankee brass—cool and analytical.

"Check out Michael," she whispered to Sam. "Very laid back for him."

Sam chuckled. "He looks like a junior member of the Yankee brain trust."

The pitching aces continued to dominate and the game stayed scoreless until the bottom of the sixth when the first hitter up for the Yankees managed to beat out a slowly hit ground ball for a single. As New York tried to scratch out a run, the Red Sox first and third basemen played in, looking for a sacrifice bunt from the next Yankee hitter. On the first pitch the batter squared and bunted the ball, harder than he wanted, between the pitcher and third baseman. But it landed in a perfect spot and, as the ball squirted by both fielders, the Yankees found themselves with runners on first and second with no outs. It was a bad break for the Red Sox.

Everyone in the ballpark knew the next batter would try to advance the runners to second and third, putting them both in scoring position. When he squared to bunt but pulled back his bat as the pitch drifted out of the strike zone, it confirmed what they already knew. Crossing everyone up, he swung away on the next pitch and hit a scorching line drive over the drawn in third baseman's head. As the ball caromed into the leftfield corner, the Yankee runners dashed around the bases. The Red Sox left fielder fielded the ball cleanly and fired it to Boston's relay man as the first runner crossed the plate. The relay man rifled the ball home on a fly as the second runner dug for the plate and slid into home as the catcher caught the ball. Safe, the umpire signaled, and the crowd went wild. The catcher turned to the ump and protested vigorously as the Red Sox manager flew out of the dugout to keep his catcher from getting thrown out of the game. When the next batter dribbled a grounder between the first and second basemen, the runner from second scored. The Yankees suddenly had a 3–0 lead.

The Red Sox countered by getting two runners on in the eighth inning. With the bullpen up and active, the Yankee ace somehow was able to rear back and get a little extra on his fastball. In a twenty-two pitch inning he managed to hold Boston at bay.

The Red Sox came to bat in the ninth inning trailing 3-0. The Yankees were three outs away from advancing to the postseason. Tony Constantine, the Yankee manager, made two moves before the start of the ninth. He replaced his weary starting pitcher with their closer and put Ryan in right field as a defensive replacement. It was Ryan's first appearance at Yankee Stadium and the TV announcers made a point of mentioning that the great, great grandson of Babe Ruth, wearing uniform number 33 in recognition of the Babe, was playing right field. But they didn't dwell on it as the drama of the moment commanded their attention.

The Yankee reliever finished his warm-up pitches and stepped to the mound as the crowd noise rose. The successor to the great Mariano Rivera was a young flame-thrower who featured a lively sinking fastball that induced a high ratio of groundballs and strikeouts. He also threw a nasty curve that could make a hitter's knees buckle. With pinpoint control, he had the kind of stuff to be an ideal closer. He was coming off an all-star year in which he had saved forty-five games with an ERA of 1.97.

But he had never pitched in a playoff game, regular or postseason. Perhaps the frenzied atmosphere or what was at stake made him grip the ball too tightly, a bad thing for a sinkerball pitcher to do. To his dismay, his fastball wasn't sinking; it was coming in straight. Even though the radar gun showed he was hurling it to the plate at 96-97 miles per hour, it wasn't too fast for the determined major league hitters, who possessed lightning quick reflexes, he was facing. The boisterousness of the crowd subsided when the first two batters hit sharp singles. As Susan glanced at the TV, the picture showed a close-up of Tony Constantine in the dugout, talking with his pitching coach.

The Yankee catcher walked to the mound to talk with his rattled pitcher. The conversation seemed to help as the closer struck out the next batter. But the third strike, a fastball that sunk in the dirt, skipped by the catcher. The runners advanced to second and third as the Yankee backstop scrambled to retrieve the ball. With one out and men on second and third, the Yankee manager walked to the mound to discuss strategy. The Red Sox player coming up to bat was their top hitter. Susan asked Sam if Constantine was going to take the pitcher out of the game. He explained that they were likely talking about how to pitch to the next batter and whether they should walk him. The pros and cons of this move included creating a force play at every base but also putting the tying run on base. When the home plate umpire walked to the mound to move the game along, Tony Constantine concluded his conversation, gave his pitcher a pat on the butt, and headed back to the dugout. The first pitch was a fastball outside by a foot. When the second pitch was in the same spot, it became apparent the Yankees had decided not to give the top Red Sox hitter anything to swing at, while trying to induce him to swing at a pitch outside the strike zone. He wasn't biting and walked on four straight balls.

Boston now had the bases loaded with one out. The score was 3-0 in favor of New York. It was the top of the ninth inning. The roller coaster was perched precariously at the top of a steep decline and Yankee-Red Sox fans knew exactly what to do: hang on for dear life. It was going to be another wild finish.

A nervous clamor pulsated through the crowd. They stood as one as the next Red Sox hitter stepped into the batter's box. The Yankee closer peered in for the sign from the catcher, went into his motion and threw a sinking fastball for a called strike. The batter fouled off the next pitch, another fastball, to go 0–2 in the count. Susan looked at Sam who was glued to the action on the field.

"He'll waste a pitch here," he said to her.

But he was wrong. Instead, the pitcher threw a mesmerizingly slow curve ball that, indeed, made the hitter's knees buckle as he helplessly watched the ball cross the plate. Strike three! Two outs!

The crowd roared and cheered as the Yankees were now one out from winning the game and advancing to the post-season. Susan squeezed Sam's arm and bounced up and down as they both stood, caught up in the excitement. Michael, who had moved next to Sam, gave him five as he lost his newly found cool.

The Red Sox batter who stepped to the plate wasn't much of a power hitter, but he didn't strike out a lot either. He had a reputation for making contact with the ball. He was a veteran ballplayer who had been in pressure packed situations before. The Yankee closer surprised him on the first pitch, though, when he came back with another slow curve that made his knees buckle, too. The crowd went wild as the umpire signaled a strike. The next pitch was a sinking fastball on the outside edge of the plate. It was a pitch most hitters would swing at but the patient Red Sox batter didn't offer as the umpire called it a ball. The crowd booed the umpire lustily, releasing some of its nervous tension. The next pitch was low and the count went to 2–1. Since a walk would force home a run, the next throw would be a key pitch. The pinstriped hurler did not want to go to a three-ball count on the hitter. The batter stared out at the pitcher as he delivered the ball to the plate, a low, inside fastball that the hitter swung at and fouled off into the stands. The count was now 2–2. The Yankees were one strike from winning the game but the Red Sox were one hit from tying it or taking the lead.

The tension thickened as the batter calmly took a few practice swings and waited for the next pitch. The pitcher went into his motion and came to the plate with a fastball high and on the outside edge of the plate. The right-handed hitter swung and knocked a fly ball on a shallow trajectory to right field, the ball never rising higher than the level of the stands. The Stadium erupted with cheers as Ryan took a couple of steps in to make the catch. But, a moment before the ball got to him, he wavered and, shockingly, held his hands out, as if to say "where is it?" As Susan watched the disaster transpiring before her she vaguely heard the Yankee announcers shout, "Buck misses the ball! It bounds into centerfield!" The ball glanced off his glove and caromed towards center field as the Red Sox runners, on the go with two outs, flew around the bases. By the time Ryan tracked down the ball, all three runners had scored and the game was tied. It was a nightmare scenario.

Everyone was shaken; the fans, the ballplayers, even the announcers. Susan went pale and sunk into her seat. Cameras panning the stands captured the pain etched on her face as the television commentator told the TV audience that this was Ryan Buck's mother and quickly recapped once again the family's story. Sam slumped silently into his chair. They sat in stunned silence. Michael walked off and stood by himself.

A few pitches later the next Red Sox batter grounded out to end an inning that would be remembered for all time. That's when the booing started.

"It's not his fault," Sam said, softly. "He lost the ball in the lights."

Susan had tears in her eyes.

"Then why is everyone booing him? I can't believe what just happened!" she said, angrily.

She looked out to right field where Ryan jogged towards the dugout as the boo's cascaded down on him. He looked completely composed but she wondered what was going through his mind. Bile rose in her throat as the all too familiar feeling of being overwhelmed and out of control engulfed her. She raised one hand to her forehead, closed her eyes, and took a deep breath.

Sam looked up at the TV monitor and watched the replay. It was obvious that Ryan had lost the flight of the ball. Because of the importance of the game, there were more cameras than usual so the play was caught from a variety of perspectives. As the announcers analyzed the different replays, one camera, located in right field, told the story. It caught the flight of the ball as it descended towards Ryan. In the moments before it reached him, the ball's downward trajectory brought its path through a diagonal background of all-white sections of fans. As they replayed that angle over and over, it was easy to see how Ryan could lose sight of the ball.

That didn't stop the fans who had already put the game in the win column from feeling angry and let down. They didn't get to see the replays those in the skybox had the benefit of watching. All they knew was the rookie missed a routine fly ball, allowing the reviled Red Sox to tie the game.

Chuck Bernard came over to them.

"Lousy break," he said. He was amazingly calm and composed. "It wasn't Ryan's fault. Could have happened to anyone. The damn white shirts were the problem."

He turned to Susan.

"Don't worry about the fans. Ryan will be fine. We'll make sure of it."

Susan smiled weakly at Bernard and thanked him. It was a gesture of pure class on his part but it didn't stop the pain she was feeling for her oldest son.

Sam tried to console her. "The game's not over yet. When the Yankees win, this won't seem as bad as it does now."

"Let's go Yankees," she said, weakly.

But the Yankees went down routinely in the ninth as they now faced the Red Sox closer.

The tenth inning was uneventful for both teams. The Stadium crowd had quieted down, as well. It was as if the wild ninth inning had sapped the energy of the fans and players. They needed to recoup their strength.

The Red Sox went in order in their half of the eleventh, and, as they took the field for the bottom of the inning, Sam got out of his seat, stretched, and went looking for a cup of coffee. He needed a boost and thought some caffeine would help. The coffee carafe was at the back of the suite where Chuck Bernard was talking on a telephone. As he poured himself a cup, he overheard Bernard say, "I don't care. Let him hit. Let's give him a chance to do something."

As he walked back, he realized Bernard must have been talking about Ryan, who was due up third in the inning. Ryan had yet to have an at-bat in the major leagues. When he got to his seat, Susan, who had said she didn't want any more coffee, took his cup and started drinking.

"Ryan's due up third," he said. "I think they're going to let him hit."

Susan shuddered. "I hope the fans are kind."

"Buck up, Mrs. Buck!" he replied. "Your son is made of tough material. He'll get past this." Then he went and got himself another cup of coffee.

The Red Sox had let their closer pitch the ninth and tenth innings. They brought in a new pitcher for the eleventh. He looked tough as he struck out the first Yankee hitter and got the second batter on an infield pop-up. He was throwing a solid 93 mile an hour fastball and a nasty slider that had a late break to it. The slider looked just like his fastball but, as it got to the plate, it tailed away from a right-handed hitter and into a lefty.

As Ryan's name was announced to the crowd, the booing started. Number 33 stepped into the batter's box, tapped his uniform shirt twice and took his easy practice swings. The TV announcers talked up Ryan's first plate appearance and the difficult circumstances under which it was occurring. Susan squeezed Michael's arm as the pitcher went into his delivery. He threw a slider that started outside but broke over the outer edge of the plate. It was a great pitch. Strike one, signaled the umpire, as the booing got louder. His next pitch was another slider, low and in the dirt. Ryan took it for a ball. The pitcher came back with a third straight slider, in the same location as the first pitch, and the best Ryan could do was foul it weakly down the third base line. The count was 1–2, a tough spot for a hitter. The pitcher tried to bust Ryan inside with a fastball near his wrists but Ryan laid off it, making the count 2–2. The hurler came back outside with the same pitch he had already thrown twice but Ryan fouled it off again. The pitcher stepped off the mound, picked up the resin bag, tossed it in his right hand a couple of times and threw it to the ground. He stepped back on the mound, peered into his catcher, and threw another slider low but over the plate. Ryan swung and fouled it to the right of first base. The next pitch was a fastball inside and Ryan fouled it into the stands. The pitcher came back with a fastball low and outside. Ryan swung and this time rifled a ball down the left field line. It was the eighth pitch of the at-bat and the fifth pitch he had fouled off. Ryan was hanging tough.

It was about then that the crowd, sensing Ryan's determination, stopped booing and started encouraging him. When he fouled off the next pitch, a fastball inside and high in the strike zone, they started cheering. The next pitch, a low slider, went streaking down the right field line, foul by twenty feet. Ryan was starting to make solid contact as he continued battling.

"The longer this goes," Sam said quietly to Susan, "the more it starts to tilt in favor of the hitter."

"Come on, Ryan!" Susan yelled. She sounded more enthusiastic.

The fans were once again on their feet. Ryan's ten-pitch at-bat had reenergized them. A chant of "Ry-an, Ry-an" started somewhere and quickly was taken up by everyone in the ballpark.

But the Red Sox pitcher was tough. He had yet to throw a pitch down the middle of the plate. His catcher went out to talk to him and discuss their strategy. They didn't have much of a scouting report on Ryan since he was new to the big leagues. In apparent agreement as to what they would do, the catcher returned to his position behind the plate.

Ryan stepped back in the batter's box, took a few relaxed swings and stared out at the pitcher. The pitcher wound up and threw a fastball on the inside half of the plate. Ryan pulled his hands in slightly and unleashed his beautiful swing. The ball went soaring off his bat, deep to right field, hugging the foul line. It was a home run...if it stayed fair. The Stadium erupted in cheers. But as the ball headed for the seats, the natural spin a left-handed hitter puts on a pulled ball made it curve. It landed foul, by five feet, as a collective moan engulfed the ballpark.

"This is brutal!" Susan exclaimed in frustration.

"I don't believe this!" Michael cried.

Ryan had reached first base, but turned and walked slowly back to home plate. As he stepped into the batter's box, the crowd took up the chant again. "Ry-an! Ry-an!"

"I don't think Ryan is going to see any more fastballs. He should be sitting on the slider," Sam said, to no one in particular.

The pitcher went into his motion and threw Ryan a slider, outside, like the first pitch he had swung at and missed. Only this time the pitch was too far outside. Ball three, signaled the umpire.

It was an epic at-bat. Neither pitcher nor batter was giving an inch. As the pitcher went into his windup, Ryan dug in and set himself.

The thirteenth pitch of the confrontation was another slider headed for the outside of the plate. While the last pitch was a bit too outside, this one was not outside enough. As it crossed the plate, Ryan glided into the pitch and let loose his compact, balanced swing. The crack of his bat against the ball could be heard distinctly against the crowd's noise. As the ball went flying out to left centerfield the crowd rose in unison from their seats and Susan heard the TV announcer in the background. "Buck hits a long drive, to DEEP left center. The centerfielder's going back, back. The Yankees win the game! The Yankees win the Division!! Ryan Buck did it! He did it!! It's a home run! Babe Ruth lives again!!"

As Ryan rounded second base, he triumphantly threw his arms in the air.

EPILOGUE

RYAN'S SEASON ENDED WITH THAT AT-BAT. THE YANKEES WENT ON TO the post-season without him. He was not part of their twenty-five-man roster and was therefore ineligible for post-season play. The Yankees won the Division Series but lost in the League Championship Series.

A month later, the Yankees sent Ryan off to play winter ball. But not before he became the toast of the Big City. Ryan's stunning comeback from the depths of despair in the game against the Red Sox had made him an instant legend.

Ryan's winning home run and celebrity made the Ruth items that went up for auction prior to the start of the World Series all the more desirable. James Dent had correctly made Susan's collectibles the cover items of his catalogue and the featured items in the auction. Going all out, Dent set Zel's diary, which was not for sale, under glass for bidders to view. The journal was opened to February 7th, 1926 and viewers could read in Zel's handwriting and in her own words, her first encounter with the immortal Babe Ruth. He also arranged with Susan to show the two photos of the Babe and Zel in Spud's barbershop.

Each of the collectibles sold for record prices. In total, Susan cleared over $750,000, after paying Standish Auctions their 20% commission. A few days later, Sam showed Susan a new addition to his card collection. It was Babe Ruth card number 144 of the 1933 Goudey set, the one Susan almost sold for $5,000 at the National Sports Memorabilia Show in Orlando. It was the card that had brought them together. He decided he had to own it and made sure he was the winning bidder.

A week after the auction, Susan took Michael to visit specialists in New York where he was fitted with the most advanced prosthetic made.

Michael met with his share of celebrity, as well. His work for the Yankees was featured in a variety of news stories and he found himself in great demand as an inspirational speaker to people dealing with physical disabilities, particularly children. Michael fell in love with the Yankee organization and the feeling was mutual. All year long he talked about New York and next summer's internship that awaited him. He also started training for a half marathon. His state-of-the-art prosthesis had opened new horizons for him making the world he lived in larger and the WTWP smaller.

Susan, Ryan, and Michael helped Sam celebrate his seventy-first birthday in early October. It was one of the happiest birthdays of his life.

Susan arranged for a private room at a swanky restaurant where the four of them could enjoy the evening in relative quiet and privacy. When the time came for toasts, Susan led off.

"Sam, you changed our lives in positive ways and helped us move beyond where we were. Without your knowledge, advice and encouragement it's doubtful we would be where we are today. I couldn't have made it through this without your support." She paused as her eyes welled up. "You are the father I always wished I had. Thank you for making room in your life for the Buck family."

Ryan and Michael stood together. Michael held a gift-wrapped box. Ryan spoke.

"Sam, we feel like Mom. This is for you."

Michael handed him the package.

Sam tore off the wrapping and opened the box. He pulled out a small trophy, about six inches high. Engraved on the front were the words, 'Honorary Grandfather.'

Sam felt his eyes fill up. He took a ragged breath and, with great difficulty, managed to hold his emotions in check.

"Seventy-one feels a lot younger than seventy." His voice had a catch in it. "Thank you." He caressed the trophy. "I'll cherish this."

He put his gift on the table and stood.

"Now, it's my turn." He reached in his pocket, pulled out a set of keys, and handed them to Susan. "These are for you?"

She took them, a puzzled look on her face.

"What are they for?"

"It seems a two bedroom unit in my building came up for sale. It was a great deal." He shrugged. "Now it belongs to you."

Susan's eyes widened. Then she started to protest.

But Sam raised his hand and stopped her.

"Just family helping family. I figure you will be spending a lot of time in New York so your own place will come in handy."

"That'll work out great for next summer, Mom," Michael crowed. "Now, if we're done with the speeches, can we order dinner? I'm starving!"

After they stopped laughing, they called for the waiter.

Before he left for winter ball, Ryan took his brother to an expensive restaurant in Palm Beach where they could get a great steak and just the two of them could have a conversation.

As they dug into their meal, Ryan brought up the subject he wanted to discuss.

"In two days I leave for winter ball, Mike. That means I won't be here next week."

Michael nodded his head as he chewed on a mouthful of steak. He swallowed and took a sip from the coke that had been served to him in a fancy glass.

"I've been thinking about that. You won't be here next Thursday."

Ryan gave a tight smile.

"Glad we're on the same wavelength."

"Don't worry yourself. I'll take good care of Mom. I plan on going to the cemetery with her and if she'll let me take off from school I'll spend the entire day with her."

They ate in silence for a while.

Finally, Michael shook his head.

"This'll be three years since the accident."

Ryan nodded solemnly but remained silent.

"You think about Dad a lot?" Michael asked.

"Every day."

"Me, too." Michael thrust his fork into the giant baked potato that was loaded up with butter and bits of bacon. "But my thoughts are less sad."

Ryan looked at him.

Michael explained. "I know he would be very happy with how we've handled things."

"He'd be proud of you." Ryan paused. "I am."

Michael smiled.

Ryan put his fork down and wiped his mouth with his napkin.

"I miss him," he said. "I wish he could see where we're at and what we're doing. Your bravery."

"And your success, Ry. He'd be going ape shit over what you've done." Michael took a moment as he ate his potato. "Speaking of bravery, I've been meaning to ask you a question. How did you get through that fly ball you missed in the ninth inning? I know it wasn't your fault with it getting lost in the white background, but how were you able to handle it? The fans booing and all?"

In typical Ryan fashion, he thought a while before speaking.

"For a minute I had this incredibly sick feeling in my stomach. I couldn't believe what happened. It made me think back to the accident and how everything can change," he snapped his fingers, "like that." He paused. "But then I realized this situation wasn't anything close to that. Nobody died, nobody got hurt. That was life and death. This was just a ballgame." He looked at his brother. "It wasn't bravery, Mike. I just got unlucky and then, with the home run, I got lucky."

Michael nodded in understanding.

"You know what Sam said after you hit the homer?"

Ryan shook his head.

"He said you're one tough son of a bitch. I think he's right."

Not so tough, Ryan thought. With the end of the baseball season, he found himself with spare time on his hands. He spent most of that time with Maggie and getting himself ready for winter ball. But there were periods where he was idle and then his thoughts gravitated to Dad. As his preoccupation with the accident continued to fade into the background, he came to realize that he still had mourning to do and damage to repair. After a couple of years of darkness he had found his optimism. But it was tempered by what he had lived through and the challenges that lay ahead.

He shook his head and mentally returned to the table.

Michael wasn't finished talking baseball.

"Key at-bat?" Before Ryan could answer, Michael continued, "I guess that's an easy one. The home run to win the game for the Yankees."

Ryan shook his head.

"That's the obvious answer. But, it wasn't the most important. At least, in my mind."

"What was?"

"My first at-bat against Bull Peters. The one where he almost beaned me."

"Chin music."

"Yeah. Chin music." Ryan paused. "I had never faced such an intimidating pitcher. It was scary. That first pitch he threw, if I didn't bail out, he would have knocked my head off. But as I picked myself up from the ground I realized I didn't feel the least bit scared or intimidated. I was angry. I wanted to do some damage in return."

"You got him good the next two at-bats."

"I did." Ryan flashed a satisfied smile. "Felt damn good, too!" He paused. "That was the key at-bat for me. It was then I knew I had no fear."

As Michael finished eating his steak, Ryan thought about that pitch Bull Peters had thrown at his head and how he felt when he realized he wasn't afraid of being hit. If only he could channel that feeling into the other parts of his life. It made him realize that chin music wasn't confined to just the batter's box.

After dessert, the waiter brought the check. Ryan reached in his pocket and pulled out a wad of cash. He selected two one hundred dollar bills and left them on the table. As they got up to leave a boy of ten or eleven came up to their table with pen and paper in hand.

"Can I have your autograph please, Mr. Buck?" he asked, wide-eyed. He stared up at Ryan who towered over him.

Ryan smiled as he looked the kid in the eye.

"Sure. What's your name?"

"Noah," the boy said, shyly.

Ryan wrote "Good luck, Noah" and signed his name.

"Here you go, Noah." He handed the paper and pen back to him.

"Thanks, Mr. Buck! My Dad says you're the next big thing! Thanks a lot!!"

As the kid turned to leave, Ryan stopped him.

"Wait a second, Noah. Aren't you going to get his autograph?" He gestured towards Michael.

Noah looked at Ryan questioningly.

"This is my brother, Michael Buck, and one day he's going to be General Manager of the New York Yankees."

Noah's eyes brightened as he handed the paper and pen to Michael.

Michael looked at his brother and smiled as he signed his name.

A few weeks after the auction, James Dent returned Zel's diary to Susan. She was surprised to learn that he discovered something all of them had failed to notice. There was another entry by Zel, written in 1948. They had missed it because it was forty blank pages after her last entry on January 30, 1927 and a dozen pages from the last empty page in the diary. James Dent, meticulous master of memorabilia that he was, had flipped through every page of the diary and, unexpectedly, found Zel's entry on August 17, 1948. It was a sad and poignant entry which, like her others, was gripping to read.

> August 17, 1948
>
> Babe Ruth died yesterday. He was 53. I have now lost the two men I cherished most in the space of one year.
>
> Babe's death took me back to St. Petersburg, Florida and 1926 spring training when our paths crossed, forever changing my life. I was moved to take out this journal from the box I had stored it in for others to someday read. Not having looked at it since my last entry in 1927, I found that reading it made that time come to life once again.
>
> Horace's enthusiasm and vigor, lost after his financial demise caused by the Great Depression, was renewed in my memory. Horace has been gone for a year and a week but the Horace I wrote about back then has been gone much longer. I miss him greatly. Horace was a wonderful father to Annie and grandfather to Sylvia, even though there was a lingering sadness about him. Tried as we might, we were

never able to have another child. I do not question why that was the case.

I never did see Babe Ruth after our dinner together in his suite at the Jungle Hotel. But I followed his career closely and cherish the mementos I have of him. He was the most unique person I ever met. I will miss him even though he has been out of the public eye for some time.

As I play with my granddaughter Sylvia I am thankful that both these men were part of my life. It is not possible to know the truth about all things. Instead, I am forever grateful for the gift of Annie and, from her, Sylvia, and all the children who will hopefully follow.

To those who read this journal, I hope you will not judge me or my actions. Instead, it is my greatest wish that you be proud of your family and your legacy.

I felt compelled to write this entry which, I believe, will be the final one. Nonetheless, not being able to see the future, I will leave a few blank pages, just in case there is cause to write more.

Susan read Zel's final entry a half dozen times. All the family secrets and suspicions were gone. The outcome was satisfying. Her love and admiration for Zel were restored.

Her boys were flourishing.

She felt healed.

THE END

AUTHOR'S NOTES AND ACKNOWLEDGMENTS

Chin Music is a work of fiction. However, real people and organizations populate the story.

The New York Yankees did conduct Spring Training in St. Petersburg, Florida beginning in 1925 and running through 1942. You can bet that Babe Ruth knew his way around the city. Robert Creamer, a highly respected journalist, did indeed write the definitive biography of Babe Ruth—*Babe: The Legend Comes To Life*. The paragraph that tips Sam as to what really happened between Zel and the Babe is an exact quote from Creamer's book. PSA (Professional Sports Authenticator) is, in fact, the leading third-party grading and authentication company in the sports memorabilia business. You can read more about them at www.psacard.com. Jefferson Airplane wrote the song "White Rabbit" and the lyrics quoted in the book.

The statistics Sam uses to support his claim that Babe Ruth is the greatest player of all time are accurate. The Babe did have a great year in 1924 and his worst year in 1925 when he came down with "the bellyache heard round the world." Ruth responded to speculation that his best years were behind him by playing spectacular ball from 1926–1931. During that six-year period his typical season looked like this: .354 batting average, 50 home runs, 154 RBIs, 146 runs scored, and an OPS of 1.20.

DeNuAc, the DNA company that does the testing of Annie, Horace's and Ruth's DNA, is fictitious. Additionally, current state of the art does not allow testing of hair clippings without the hair root attached. I used dramatic license, referencing "new technology," to make the DNA tests possible. All mistakes, of omission or commission, are mine.

I would like to thank the following people, without whose help *Chin Music* would not have been possible. Dr. Cynthia

Harris gave me tremendous insight into the emotional after-effects of a catastrophic car accident like the one that struck the Buck family. Allison Dickens' editorial suggestions and expertise brought the story together and got me across the finish line. Thanks to Jen Miller, a brilliant author, for recommending Allison to me. Jason Feifer, for his support throughout. Anthony Mattero, literary agent, who got me two-thirds of the way there. Claire McKinney and Paula Balzer, public relations and marketing pros, for their unstinting efforts in helping me bring *Chin Music* to the reading public. Charles Salzberg for his wise counsel, his recommendation of Claire, and for teaching me how to write a pitch. A special note of thanks to Larry Bilsky who caught two baseball-related mistakes in an early draft.

Special thanks to Michael Goodman, Bob Haupt, Warren Albert, George Liss, Herb Zarkin, and Larry Bilsky who took the time to read and reread multiple drafts of *Chin Music* and provide useful suggestions. To Michael Renbaum for letting me swing a Babe Ruth bat and whose passion for sports memorabilia is contagious. Thanks to all my friends and family who encouraged me to keep at it. A special call out to my buddies at the Old Course for their comments and support.

To my wife, Janet, who has been my partner on this four-year journey and whose suggestions made the story better, I thank you for your unwavering support and love. I love you with all my heart.

A special tribute to Heather, who we lost ten years ago. I believe she would be proud of the story I wrote.

A final tribute to my father, who instilled in me a love of baseball that continues to grow.